Scr

Written by Ray Carpenter
Illustrated by Doreyl Ammons Cain
Edited by Dianne Yount

Catch the Spirit of Appalachia, Inc.
WESTERN NORTH CAROLINA

First Edition 2011

Layout by Amy Ammons Garza
Edited by Dianne Yount
Illustrations by Doreyl Ammons Cain

Note: The poem "Forgotten," listed on page 93, is the recipient of the Editor's Choice Award, August 2004, awarded by poetry.com and the International Library of Poetry.

PUBLISHER
Catch the Spirit of Appalachia, Inc.
Imprint of Ammons Communications
SAN NO. 8 5 1 – 0 8 8 1
29 Regal Avenue • Sylva, North Carolina 28779
Phone/fax: (828) 631-4587

Library of Congress Control Number: 2011941418

ISBN: 978-0-9837382-0-6

Dedication

To
Zella Sparks Carpenter
Elder, United Methodist Church

November 21, 1941 – November 25, 2010

She taught us what was most important in life through her tireless service to others. Her life was rich with family and friends. She taught us to remember our best times and highest moments and live in them to give us joy and happiness. Zella left us with an example of a life lived in love and service for Christ. Her thoughts and vibrant witness remain to inspire us and call us to live beyond ourselves as we love the Lord our God with all our hearts, with all our minds, and with all our soul and to love our neighbors as ourselves.

Zella, my wife and my dream, it was an amazing 45 years; and when I wake in the morning, my first thought is how fortunate I am for having spent those years with you. I thank you for that.

May God hold you like the lovely and fragile Luna Moth and carry you to safety, away and out into a new growing space—not too loosely, lest you escape into a greater threat, not so tightly that you panic and self-destruct, but so gently and securely that surely you feel cradled like a baby floating under her mother's heart. A blessing for one well loved.

Her memory remains alive and on this earth. It takes shape in my daughter-in-law, a wife, a mother and a United States Marine officer, twice deployed since 2005. My wife's humor and kindness are visible everyday in my granddaughter Aiden. Zella's individuality and toughness appear in my other granddaughter Autumn. Marvelously, sometimes the characteristics show up on different days in both children.

Keep joy, happiness and contentment...
Au revoir, Zella, my love.

For my granddaughters

Aiden Laurel and Autumn Kai Carpenter

Acknowledgements

Amy Ammons Garza and Dianne Yount, my editors, for working so tirelessly to edit a book from my mountain of words. I cannot fully express my gratitude for your exceptional generosity, your faith in me to finish the writing, and your superb guidance. My special thanks to you.

Doreyl Cain, my illustrator, for your drawings and paintings that interpret my scribbles and turn them into artistic visions for the book. My appreciation and thanks for making the book beautiful through your special gifts as an artist.

Barbara Ann Bish, my philologist, for teaching me new words and for tolerating my endless lateness to deliver chapters of the book for you to review. Thanks for your friendship and encouragement during this writing.

Prologue

I began a work of art, writing the story of my life, in Graham County, North Carolina, where I grew up. Somewhere in this enchanted forest where all kinds of sweet flowers grow on rocks, where bright green moss and ferns abound, where pale pink starry flowers grow, and soft bellied gentian grow more blue than the sky at its deepest, and where pure white transparent lilies nod in the soft breeze—I began creating my story. And here, yellow and purple butterflies dart hither and thither to repair everything. Here where the sky sends down such pure light, the water is the purest, and the birds sing the sweetest melodies far into the soft white moonlight night, I began to write this book.

A lot of my friends jolted their memories and shared their stories to help me write my memoir. I had forgotten a lot of things until I started the research to write my story. In many ways, to bring back the memories was like spending a daily walk, for more than a year, to the office of a psychiatrist to sit on a leather chair to get help.

To recall what it was like living there seven decades ago, I went back. With one sweep of the living tableau, I saw the past, the face of today, and the promise of the future. It wasn't the dust heap called history. I made a base on which the spirit of my dreams would stand, and around its rim I carve the figures, in prose and poetry, of many dear faces with their hands raised to beckon all generations to come see life unfold when I was young.

I'll tell you about my boyhood home at the end of an old dirt road, about what it was like living there in times past, about a way of life that was so different from early scribbles, about patched overalls, hickory withes and discipline in a time at the end of the Great Depression.

I returned to my birthplace and walked the rutted, dusty, old road on Mill Creek that I walked as a child. I drank from the natural spring on the land where I lived. I bought Tastee Carmel bars at the general store, a hangout place in my early years. I went back and knelt at the old wooden prayer rail in the sanctuary that was my childhood church. I walked the halls of my grade and high schools. I found some of my classmates and teachers that I hadn't seen in years and laughed with them about things that time and other things in our lives had all but erased.

I'll tell you about magnificent ships pitching in storms; the sea; the sky; the sun from Gibraltar to Istanbul, from Arabia to Tangiers; heat, rock, dust, red-brown land as old as time and the sea—even older; and about some of the brassiest, bawdiest night clubs and women in the world. I'll tell you about the crowded Sampans of Tokyo Bay, my college years, my career, and my family.

My story is written candidly, set during hard economic times, and describes my way of life, the way it really was, so you may feel a part of it and experience my struggle to survive. I have included the tears as well as the laughter. My purpose in writing this story was to make our ancestors come to life as real people, experiencing hardships, joys and sorrows, successes and difficulties, as we all do.

My story is not an encyclopedic collection of everything but rather a selection of remembrances that highlight my life. Its episodes are written using family stories and events in my time that I want to pass on to future generations, not only for their interest but also for their didactic value. It is not a genealogy, although some stories do go back to older generations in my family.

I am writing my memoir at this particular time in my life so I can reflect on my life with greater serenity and objectivity. Children, have fun reading my story! I hope this little book will inspire you to write your own memoir so you, in turn, can hand it down to your children.

With love,
Ray Carpenter
June 1, 2011
Robbinsville, North Carolina

Old Houses

I
think
old houses
are like
grandmothers,
with lilacs for their
purple ribbon bows,
Their upper windows
square as spectacles
And most of all a look...
as if they watched the road for someone,
gone so long ago that only they remember
Who it was and why they wait there
patiently all day....

Contents

Poetry & Illustrations

"Catching" Babies

Scribbles

by Ray Carpenter

Fifth of Twelve

Now and then a poor woman in my community would simply drop another new baby. She would "catch it" herself, snip and tie the cord, clean herself and go back to the field the next day to hoe. Things change, but the bees and butterflies still perform their ordered destinies to eat and propagate their species.

Mine was not a do-it-yourself birth. I was the fifth of twelve children. No signs appeared in the heavens, none that anyone recorded. There were no thunderclaps representing the fall of Adam and Eve; no blazing-tail comet flashed across the sky; lightning showed no spider veins or liquid claws; nor was anyone in the county born with webbed toes or club feet.

Court records showed only one birth: a son born to Henry and Rilla Carpenter on March 18, 1935, in Graham County, Mill Creek, Robbinsville, North Carolina, at five minutes past midnight—about fifteen years before television would make mountain people aware of another world. On that creek, in that county, that hour, that date, a Romantic was born without a birth mark!

At that late hour, another Pisces was added to the world population, another human baby was born.

1

I was no different from other human babies except for a congenital hole in my right eardrum, asthma, and thrush. A normal baby: a weak, helpless little creature; a postpartum wrinkled-up fetus; a poor child soft-boned and unable to support myself on fragile legs, unable to focus my eyes, wet and befouled with my own excrement, crying for a clean diaper and suckle to satisfy my lingering hunger.

For a moment, I screwed up my face, frowned, and wrinkle-grinned at the same time as I spat and poked out my tongue at the corner of my toothless mouth. I laughed and howled by turns and cried for the stars but stopped crying when I got my mama's teat. As the days passed, my baby hair fell out and grew back in long and blond. My eyes changed from a shadowy blue to a light green and no longer required felicitous cleaning. Rolls of baby fat stayed around my middle a little longer, but I began to hold my head up, roll about, and burn off the fat. My belly-button bud healed, dried, and dropped off, leaving less chance for infection.

Thinking back, I remember being told I was caught by midwife Julie Farley at the foot of Mama's bed in the living room of an old, frame, clapboard house on Mill Creek, eight miles northeast of Robbinsville.

When Mama came to her birthing hour, Julie came, wearing her sun bonnet, with a change of clothes: clean cotton bloomers, outing flannel petticoat, one long calico dress. In her frayed valise, she brought a few medical supplies, including a bottle of Lysol, a tiny set of hand scales to weigh babies, some bandages for belly bands, a hand brush and a cake of soap, a small pair of scissors, and a spool of cotton cord tape for tying the umbilical cord. She stayed around a few days after my birth while I was unfolding and Mama was recuperating.

Years later, Julie helped me to better understand catching babies. She said, "I gave no medicine even when your mother was in pain. Sometimes I gave her black gum bark tea and a little castor oil after each of her babies were born. Some old granny women did give expectant mothers a pinch of snuff to bring on labor pains. I never did.

"Your Mama always went nine full moons. I believed the moon had everything to do with the time a baby was born," she said. "I put my faith in the Lord that he would see your Mama through. Lives hung in the balance. I always had prayer before I went to work to bring the baby. Out of the hundreds of babies I delivered before I kept records and the hundreds of babies I delivered after I kept records, I never lost a mother or child, and I thank the Lord for that."

Julie continued, "I never rode a mule or horse but always walked with a lantern in my hand when dark came. Expectant mothers in the county depended on me. I braved the elements and wild animals. I was not afraid of the dark. There were no doctors, and I answered the call when and where I was needed. Many times I stayed up all night to assure the expectant mother about the time between her contractions and the different intensity levels of them. It was tiring but joyful when I saw the smiles on the faces of family and friends and they knew the new baby and mother were out of danger.

"Many of the couples were young and had no money to pay me. I delivered babies for nothing. Sometimes I was paid two, three, or four dollars. After I was licensed as a midwife by the agency in Raleigh and kept records, I received twenty five dollars, the amount the state allowed me to get.

"Law me," she exclaimed excitedly, "I was glad to get that amount."

In addition to caring for the newborn baby, in those days midwives normally did the cooking and cleaning. Julie did neither. She ensured the house was spotless, and any person sick in the house was confined to a separate room. She mixed natural herbs and doctored them. She did not tolerate a dirty or germ-filled house to birth the new baby. She meticulously dressed me. No one but her could wash my head. She protected the soft spot. Soon it was covered with my hair and closed completely as I grew older.

Julie rarely spilled things on her white apron but changed it after my bath and baby powder dusting. She ate small amounts of the right kinds of food but liked to use a pinch of dental snuff between her cheek and gum. She always drank a glass of brandy after her evening meal.

Julie was a large woman, standing almost six feet tall. Her eyes were dark blue and sharp. Her face was creased with tiny wrinkles, but it was a sensitive, appealing face. Her slender hands belied their age and their labors, and a gold band on the finger of the left one encompassed a lifetime's fidelity.

No doula helped with my birthing, but Aunt Nora, mother's beloved sister, kept clean, sterilized wiping towels, hot water, a small wicker basket with a little white cotton blanket, and a narrow white strip of cloth for my belly-button band (with a small latch pin to fasten it) all at Julie's fingertips during my birth.

A small, unpainted handmade cradle sat in the corner of the bedroom, already made up with a brown and yellow cross-stitch quilt. Embroidered with the same stitch in the center of the baby's quilt were the words: "Babies are great gifts, you will be one." Julie brought this for me.

Mama's one last push got my body out. Immediately, Julie cleaned me up, dressed me in a cotton gown with a drawstring at the bottom, removed me from the wicker basket and placed me in the cradle, and gently tapped it to start it swinging. She later told me that I was the twenty-third baby she caught in the last two years. She whispered softly that I was a doer: a screamer, sleeper, eater, guzzler, licker, smacker, whiner, laugher, simpleton, and a chewer of my toe.

She finally admitted to me, along with Mama chiming in, that I was a little tender thing all blubbered with slobber, a hanger-on to my mama's dress tail when company came, a scrambler for the hot flat iron, a creature of habit because I always placed my tiny left hand on Mama's breast as I suckled and held her finger with my right hand. I was a beloved fool, even when I slept.

As I grew up, Mama told me stories that made me laugh and, sometimes, caused me to cry, but I learned from them. She broke into telling stories about her life. She spoke more to the side than directly to me to say, "I have another story to tell you."

For some reason, the flapping of clothes from the outside clothesline inspired these stories as we gathered our clothes and dropped large wooden clothespins into a drawstring bag to protect them from the weather. She talked about her life, her love of each of her children with different personalities, her successes and failures, her hard work and the hard times she lived through. Often she talked about marriage, birthing babies, God's graces, and about sparking.

Her side stories were eloquent. "Henry and I met

at a corn shucking one Saturday night," she said. "By local custom, after he found the red ear of corn, he had the choice to let it be good luck or to pick his girl."

More to herself and almost as an afterthought, she said softly, "I wonder why we two met? I wonder what brought us together in this place, in this time without a cause." She smiled and continued her thought, "Perhaps it was luck and maybe it was fate or divine intervention."

Playfully she continued, "Cupid's arrows, Venus's magic, serendipity, synchronicity—all are used by master poets to give reasons for love's simultaneous occurrence and help understanding, but they are not the final answer."

She continued, "He chose me out of several girls there! I was an excited and happy fifteen-year-old and he was the happiest twenty-one year old on the creek that night! He had been winking at me earlier with his beautiful brown eyes and, to be honest, I had been flirting with him even though I didn't know him."

Suddenly her thoughts flashed back! "When I was eleven years old, Papa kept me out of school to work. I really liked school and to learn, and wanted to go so much, but at that early age I did hard work for Papa," she explained. "He was driven to work, a taskmaster, a domineering father.

"Economic depressed times created hard times to live. It was a struggle to survive. I did all kinds of domestic chores in the house, including cooking, cleaning the house, washing clothes, ironing, milking cows, and manual labor in the field, including hoeing and carrying manure to fertilize crops from dawn to dusk. Papa took me to a logger's camp to cook when I was twelve years old. I caught bream and cooked them for the loggers. I wanted so much to go back to school, but Papa kept me working. I wanted to change my life and get away from the relentless pressures Papa caused by his insistence that I work. Perhaps the necessity to change brought Henry and me together.

"He was strong. I liked for him to hug me. He was a clean young man. He always kept his black hair neatly trimmed. When he called on me, his clothes were threadbare in places but always clean. I liked to smell his faint body odor and especially the scent of cloves that he occasionally used. I thanked him for the simple gifts he gave me when he came to call on me. His gift of a small locket shaped like a heart on a small, linked, silver chain was my favorite. I wore it for years but lost it.

"By the time the corn shucking ended, we were holding hands. He hugged me again and, as he was leaving for his home, he kissed my hand and whispered, 'I want to see you again.'

"'Yes,'" I quickly answered, still smiling. "No, no we didn't kiss in the mouth," she laughed. "We both chewed tobacco and dipped snuff and didn't give it up. We learned things about each other," she said, as she became more solemn. "He helped me carry manure from the end of a cornfield where it

was left in tote sacks after a barn cleaning. We strapped the totes to our backs so we could use our hands to fertilize corn hills in the furrow rows. It was hard work and most unpleasant on a hot day when we were downwind of the manure pile and got it on our hands as we worked. Our work together that day in the field was not a typical outing for us, but we learned about each other's willingness to work, which was important to our future life together.

"As he was leaving the field, he smiled again and said, 'You like to work with your mind and with your hands; with your hard work and mine, we could have something together.' I never forgot those words," Mama said.

"Any job he could find, he would work to make a dollar. Money was scarce and many families were near starvation. The Great Depression destroyed the economy in the county, and he worked ten hours a day in the woods, cutting timber and pulling logs with a groundhog skidder for ten cents an hour to survive. We got to know each other better. I finally got the courage to ask him if he was a woods colt. In his usual down-to-earth manner, he answered clearly, 'No as far as I know there is no incest or miscegenation in my family.'

"'Are there any illegitimate children in your immediate family?'

"'Not that I know about.'

"'Good,' I said, 'mine either.'

"I lowered my voice and asked, 'What are your politics?' Without hesitation he replied, 'I never sell my vote. Honor is one thing and money is another. To be honorable is more important to me than money.'

"'Are you a Christian?' I asked. He hesitated a

moment and answered, 'No.'

"I told him to keep his mind on the Lord and off betting on cock fights, the liquor and beer bottles, cigars, and girls' ankles if he wanted to live a better life. He laughed and told me that I was beautiful, just beautiful!

She was silent for a moment then shook her head. "Another year passed," she continued. "He was twenty-two and I was sixteen. We were married July 5, 1925, in a frame building used as a church located at the ford on Cochran Creek. After our marriage, my father, Oliver Orr, gave us a small house to live in across the meadow from his. We lived on Cochran Creek for two years. Our first child, Leonard was born on March 7, 1927. He was a great gift!"

"Was Leonard's birth assisted by a doctor?" I asked.

"Lord no, son," she replied, more pensive now. "There were no doctors in the county to catch babies in those years. He was delivered at the house by Magnolia Jordan, a midwife who rode a white horse around the county catching babies. We moved from the ford on Cochran Creek to Mill Creek."

Eleven

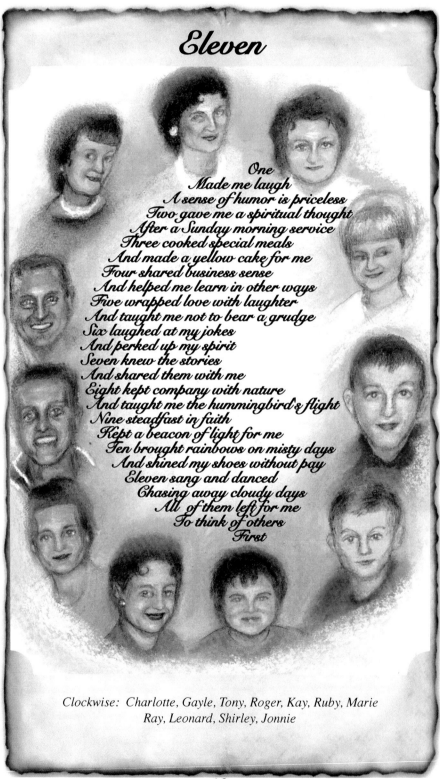

One
Made me laugh
A sense of humor is priceless
Two gave me a spiritual thought
After a Sunday morning service
Three cooked special meals
And made a yellow cake for me
Four shared business sense
And helped me learn in other ways
Five wrapped love with laughter
And taught me not to bear a grudge
Six laughed at my jokes
And perked up my spirit
Seven knew the stories
And shared them with me
Eight kept company with nature
And taught me the hummingbird's flight
Nine steadfast in faith
Kept a beacon of light for me
Ten brought rainbows on misty days
And shined my shoes without pay
Eleven sang and danced
Chasing away cloudy days
All of them left for me
To think of others
First

*Clockwise: Charlotte, Gayle, Tony, Roger, Kay, Ruby, Marie
Ray, Leonard, Shirley, Jonnie*

Four Brothers, Seven Sisters, and Me

Leonard, the first child, was born on Cochran Creek, March 7, 1927, and delivered by Magnolia Jordan, who rode a white horse to houses around the county catching babies. After him came three sisters: Marie, born in the old Floyd Carpenter house, on September 13, 1928, and delivered by Julia Farley, another midwife catching babies at that time; Ruby, born October 24, 1930, at home on Mill Creek and delivered by Julia Farley; Ruth, born October 30, 1932, at home on Mill Creek and delivered by Julia Farley. Then came two more boys: Ray born March 18, 1935, at home on Mill Creek and delivered by Julia Farley; Ralph, born on February 18, 1937, at home on Mill Creek and delivered by Julia Farley.

After that came four sisters: Shirley, born September 26, 1939, on Mill Creek at home and delivered by Julia Farley; Charlotte, born November 20, 1941, at home on Mill Creek and delivered by Julia Farley; Gail, born June 25, 1945, at home on Mill Creek and delivered by Julia Farley; Kay, born October 4, 1947, at home on Mill Creek and delivered by Julia Farley. Mama was older, but two more brothers came to be part of my beloved family: Tony, born March 13, 1950, at the Andrews Hospital and delivered by a pediatrician; and Roger, born February 16, 1953, at Robbinsville, Parrette Clinic, with Dr. Nettie Parrette attending.

Life was primitive, simple, and slow-paced for me. My sisters, Shirley, Charlotte, Gail, and Kay, played tag, made mud pies using zinc top fruit jar lids under an old pine tree at the end of a corn field and had fun making dolls from cucumber tree leaves.

Television finally came to Yellow Creek. Shirley, Charlotte, Gayle, and Kay couldn't wait until Saturday night to visit Hoover and Alma, neighbors who lived about two miles away up the creek and invited them to come and watch different programs on their set. "The Life of Riley" was a favorite program. Charlotte especially enjoyed watching it. Sometimes, when it was late at night and cold, Alma brought them home.

Ray with Charlotte and Shirley

Entertainment had changed! For them, it went from making leaf dolls and mud pies to watching television, and it never went back to playing hoopoe-hide and aunty-over.

My favorite thing was to go fishing with Shirley. She knew the time I finished my work in the fields on Saturday afternoons and had taken the gears off the horses and fed them. She was ready with her small cane fishing pole, line, hooks, bobbers, night crawlers, and her little stringer to string fish on as she caught them. She would get excited and her beautiful brown eyes sparkled with the anticipation of hooking a big rainbow trout in Yellow Creek.

Shirley also would bring some matches to build a fire and a small aluminum skillet to cook fish to eat with cornbread beside the creek. I would clean and cook the trout we caught.

I remember one day as we sat down to eat the trout, Shirley opened her brown paper bag and all she had in it were two small, white, wrinkled cucumbers. "Ah! shucks! I forgot the salt," she said, as she kicked the bag under a tree. She laughed with a warm smile as we left the creek bank with a string of eight trout to go home just before dark and said, "Salty cucumbers are better to eat with green beans and tomatoes."

I watched Shirley grow into a beautiful young woman. Her big moment came! Edwin Estes, her beau, came to the old house on Yellow Creek to pick her up on their first date. She was ready to go and came around to ask her date in. Dad was sitting on the couch with his old socks and shoes to the side, soaking his feet. The night air sifting over and around them carried the sour odor of sweaty socks and un-washed feet in the living room. Shirley pinched her nose. "Is this really necesary?"

Dad only grunted, "Hello." Shirley was so embarrassed that she turned red. Her beau said, "Shirley, are you ready to go?" She never understood Dad's ways but never disowned him. Neither did that beau ask her for a date again.

Charlotte listened to music on the radio and would often dance with the tune being played. Dad would not allow loud noise around the house, and she quickly turned the sound down before he came around to turn off the radio. She had a warm and sweet spirit. Her deep, lustrous, brown eyes commanded love and respect. To know her was to love her. I miss her and remember her in the winter as snow walks down from high peaks and covers the leaves of gold. I remember her in the stories that are told and miss the German chocolate cakes she baked.

I played marbles, hoopoe-hide, hopscotch and aunty-over by throwing a ball over the roof of the house. Later, I played jackrocks with a sweet friend, Lorene Jones, by throwing the jacks on the floor and picking them up on the required first catch of a bouncing small rubber ball. She won the game most of the time. I enjoyed playing solitaire and Rook as I grew up. I was too embarrassed to play jacks and marbles the rest of my life. I rolled dice a few times for money but never said anything to Dad and Mama about it. I played five-card stud poker but never won much money.

I joined my family at the dining table. I talked about the good things as well as the bad things that happened to me that day. Dad always wanted to know if I got a whipping at school. He wanted to know so he could give me another whipping.

I helped Mama make a bed tick from wood shavings. I made a feather bed tick from goose feathers and put it on top of the bed tick made from the shavings. Mama made me a homemade quilt and put it on top of the feather bed. I kept warm on cold winter nights when wind blew the snow and ice through cracks in the wall and up under the shingle roof and floors not underpinned.

A poor family lived around the mountain from me in an old wooden clapboard house with cracks in the floors. A baby was always on the way to join its seventeen brother and sisters. The floors were made from split logs called puncheons. At harvest time, Mama asked me to load up my old Model A pick-up truck with sweet and Irish potatoes, cabbage, turnips, and beets and take them to the family who lived around the mountain.

One evening, after dark, I was there unloading the vegetables I brought them. It was time for their mama to put the children to bed. She lifted up a puncheon and placed two small children in what looked like a nest made with goose down, leaves, and straw where the puncheon had laid. It was the only place not taken. The children were then covered with a ragged old blanket, and that's where they would spent the night in their nest. The next morning the children were taken from their leafy bed and the puncheon was slid back in place. When I got back home, I told Mama what I had seen. We were saddened and began to cry. Their dad was away in prison.

Pa Carpenter gave Leonard a red- and white-faced heifer calf. Pa and Ma loved Leonard, and I knew that he was their favorite grandchild. They wanted him to have milk and butter. The calf grew into a beautiful cow that gave gallons of milk for me and my siblings. Marie churned the milk and molded the creamy, yellow butter from her milk in a wooden half-pound butter mold with roses etched inside that made the butter look like a work of art. All my siblings liked the butter on Mama's light and fluffy hot buttermilk biscuits with honey, jam, and jelly. Hot applesauce was my choice when I had her hot biscuits and butter.

Pinky was my favorite cow, and my job was to feed and care for her. She produced other heifer calves that grew into cows. Sometimes the cows got off schedule giving milk so they could have their baby calves. This break in the cows' schedule caused a shortage of milk and butter. When times were rough and the supply of milk and butter ran out, Marie bought milk from Garland and Icey Lloyd for twenty cents a gallon and brought it home. One thing that Icey did to help families survive was run a monthly tab for them and forgive their debts at the end of the month when families found it impossible to pay.

I helped Dad clear trees, stumps, and roots from about four acres of the land he bought to use for a corn patch, garden, and a pasture for two fawn-splashed, white jersey milk cows and Pinky. The fertile soil was black loam but most of it was not suited for farming because of steep hills and rocks. A pig pen for fattening hogs to be slaughtered at the first frost and a small lean-to barn for horses and cows were about three hundred yards off to the left of the house.

On the other side of the old dirt road, less than two hundred yards away behind some trees, was an outhouse. Mama wouldn't let Dad build it closer.

At the end of the garden stood the chicken house with hen's nests running the length of both sides. It was built from slabs cut from logs at a local saw mill. Over two hundred laying hens grazed free in an open lot. Ruby and I gathered baskets of eggs. Mama let me sell some eggs and keep the money. On

Sundays, Mama had me kill three or four pullets and we had fried chicken for lunch.

Alex Phillips, my great uncle, built the frame clapboard house. Money and materials were scarce then, so he used rough, unfinished lumber from a sawmill down the road and four-inch-wide, fourteen-inch-long oak shingles split with a mallet and froe from oak blocks. The shingles were beveled on one edge, fitted one on top of the other, and nailed down for the roof. There was no plumbing or electricity. Windows were unsealed and doors ill-fitted, and there were no screens on the door or windows. The lower side of the house was high off the ground on its rock foundation. On cold winter nights, wind blew snow and sleet through cracks in the bedroom, and children sleeping there had to bundle to keep warm.

Outside the house, steps from the ground level up to the porch were at a steep angle and had no banisters. Inside, a monkey ladder nailed to the wall led from the living room upstairs to an unfinished alcove with a bed and a small space where children could play. A large rectangular room, a later addition, ran the entire length of the house on the upper side and was used as a combined dining and living room. One bedroom was out of place because it was between the dining room and kitchen and the living room. The living room was small and crowded. A pot-belly, wood-burning stove and Dad and Mama's bed occupied this room. Alex later built standard stair steps and re-moved the monkey ladder. Around the porch at the back of the house, he built a room on the porch to store pork and beef when hogs and calves were slaughtered.

Dad didn't have a car to drive from Mill Creek to Tapoco to work. Gardner Williams rented him a house on Meadow Branch across from Faset Jenkins grocery store and within walking distance of his work. Gayle was a baby and Leonard left for the Army when we lived there. I walked to Bears High School each day with my sisters and walked home for lunch. The school was named for Mr. Bears, an engineer for Alcoa, who wanted his children to have a school in the community and was instrumental in getting the school built and staffed with good teachers. Dad bought a car and, after four months, moved back to Mill Creek. Dillard and Marie later bought the school property. They renovated the old school building and changed it to a dwelling. Now Marie lives there.

Mama dropped me off at Papa and Mama Orr's house to spend the day with them on Cochran Creek. They treated me like a prince, and I always enjoyed spending a day at their house. Their house was across the meadow from the creek. Earl and Winnie Blair's house was up a narrow trail behind the tobacco barn. Papa Orr bought me a little red Flyer wagon that I could pull. I was proud of my wagon and often used it as my bed.

On a warm spring day, I pulled my wagon under a large maple shade tree in the front yard and went to sleep. Earl Blair came along, grabbed the tongue of my wagon, and pulled it toward his house. I awoke, frightened and crying because I could only see his back, his old black coat blowing in the wind, and his old crumpled felt hat. I thought a vicious killer was kidnapping me.

Shivers ran over my body! I could hear each beat of my heart as it pounded in my chest. Earl was whistling "Pennies from Heaven," a popular song, so loud that he didn't hear me crying or notice when I jumped out of the wagon and ran.

Seeing no sleeping boy in the wagon when he got home, his whistling suddenly stopped. Fear hit him. Sweat glistened on his face and upper lip. He rubbed his empty hands together, and, with panic-stricken eyes, began to scream. Then a hysterical Winnie joined him in the hunt for me. They looked in an abandoned privy hole at the end of the field, behind haystacks, in ditches along the tobacco field, and in the swift currents of Cochran Creek with no success.

"He is lost, he's lost," Winnie kept crying out. Both of them were running around calling out for me. Papa Orr knew something was wrong and ran to join them. After about an hour's search, they found me in the tobacco barn, on the hay, fast asleep. Papa Orr, most relieved, dried tears from his eyes and softly commented, "This boy is the only person around here who knows what he's doing." He took my hand and said in a gentle voice, "Let's go, son," as he pulled my wagon and led me back to his house.

It was her thinking of others that made me think of her. She was made of sunshine and snow. On warm or cold days, her bearing had a meaning, her movements a grace. I praised her as charming but some asked me what I meant. I smiled and said, "The charm of her presence I feel even when she goes." She had great warmth, wit, and humor and made me laugh. She pushed her point and backed it up with common sense during fun times with her. Sometimes, she would fly off in a huff. That was my Aunt Nora!

One Sunday after church, I asked her what she thought abut the minister's sermon. With sarcasm in her voice, she said, "I prayed for him the first hour but didn't give a damn what he said the next hour. I wanted him to shut the hell up!"

A lady from out of town moved across from Aunt Nora's house on the other side of East Mill Creek. Aunt Nora welcomed her and gave her some hot applesauce made from her early red June apples. "It was delicious," the lady kept telling Aunt Nora. Later, Aunt Nora decided to take her some fresh red June apples so the lady could make her own applesauce. Aunt Nora explained to her how she made the applesauce three or four times. As Aunt Nora was leaving her neighbor's house, the lady followed her to the door and asked one more time how Aunt Nora made the tasty sauces.

Agitated, Aunt Nora replied, "Eat the damn apples raw; they're pretty good that way!"

When I wanted a laugh and rice pudding, I always went to Aunt Nora's house when I was growing up. I knew I would get the best!

The Farmer

The farmer walks in his field
And loses all his winter fear
He turns his soil to the sun and rain
And with it turns new hope again
To all the changes of the year

The waiting stillness of the field
Has ended his winter strife
He reads the promises of old
Upon the breathing heart of life

The team is conscious of his wit
Cause he never lets them rest a bit
He plows his furrows round by round
And plants his seed in the fertile ground

A Walk That Changed My Life

I attended Rock Springs Church, which early in its history doubled as a one-room schoolhouse. Nothing fancy, just a clapboard frame, rectangular structure heated by a wood stove with a solitary vent pipe through the roof. I did not go to school there but Mama did. It sat on a bank of the Cheoah River downstream from Santeetlah Dam, surrounded by the high Smoky Mountains of Western North Carolina. Cool, clear water from a deep underground source ran freely on the upper side of the unpaved driveway and parking lot. A large brown dipper made from a hollowed-out gourd suspended by a leather strap hung on a nearby limb. Everyone, except those with mysophobia, used the dipper to dip water and drink from the spring. Drinking from a community dipper was unsanitary but water from this dipper quenched many a thirst of school children and churchgoers on a hot day, including mine. The toilet was outside, up a trail and out of sight from the church. During World War II, parishioners from the church brought their lunch baskets to the spring, spread tablecloths on the ground, and continued to pray for the nation and the servicemen and women long into the evening.

Affinity and consanguinity were evident throughout the membership of the church. I knew everyone by their names and was related to many of them through marriage or blood relationship. The church roll was made up of about sixty names, though on an average Sunday only half that many attended service. Our family, twelve altogether, took up an entire bench at Rock Springs Church. I can't remember when I didn't attend church there while growing up in the community. When I was older, Mama told me I went to church there before I was born!

The small congregation, though sincere in its hymn singing, boasted little musical talent. One Sister-in-Christ who took piano lessons, was by default our music director and pianist. Other pianists who played music in the church now and then played by ear. Each year, when people's gardens came in and there were plenty of vegetables to go around, the church had all-day singing and dinner on the ground. I always liked the dinners best. One Brother-in-Christ sang, "It is Well With My Soul" a cappella and I felt up-lifted.

The choir consisted of six women, two of whom were suffering from presbycusis, but Brothers- and Sisters-in-Christ prayed for them and they sang in spite of that. Two men in the choir were good at singing duets but sang off-key when they accompanied the choir. The pianist's hymn selection grew by neces-sity from the small patch of common ground shared by the songs she knew she could play on the piano and those the congregation was capable of singing. Rock Springs Church did not use a definite planned order of worship service because most members be-lieved that the Holy Spirit inspired spontaneous singing and preaching. The first time I attended the Methodist Church in Robbinsville with a girlfriend, I was surprised by the complexity of the melodies the organist played and by the sheer tuneful competence of the singing. Until then, I didn't know that it was possible to worship God in cadence and keys shown in song books. Methodists always do their service by a printed order of worship in the bulletin so the parishioners can follow the service.

In the years since I left, Rock Springs Church has moved from the old location below Highway 129 to a new location above the highway, built a new building, and became the Santeetlah Baptist Church. The one-room school is no longer a part of that church. Two things did not change: the people there have an abiding faith in Jesus Christ, and the congregation still sings out of both the rounded- and shaped-note editions of the 1940 *Broadman Hymnal*. Though I heard the songs in the *Broadman* sung well only once a year—on Homecoming, the third Sunday in May, when the church overflowed with visitors and our musical shortcomings were hidden inside a joyful noise—they have always been the songs I love best. I would be hard-pressed to recall even a single sentence from the hundreds of homilies I heard growing up at Rock Springs Church, but I can sing from memory at least one verse from each of the hymns we sang from the *Broadman.*

It was rare even to hear someone call out "Amen" except during the summer revivals when preachers visiting Rock Springs Church preached every night for a week or sometimes two. The Holy Spirit sneaked in through the open windows and moved silently through the church. During revivals, even the most staid members of the congregation allowed themselves to be overcome by the Spirit at least once. Spiritual renewal was as necessary to the people of Rock Springs Church as breathing; but once revival was over, the men and women I knew best, fortified by grace for another year, simply went back to work. And if, before the time for revival came again, they suffered crises of faith or began to doubt the rightness of the paths they had chosen, I never heard them say.

Because the people of Rock Springs Church were by nature circumspect, we sang "Just As I Am," the traditional Baptist hymn of invitation, only during revival week when the public displays of religious emotion were likely to be sparked by the song we all loved to sing together just before the preacher's homily.

Rock Springs Church was opposed to instrumental music in the church. Music of this type was considered a desecration of the Sabbath and God's house. Stringed instruments in particular were considered in poor religious taste, if not completely evil. The organ and piano fared better, but there were still those who thought the only acceptable way to praise the Lord was by voice. A memorable story surfaced about a young man who played rock 'n' roll in another Baptist church in the neighborhood. Back then, the church was never locked. He was inside the church picking his guitar and playing the piano, entertaining his young friends with Elvis' "Heartbreak Hotel," and Jerry Lee Lewis' "Whole Lot of Shaking Going On."

"This type of music is not acceptable; it is the devil's music and I won't allow you to play this music in the church," the deacon told him. The outraged deacon turned the young man out of the church. Today all the Baptist churches in the country permit stringed music to be played in the church. What a change!

At Rock Springs Church, religion was of the emotional type, both as to preaching and the reaction of the congregation. Homilies were invariably laced with fire and brimstone. Some of the common themes of homilies were dancing, drinking, smoking, playing cards, rolling dice, and the use of cosmetics. The church set high standards of conduct for its members. Members were often turned out for unbecoming

conduct such as having babies out of wedlock, back-
sliding, showing too much skin, wearing skimpy
shorts, laying out all night with a member of the opposite sex who was not a spouse, adultery, fornication,
shacking-up, drunkenness, cursing, gambling, telling
lies, and backbiting. I remember one incident of a
standing member of the church being turned out for
drunkenness. One of the men, a deacon working on
the committee that did the evaluations and made the
decision to turn people out of the church, was later
known to be the seller of the moonshine to the
member that he voted to turn out of the church for
drinking.

Another practice of the early Baptist church, and
indeed most Baptist churches in the country today, was
the baptizing of converts in the creek or river nearby.
One of my best friends got baptized in the same eddy in
the Cheoah River that I did. Women always pinned their
skirts between their legs with a latch pin to keep them
from catching air, billowing, and floating above their
heads. Men just wore their pants and shirts. The
preachers instructed my friend to cross his arms on his
chest and immersed him in the swirling eddy. He came
up shivering with the preachers wiping his face and saying, "Amen." His many friends and churchgoers standing on the bank gave thanks to God for a new brother in
Christ. "They kept singing 'Shall We Gather at the River'
and 'Where He Leads, I Will Follow' and praising God,"
he explained to me. My friend told me that he kept feeling something wiggling in his shirt pocket. When he
changed shirts behind the trees by the river, he discovered a minnow that had found its way there! Later he
told me that he believed that one minnow to be the Father, Son, and Holy Spirit, the Trinity. He returned it to
the eddy.

Being poor and practicing a fundamentalist religion went hand-in-hand in mountain churches in Graham County where I lived and grew up. It has been as much as, or more of, an influence on my life than everything else I've done. My thoughts and actions are often ruled by the Baptist Church teachings I learned early in my life at Rock Springs Church. Churchgoers there are passionate about their faith like no other place I know. I felt the spirit and pulsating excitement at Rock Springs Church myself! Witnessing, testimony, praying and shouting. No wonder some mountain churches are called shoutin' churches! Now, it's hard to get people to tell you their religious beliefs. Back then, when I was growing up, it was impossible to keep people quiet, as they encouraged the preachers through their homilies with shouted praise and amens.

Maybe Mary Onley came from a farm or some poor family, or perhaps some remote district of Rock Springs Church. No one there, including me, knew why she came; Pastor Gardner Williams brought her to church. Perhaps she had a checkered past. Everyone knew she had money at the local bank and lived well. Even now her wit, humor, and deep lustrous eyes with almost transparent irises of blue have helped her to earn respect and to live a more polished life.

A preacher at Rock Springs Church brought out the best in Mary each Sunday. She was an honorable woman in all her deeds and a faithful member of the church. On a particular Sunday, I was most observant of her because I loved her as a Christian. Miss Mary was moved to tears and to action by the preacher's enthusiastic homily about the fishes and loaves. Suddenly, she began to shout! In her high top shoes, her small feet began to shuffle to the aisle. She seemed to float up out of her pew, waving her little white handkerchief in front of her face, and, keeping her eyes turned toward heaven, she sang her favorite hymn, "Amazing Grace." She began her song in ecstasy, singing God's praises and walking down the aisle to the front of the church, still waving her handkerchief when she knelt at the prayer rail to finish her praise. Just as suddenly as she had begun, she returned to her seat. She never shook anyone's hand, including the preacher's. No one complained about her mysophobia. The preacher said to her, "Miss Mary, it was good to see you in the Spirit today when we took the wine and bread." She smiled a warm smile and said in a quiet, gentle voice, "Yes, preacher. I had a nibble...just a little nibble today."

No producer or director has ever dramatized the emotion, power, or actions that came from God's Bible- whopping preachers at Rock Springs Church. They had a charisma unmatched by modern orators. Whether or not one believed them, it was impossible to ignore them. No one listened to a charged-up country Baptist preacher and fell asleep. The preacher got your attention and emotional involvement with little more than the power of vocal inflections. His voice would rise to a high crescendo and fall to a whisper all with enunciation and pronunciation worthy of any great orator. Whether or not it was good preaching or teaching, there was no disputing it was memorable.

I listened to those preachers rile the people with their homilies, stomping back and forth across the platform with their pant legs shaking and beads of sweat standing on their brows. They would utter warnings about hell so convincingly, I could almost feel the heat. About every ten minutes, the preacher would scoop a dipper of water from a bucket and swill it down with such force, it's a wonder he didn't strangle. He would be in such a hurry to get that water swallowed so he could get right back to preaching. He would shout out his sentences with little time for inhaling. When he finally took a breath, he was almost suffocating on his feet; his desperate intakes of air sounded like a wind tunnel swishing into his lungs. Each breath was gasped as if it were his last. Then he would go right back into another thirty-second sentence that would deplete him of oxygen. His shirt would be wet with tears, sweat, and drinking water he had excitedly sloshed all over himself. He would jump from the platform and land two or three rows into the aisle. The congregation would heat up to a fevered pitch as the people leaped from their pews, running and dancing and colliding in the aisle, all in praise as a testament to their faith.

One of my favorite preachers at Rock Springs Church was a small, wiry man with a high, booming voice who spoke with power, passion, and sweat. He came prepared to preach on the devil, made the points of his homily succinctly, called for sinners to come to the prayer rail, prayed with them, and concluded his service at noon, as was his custom, a blessing in itself since we were all in need of food and drink.

On one particular Sunday, his face was bandaged up with two or three small, narrow band-aids crisscrossed over cuts where he had nicked himself with his straight razor while he was shaving. The dark blue suit he had on was well-worn but neatly pressed and accentuated by a flat-ironed white shirt and dark blue tie with white stripes. His gray felt hat that showed marks of old sweat around the sweat band was always on his head straight as he walked across the parking lot to the church. He always stopped just inside the door, removed his hat and said a short prayer to himself before entering the sanctuary. As he started his homily on this Sunday, he removed his coat, loosened his tie and rolled up his sleeves. "The devil," he said in his powerful voice, "is loose today. People must turn away from the devil and his spiritual powers," he continued. "Evil, destruction, and death are the results of the devil's evil power." Suddenly, his hands went up in a gesture to show the devil's rising temperature. He said, "I pray daily for God to raise the devil's temperature so high that it blows off the devil's head!"

People didn't just go to church at Rock Springs Church; they **had** church! It was a social as well as a spiritual gathering for poor mountain people. There was no admission fee. People put what they felt they could afford into the offering plate. No one asked them for a pledge as they do now in modern churches. All the members knew one another and their children. They knew what neighbor was about ready to give birth to a new baby, who was sick and shut-in, who needed prayer, when the next barn-raising would be, who needed a ride to the doctor or the grocery store, and who was lonely and bereaved. Interestingly enough, they also knew all the people needing a church home and people who were sinners in the community, making frequent contacts with them to encourage them to come to Rock Springs Church.

They responded! They believed church was the place to open your heart and take off your shoes. About every three months at Rock Springs Church, there was a foot-washing service. The members removed one another's shoes and socks and literally washed their neighbors' feet, calluses and all. We did that because Jesus Christ had washed the feet of His disciples. Can you imagine people in today's sophisticated churches being so humble that they would remove one another's Rieker shoes and Hanes socks to bathe another's pedicured feet?

People at Rock Springs Church took their religion seriously. At a time when thousands of American soldiers were fighting the communists in Korea, one churchgoer cut off the little news being received about the war by smashing a neighbor's new television with a hammer. His reason was that God didn't mean for man to have something as mysterious as moving pictures inside a cabinet. The television was worldly and therefore sinful. On July 21, 1969, the American astronaut Neil Armstrong became the first person to set foot on the moon. With the words, "That's one small step for man, one giant leap for mankind," he explored the moon's surface, accompanied by his fellow Apollo astronaut Edwin "Buzz" Aldrin. Images of this historical moon walk were flashed across the world by television. At Rock Springs Church, churchgoers said, "Nothing is written in the Bible to support man landing on the moon; that is not part of God's plan." They adamantly said, "It didn't happen, Hollywood producers faked the entire event."

During summer, when the mountain air was heavy and unstirring, the one-room sanctuary was cooled by the breeze that came off hand-held fans made by churchgoers. The soft sighs from the paper fans stirred the scents that were as much a part of the church house as the pew Bibles. There was the oily smell of paint. It had been spread layer after layer by churchgoers on the yearly cleaning days. On the wooden pews, undisciplined boys carved their initials and added their girlfriends' initials with their bone-handled pocket knives. There was the scent of Aqua

Velva aftershave that failed to cover body odor among the hard-working members. One member, as if by calling, handed out Dentyne chewing gum before Sunday school so there was always the scent of the gum mixed with chewing tobacco, pipe, cigarette and cigar smoke. Often enough, this gum ended up an ugly glob underneath the pew. Nowhere in the thirty-nine books of the Old Testament or the twenty-seven books of the New Testament is it written that Baptists must chew tobacco, dip snuff, chew gum, or smoke, yet the member at Rock Springs Church continued to hand out gum until he died and went to be with his Savior. I smelled so much Dentyne gum in my growing-up days that I never buy it today! Neither do I smoke. Mama was pleased that I didn't chew tobacco, dip snuff, or smoke.

Rock Springs Church didn't really have a pastor. "Pastor" implies someone on full-time salary, whose main task is calling on people in the membership. We had preachers. Many had no ordination from any denomination. Many had no formal biblical training. Instead, they occupied the pulpit because they said God told them to do it. They said they were called to preach, and preach they did! During their homilies, they would tell you what God had told them to tell you; sometimes it was about you and your wicked ways. They gave the congregation hell! Hell in word-pictures, hell in the colors painted in words, hell in images of terrible beasts and lasting images of a burning lake of fire! Those preachers preached what other churches later called a "fear gospel." Their message was built on fear. If you feared God enough, you would repent of your sins. If you did not repent of your sins, you were going to hell to spend eternity. "And eternity," the preachers whispered, "is like a circle. It never ends." Terrifying? Yes. Was all that real gospel or fear motivation? I wondered many times what that preaching and teaching did to me. For certain, I never forgot it! Sometimes, during the night, I recalled the images and was afraid. If your only exposure to fundamentalist preachers has been the smooth country preachers on direct television, you have no idea what fired-up evangelism is really like. To a small boy growing up, it was fearful but fascinating.

If I had raised then the religious questions that I would have later in life, I would have been scolded by church leaders for letting the devil get into my head and turned out of the church. I grew up in a Christian church, and my expectations for healing, for example, are not unusual. I was taught that God could heal, just as surely as I was taught that Jesus Christ died for my sins. How many of us question what we were taught when we were young, especially if we were also taught that questioning is sinful?

Bible scholars agree that when Jesus Christ was twelve years old, it was His year of decision. Mine too. On Wednesday morning, May 4, 1949, Jeff Millsaps, my faithful neighbor, picked me up in his maroon 1941 Plymouth to take me to Rock Springs Church to the revival meeting that preachers Harold Jenkins and John Patton were holding that week. I missed Monday and Tuesday services because it was springtime and our garden, plus the corn, potato, and tobacco acres, had to be plowed so we could plant our crops. I had borrowed Oliver Orr's team of horses to plow, and they had to be returned to him by the end of the week. Church was a secondary priority that week. Mama encouraged me to go to church with Jeff but did not pressure me to go as a sinner. She wanted me to make up my own mind about becoming a Christian and joining the church. I am most thankful that I went to the revival with Jeff. No one dragged me to the mourner's bench that day, as was the case with some sinners.

Preacher Jenkins preached about sin that day. He was against it. He came to the end of his homily, much like many other homilies, except his message that day was special for me. The thing that I remembered most about his homily on sin was that if one is a Christian and asks God to forgive his or her sin, then God would do it. He explained that everyone sinned and fell short of the glory of God. I recall his pleading, as he always did, for sinners to come to the altar and accept Jesus into their hearts. On the way home, Jeff asked me if I was lost, as he put it. I answered that I wanted to say my prayers and ask God to help me understand. I also told him that I wanted to discuss all my thoughts that had occurred in the revival with Mama, Daddy, and Oliver Orr because becoming a Christian was very important to me. My opportunity to talk with them came after I got home that day. I wanted to return to Rock Springs Church on Thursday, at 10:00 a.m., when the service began. Something was amiss with my soul!

John Patton closed his homily on Thursday with an altar call. Suddenly, I wanted to walk to the altar where I had seen sinners go many times before. I didn't know that my struggles were apparent until the couple standing beside me stepped back so that I could reach the aisle. I was torn between going to the front of the church, where the preachers waited to receive those of us called by Jesus, and staying put because I was afraid. I was conscious of how small I was before God and in the eyes of the people I had known forever. The tugging that made little sense to

my mind was pulling at my very soul. The congregation quietly sang "Softly and Tenderly, Jesus is Calling," a hymn I will never forget, as I made my way
down the aisle to that old wooden prayer rail where
the preachers and all those present fell on their knees
with me to pray. John Patton leaned over and I whispered into his ear that I wanted Jesus Christ to be my
Savior. At the moment, I felt the unconditional love of
God rising up from the hymn, the song of Jesus'
perfect love. I reached out my hand to all my friends
around me in Christian brotherhood, fellowship and
love. I will tell you, it was the most important thing I
have done. When I knew I had a new brother or sister
in the family, when Dad bought ice cream at Pearly
Odom's general store and brought it to me in the field
on hot days where I was plowing tobacco, when he
brought me a collie puppy I named Jack...these things
I cherish, but nothing compared with the joy and soul-
jarring emotions I felt when I asked Jesus Christ to be
my Savior.

The other thing that struck me that spring morning was the sight of Harold Jenkins, John Patton, Oliver
Orr, Jeff Millsaps, and Mama, along with many other
friends and members of the church, all on their knees,
crying and asking me to join them at the altar. They
loved me and were afraid I would die without being
saved, that I would be lost and spend eternity crying out
in hell for God to save me. At the end of the revival, I
was baptized in a swirling eddy in the Cheoah River,
along with twenty-one other converts to the faith, and
joined the church. One of the converts was my friend
who pulled the minnow out of his shirt pocket!

On November 27, 1959, after my hitch in the
United States Navy, I came once again to Rock Springs
Church. I had to unlock the door that was never

locked when I was attending church there. I walked, as I had on that spring day in May 1947, down the aisle to find the exact spot where I had knelt down at the wooden prayer rail and accepted Jesus Christ as my Savior. Initials of boys and girls were still carved in the wooden pews. Breezes came through the open windows and the buzzing natter of insects still punctuated the quiet sanctuary. In that moment, I found myself wishing for the scent of tobacco smoke, chewing tobacco, sweat, and Dentyne gum.

In Hugh Lofting's book, *The Story of Doctor-Doolittle*, the monkeys find the extraordinary two-headed animal, Pushmi-Pullyu, and bring it to Doctor Doolittle. He is puzzled at the sight of the strange creature and asks, "What in the world is it?" Dab-Dab, the duck, exclaimed, "Lord save us, how does it make up its mind?" Unlike Pushmi-Pullyu, I made up my mind that Jesus Christ would be my Savior years ago in a little country church.

I still get questions about God and my belief about eternity, the ultimate reason for being a Christian. God is unchanging, people change. Beliefs differ, beliefs change. There is something to a belief in God that survived two thousand years, a belief that has been triumphant through cultural and religious changes including abuses, and a belief that has sustained me through the years. Through faith in Jesus Christ, I believe in God: a God I can ask to forgive my sins, a God I can pray to, a God I can ask for help, a God that gives me hope. There is a heaven, I believe. What peace I missed here on earth will be made up for in heaven because of my decision to become a Christian at the old wooden prayer rail at Rock Springs Church at the end of John Patton's homily.

My non-Christian and my Christian friends still ask me about the practical benefits of being a Christian. I tell them about the difference Jesus Christ has made in my life. I tell them that He gives me courage even in failure, lack of money, pain, sorrow, depression, waiting, illness, and disappointment. I share with them what I learned from my family, my church, my relationship with other Christians, small groups and critics.

From failure, God taught me that there are few positions in life in which difficulties have not been encountered. These difficulties are, however, my best instructors because my mistakes often form my best experience. I learn wisdom from failure more than from success. From lack of money, He taught me that every dollar in our keeping belongs to God and must be used so as to best promote the interests of His kingdom. It taught me the greatest thing that I can do for God today is to consecrate everything to the Lord. From pain, sorrow, and depression, God taught me that I should bury sorrow because everyone has their share of sorrow. I need to bury it deeply and hide it with care. I need to bury my sorrow and let others be blessed, giving them the sunshine and telling God the rest. From waiting, God taught me that God's timetable is different from mine. I must respect God's timetable to answer prayers and all other things of God. From illnesses, God taught me that He is the great healer of physical and mental illness. All are mortal, no one is immortal and all will face illnesses and eventual death. Skills, medical technology, and knowledge to treat illnesses are also gifts from God. From disappointment, God taught me to pay as little attention to the disappointments as possible! Plough ahead as a steamer does, rough or smooth, rain or shine! To carry my burden and make my port is the point! From my family, God taught me love and unity. My church showed me that it is my mission and my relationships that are a must. Without relationships with God and people, I would have no purpose; small groups offer a sense of belonging and love. From my critics, I learned when criticism is constructive and when it is condescending and better left unsaid.

I have written about life and death, heaven and hell, and eternity and concluded that what eternity is, and in what form I come to it are the unanswerable questions. I believe we are in some manner cherished by our Maker—the One who gave us this remarkable earth has the power to still further surprise that which He caused. Beyond that, all is silence. Yet the desire to know never ceases nagging my soul.

Eternity is an unseen world. My existence between no beginning and no end has almost come to that odd fork in my life's road, some say eternity. Toward an unseen world, my slower pace takes sudden awe, my feet reluctant step. Before are rail fence rows, but between are level rows of the dead. No hope for retreat, no detour, behind me a secured route, eternity's victory flag before me, and God eternally. After these thoughts, a wonderful warmth fell over me and I became still.

Mill Creek

When the Cherokees, by treaty, gave up a section of the Smoky Mountains in Western North Carolina, later known as Mill Creek, the state sent in a team of surveyors who made detailed maps of the area. The maps were filled with notations of the quality of the land such as bottomland; hilly, steep mountain; and timber-covered. These maps were then marked off in large plats with enough acreage for a farm and also contained some forested land. The maps were then placed in the county courthouse so that a settler or land speculator wanting to make a claim could show the official where his claim was and have his claim recorded so no one else could claim his land. He would make a down payment with the understanding that the balance had to be paid within a certain time.

Most of land in the Smoky Mountains was first claimed by land speculators rather than by settlers. These wealthy men bought thousands of acres from the state and then sold them to settlers at a profit. The land was priced according to its quality, with level bottom or valley land going for the highest price, from $3 to $1 per acre; and steep land, unusable for farming, often going for 50 cents an acre. Eventually, when most of the desirable land had been bought, the state would greatly reduce the prices, almost giving it away. Money from the land sales was sent to the state's treasury. These were called grants, which does not mean that the state granted or gave away the land, but that the purchaser was granted the right to buy the land from the state. After a settler had made his land claim, he could then hire a surveyor to survey his land and place stakes, or make marks on trees at the corners, or metes and bounds, which staked out the land. This was written up and placed in the county courthouse land office or Register of Deeds.

In the Carpenter family's collection of papers is an 1858 title from the state that lists Levi Carpenter, Pa's dad, as buying bounty land, which means he bought it from the state rather than a land speculator. In 1898, Pa bought 86 acres from the state for 50 cents an acre. Arthur Garfield Carpenter, my grandfather, "Pa" as I knew him, bought steep land, very rocky and unfit for farming, for 50 cents an acre on upper Mill Creek through a land-grant purchase. He divided it into parcels for three of his sons: Henry, Floyd, and Clay. He was fair with his four sons, and helped Alfred buy his property, located off Tallulah Road, from Otis West. A small rill running through this property provided coolness for the springhouse that Alfred and Sarah Jane built. The road going by the property was changed from a rural route to a new name, Carpenter Hollow, for better identification of that area.

Pa kept several acres of the land he purchased on Mill Creek for himself. He cleared trees and stumps from about five acres for an apple orchard, viticulture and pasture for livestock. A steep hillside off to the right of the property was used to grow corn, clay peas, cornfield beans, and pumpkins. Flat bottomland of fewer than two acres laid along the dirt road that ran up Mill Creek and was used for a garden, a potato patch, and a hay field.

Grapes hung in golden clusters on Pa's grape vines in late September. They were irresistible when I walked up the old dirt road on my way home from school! I grabbed big bunches. Pa threw apples at me, chased me, and, when he caught me, he grabbed me by the nape of the neck and my belt and told me I was going to split hell wide open, His face reddened as he said, "You are no good for stealing my grapes." He told Dad, and I got a whipping for grabbing Pa's grapes.

Pa built a wooden barn with a tin roof, a hay loft, a corncrib, and a stall for his beautiful, fiery black mare Nell, a work horse. On the lower side of the barn, he built two stalls for milk cows. The wood barn still stands with a rusty roof, a stark reminder of his struggle to survive during the depression years.

When they were children, Leonard and Marie used Nell to pull large dead trees from the mountain to the wood-yard to be used for firewood. One day the single tree came loose, bumped Nell's heels and frightened her, causing her to run. Leonard, holding on to her lines, was dragged down the mountain and onto the old dirt road. He was skinned from the top of his head to the bottom of his feet and his clothes torn off. He was bleeding from scrapes and cuts. Pa grabbed Nell's reins to stop the runaway horse. Leonard was badly hurt and rolled into the ditch with closed eyes. Marie, scared badly, stood close to Leonard, wringing her hands and crying. Pa checked Leonard to be sure he was alive. He kept saying, "Damn, Damn, Damn. From now on, leave Nell in the pasture."

One day Pa was reaching for corn in the corner of his corncrib to feed Nell, and a large copperhead snake, hidden under the shucks, bit his hand. He ran to the garden, grabbed his hoe, ran back to the barn, and killed the snake. He almost lost his life, but finally Doctor Maxwell rode his own horse over to Pa's house, doctored him for snake bite, and Pa recovered. Scars left on his hand by the snake's fangs were visible as long as he lived.

Pa was not a farmer; rather, he made a living working in logging camps as a lobby hog. Uncle Floyd did all the farm work on Pa's farm and used Nell to plow Mama's garden, potato patch, and cornfield along with his own fields. Uncle Floyd broke his double shovel plow many times on the rocks. He had no money to get it fixed at the blacksmith's shop or to buy a new one. I helped him wire it together and he continued to plow the fields.

One of the things that I was always pleased to hear was, "We are in the short rows now." Short rows were the last rows in the field so that meant plowing and hoeing were finished for the day. Lunch was served by the family that owned the corn field. Food of many kinds was piled high on the table. A hungery weed-puller enjoyed a feast! The work exchange was special, and the hard work got finished. Families helped each other. The older children hoed and the younger ones pulled weeds. Everyone worked. Jonnie didn't like to hoe, but she worked hard in the house, cooking and tending babies. She took care of Ralph when he was a baby. He had dark brown eyes and beautiful golden hair that bounced in Fauntleroy curls. She loved him so much. He was a sweet and beautiful baby brother. Mama worked in the fields from daylight to dark and Jonnie carried Ralph to the field so he could suckle. She always carried him back to the house instead of letting him sleep on a pallet under a shade tree at the end of the field. She feared that a bald eagle would swoop down and carry him away in its talons.

"The old family cat got in Ralph's face and it was difficult for me to get the baby to sleep," she mused introspectively.

Jonnie ironed her clothes with an old flat iron heated on the wood-burning stove. One day the hot iron was left on the stairsteps, and she pulled it off and burned her foot severely. To this day, a burn scar is still on top of her foot. She was around the wood-burning stove in the living room and got burned on it when she was growing up. "I hated the stove," she said. "I burned my arm." I was always bumping into the stove and getting burned.

Jonnie and I opened a small stand on the end of the porch to sell butter. A good idea, but the butter melted before our first customer came along. The "open for business" sign had a short life. "Oh well," she said, "some businesses go down the drain, others go up in smoke, but our business melted." When our business failed, we climbed into the swing at the end of our porch to read stories. I touched the porch floor with my toe and the swing gently swayed once more.

Sanitary conditions were deplorable. Open privies were smelly. Flies crawled around everywhere, and some died on a twisted fly catcher hanging over the dining table. There were no screens on the windows and doors. Bed ticks, fleas, chinch bugs, and mosquitoes had to be killed constantly. Body and head lice were parasitic on my skin and in my hair. Mama kept me out of school several times over the years to rid me of the pests. Given the absence of basic hygiene in Graham County, there was a high rate of infant mortality. My sweet brother developed pneumonia in his left lung, but Doctor Crawford mixed his own herbs and doctored the disease. There was no penicillin or other powerful antibiotic drugs to fight pneumonia then, and Ralph developed the disease in both lungs, ran a high fever, became dehydrated, and died. With deep sadness, I truly miss him, always thinking about the brother that I didn't get an opportunity to know.

Roger was a special baby, my kind of brother! Red hair and blue eyes. He was beautiful. Mama got kidded that he was a woods colt because he was the only redhead in the family. When I left for the Navy on January 2, 1955, he was all boy and grabbing everything. I knew I would miss him. The first thing he wanted to show me when I came home on leave was a baby deer. The game warden at Tapoco fed it milk from a baby bottle and raised it. Some hunter had killed its mother. The spotted fawn ran loose in a fenced lot at the warden's house. Roger and I drove down to the warden's house to see the deer. I made a picture with Roger standing by the deer, and he never forgot that. I loved him, and he gave me a hug and kiss before I left again for my ship. The warden took the deer to Slick Rock Creek and turned him loose so he could run free.

I pushed entrepreneurship early in my life, especially after I bought my first car, forgot about puppy love, and began dating girls. I wanted to look my best and be well-kept for my gal. Gayle and Kay, my beloved sisters, were eager to earn money. Good salesmen promise the world but seldom live up to their end of the sale. I was no different. I bargained with them to shine my shoes and iron my shirts and pants. I offered to pay them 25 cents each. They countered me with 35 cents, explaining that shining shoes and pressing clothes was hard work. After haggling for a while, I made them a final offer of 30 cents. They took it. They did a good job with the work for me but I paid them nothing. They let me know all along that a promise made was a debt unpaid. Years later, I gave Kay the money to pay for her trip to Raleigh with the Beta Club and, off and on, I gave them both a bill with

Lincoln's picture on it. I felt better after that.

Jonnie finished all the requirements for a high

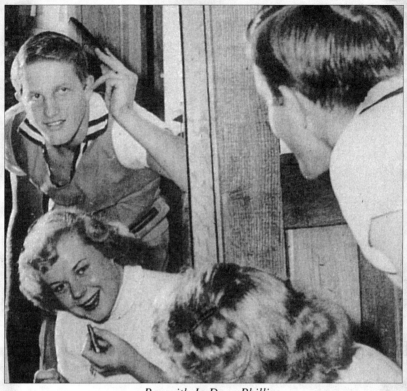

Ray with Jo Dean Phillips

school diploma a year early and began work at Tapaco Lodge when she was fifteen years old. She saved her money for tuition, Marie gave her two hundred dollars to enter college, and her dream to attend Piedmont College in Demorest, Georgia, came true. She had fifteen dollars in her purse when Uncle Claude Eisenhower drove her to Topton Bridge to catch a Trailways Bus to Washington, D.C., to find work. Uncle Claude said to her, "Jonnie, you will be back home in a few days."

"No, I'll not be back to Graham County to live," she answered Uncle Claude. Jonnie found work in Washington and was promoted to manager in her job. I always respected my sister for her independence and earning her own living. Mama and Dad were proud of her for her accomplishments.

I worked hard on the small patches of land growing corn, beans, peas, potatoes, onions, cabbage, carrots, beets and other garden vegetables. I made extra money gathering moss, yellow root, lady slipper, Mayapple plants, and other herbs. Granny Stevenson, a wise woman with long reddish hair who stayed a few days each year with Ma and Pa Carpenter, made medicine from the herbs to treat many diseases for poor people living on Mill Creek. Eller Carpenter, my grandmother whom I called "Ma," had a root cellar. She gave me space to keep some vegetables. One unique way I preserved vegetables was to dig a big hole in the ground with dry straw in the bottom, put the potatoes in the hole, and cover them with about a foot of dirt. I buried turnips and cabbage in a trench with their roots sticking out. This unique method preserved the vegetables for the cold winter months.

Ma was a wonderful teacher. She taught me how to smoke apples with burning sulfur and how to dry green beans for leather breeches. She taught me how to use wooden barrels to preserve pickled beans, kraut, and bleached apples. I helped Mama wash clothes on a scrub board and boil them in a big black pot down by Mill Creek. Mama taught me how to cook hominy and remove the corn husk with red devil lye to leave a delicious white grain of corn. The work ethic and things I learned working and growing up on this small rocky farm and the love that I learned for all of God's beautiful things I grew served me well—and continue to serve me well even today.

I took a bath on Saturday, or when I worked in the fields, in a wooden washtub with warm water heated on a wood-burning stove or by the sun. Mama always got my warm water ready and had big bars of white Ivory soap for me to use at bath time. She left towels, wash cloths, and the Ivory soap in a small storage house next to the house. There was no running water or bathroom in the house.

She made tea from yellow root, sassafras, boneset, and other herbs that helped me when I got sick. "Work never hurt anyone" was an axiom Mama lived by and frequently used to teach me to work. I appreciated her humble expression and teaching more and more as I grew older and worked beside her in the corn and tobacco fields.

Once, I took Tony with me to the cornfield to plow. He was happy when he got to ride the horse with me. I put him under a shade tree when he went to sleep. I forgot him, and the horse almost stepped on him in the high weeds at the end of the corn field by the pipeline on Yellow Creek. I never took him back to plow again.

Ray and Tony

To this day, I still don't know what happened one day when Tony was three years old. He was playing around a little old Model A truck I hauled wood in from the mountain to our woodyard. I came from inside the house and got into the truck to back it up to get another load of wood. I was unaware that Tony was on the other side of the truck. Suddenly, my sisters and Mama were screaming! Tony had fallen off the running board onto the ground on the opposite side of the truck as I was turning the wheel. Some way he ended up under the truck. I never saw him. The wheel missed him and he was unhurt! He was crawling out from under the front axle. Mama and my sisters were crying and looked as pale as ghosts. Mama thanked the Lord that Tony was not killed. I thank the Lord that I didn't accidently kill my brother.

My life was primitive but fun. I read books by kerosene lamps, carried cold water from a spring, drank water from a family dipper, slept on iron beds with metal wire springs using goose-down pillows and feather beds. I slept with three or four of my brothers and sisters in the same bed until the age of accountability. After that, I got my own bed. When my friend came home with me from school, we slept foot to head across the bed like stacked wood. Girls, friends of my sisters, came home with them.I gave them my bed and slept in Mama's room on the floor on a pallet.

Mama was up at four to get Dad off to work. She cooked on a woodstove with a warmer box by a smoky kerosene lamp or candle. She baked big pans of fluffy biscuits and cooked eggs, gravy, ham and streaked meat, a big pan of apples, and big pans of sweet and Irish potatoes. Coffee, milk, and butter were served with jellies, jams, applesauce, and fresh honey. I sat with my brothers and sisters around a long, wooden, homemade table covered with a vinyl cloth. With our hands clasped, we said grace and enjoyed eating together.

One day a truck from a local furniture store in

Robbinsville brought us a new dining table and living room suite. Mama was pleased, and I felt better when company came. Marie bought the furniture so Mama would have something nicer in her house. Dad paid her back for the furniture. She was pleased with her job. She remarked, "Now Papa Orr can't work me to death cooking, hoeing, washing clothes, ironing, and all the other hard work he had me doing for nothing."

She worked four years after she and Dillard were married and before Karen was born. She didn't make much money and Dillard was just getting started with Alcoa. Twenty-eight dollars was taken out of his pay check each month for rent on the little house they first moved into on Yellow Hammer Branch. Marie came to the house on her days off and helped Mama can vegetables. I was always pleased when she came home; she gave me a handful of money when she came.

Pa told me that he worked on a logging job on Squally Creek and said, "My job was to keep the logging camp, feed and water the horses at 4 a.m., and have them ready to work at 7 a.m. I also made the beds and swept the floors. One nasty job I did was to apply kerosene to the bedding to rid the beds of chinch bugs," he continued with a frown on his face. "Um," he shuddered, "I took a drink of likker before and after that job." He winked, "No, I didn't have the wonderful smoky-flavored Scotch whisky the Scots made, or the Irish whiskey made in Ireland, or Bourbon whiskey made in Tennessee and Kentucky to drink, but I drank moonshine likker. It was known around logging camps in Graham as corn-squeezing or pop-skull."

Dad paid less than one hundred dollars on the land-grant debt and nothing for a house that was on the property on Mill Creek. The sons all had agreed to pay their portion of the debt owed on the land to the state. A land-grant marker visible on a large tree, now rotten and gone, below Uncle Floyd's old house, marked the metes and bounds, a humble way of life, and a pioneer beginning for my family.

Dad, Mama, and Leonard, after leaving the ford on Cochran Creek, moved into the small house located below Pa's house on Mill Creek that Floyd and Ardell had lived in. Gone now is a wisp of blue smoke from the wood stoves of Uncle Floyd's hand-hewn house; gone, too, are the men who used the axe, froe, crosscut saw, notch and mortise, tenon, joist and rive to build the pioneer house. Sounds of children playing in the yard; the smell of cornbread, fried potatoes, clay peas, and collard greens; and the warmth and love that came from the old house still reminds me about the simple and beautiful lives who once lived there. It was like a grandmother with lilacs for her purple-ribbon bows. Its upper window, in the alcove, was square like spectacles. Most of all a look, as if it watched the old dirt road running up Mill Creek for someone, gone so long ago that only they remember who it was and why they waited there patiently all day.

Gone now is the dusty, rutted, dirt road that I walked down and crossed Mill Creek on a narrow log foot bridge in front of Ross Wiggins' house to catch the school bus where it turned around at a large pine tree about half way up Mill Creek. I watched for a shadowy figure, a crippled man, in the window of the Wiggins house. He would sometimes chase my two beautiful sisters, Marie and Ruby, when they were teens and frighten them when they were walking home after school, up Mill Creek and past his house. I can still hear his manic laughter as I walked by the front door of the house. I caught glimpses of Ross, his dad, but walked on home in trepidation. No one was really sure about his mind or stability. He wore high-top leather boots with his trouser legs stuffed in them during summer and winter with the laces drawn extremely tight. His actions were disjointed. He had frayed nerves. His speech was jerky and broken. Shivers ran through me one day when Ross stepped out from behind a tree in his yard, laid his shaking hand on my shoulder and said, in a trembling voice, "Here's an apple for you."

In a frightened voice, I said, "No, No," and I ran all the way home. Ross had served years for killing his father and was out of prison on parole.

Later, as I grew up, I was blessed with more sisters and brothers, and we moved into a larger house above Uncle Clay's house. The old dirt road ran behind his house, and a log foot bridge crossed Mill Creek over to my house. Rain, snow and ice made the rough-hewn log foot bridge slick, but I never fell into the creek.

Sometimes Ruby and I got off the school bus where Mill Creek and Tallulah roads intersect and went to Fred Martin's small grocery store to buy saltine crackers and peanut butter so we didn't have to pack biscuits and jelly for our school lunch every day. I pointed to the Tastee candy bars, and Fred put a quarter's worth in a small brown bag and handed them to me. My favorite soda was NuGrape, and Ruby bought me some peanuts to put in the bottle. I shook it and it always spewed out, much to my dismay.

At that time, Columbus Anderson and his family lived in the last house on Mill Creek; the Jackson and Wilson families had lived there before Anderson. The Anderson family moved out, the small clapboard house rotted and crumbled over time, but parts of it continued to stand in a dilapidated condition for years.

My last year in elementary school, I was looking

SCHOOL DAY
1942-43

through an old picture box upstairs and found inside it a small matchbox that contained a black and white first-grade photo from my 1942-43 school year; wearing bib overalls. There was also a picture of the old house. Stuffed into the corner of the match-box, I also found a small, crumpled piece of old, lined, tablet paper with verses scribbled on it in a handwriting so peculiar that it seemed as if the writer might have taken lessons by studying the famous fossil bird tracks in the Pyramids of ancient Egypt. The date was un-readable, but it was my handwriting. And, in one corner of the crumpled paper was a legible note which read: "For Mrs. Blankenship's Fourth Grade English class, at 10:00 a.m., September 8, 1945." A talent I had always wanted to find, long ago, so long ago. A talent anchored in the harbor of my dream. But, now at last, it's no longer long ago, and my dream came true.

The old writing on the crumpled paper I found was one of my earlier attempts at writing scribbles. A simple title, a simple scribble:

No More...

Raindrops beat a steady,
pat-patty-pat-pat
on the shutters of my memory,
a vine tangled path,
led to a crumbling old house,
unkempt yard imprisoned,
by a rusty lock and chain,
beyond a fallen woodshed,
two crumbling barns form
 a triangle,
I close my eyes to hold
the scene: only silence,
no cows chewing their cuds
stand with locked knees,
puffing steam,
no children cried,
no butterflies repaired,
no flowers leaned
upon fences...
after the rain.

Many times I picked blackberries from the briers that grew up around the old garden and potato patch. I was always curious as to why everyone left the old house to rot. After all the years, there was still the homey smell. When I turned the small, crumpled piece of old, lined, tablet paper over, I found another scribble in my handwriting so faded that I had to guess at when it was written. Perhaps it was written when I was in the fifth grade because I could see a particlular word, Denton. If that is accurate, I wrote the scribble in 1946 for an English class. Blain Denton, my fifth-grade teacher, never marked my paper. I can only speculate that the date is correct. This time, a simpler scribble with a simpler title, a doggerel rhyme, but somehow a beautiful effort for a young scribbler.

This Old House

Be of brick, wood or stone,
this old house heard many a song,
from a bird on distant tree,
come to it faith, hope and charity,
with the shutters old and gray,
and the paint that faded away,
nails are drawn from boards askew,
leaks come with the morning dew,
windows are broken by boys at play,
steps have rotted from many a day,
each board, each nail played, it's part ,
played it well, until the smell,
the homey smell was gone.

Mama sent me there one hot morning to pick her a bucket of berries to make jam. I wanted to stay home and play. When I got to the berry field, I gathered maple leaves and filled my bucket, but picked enough berries to cover the leaves and round out the top of the bucket. My play time was cut short that day. Mama called me inside the house, handed me the bucket, and smiled warmly as she said, "Maple leaf jam is not what I had in mind. Go fill the bucket with blackberries so I can make blackberry jam." I minded her and left for the berry patch to pick blackberries. I gathered no more maple leaves that day.

An Act of Kindness I Never Forgot

When I was young, I stayed with Papa and Mama Orr during the summer until school began in the fall. I slept on a small rollout bed with a straw mattress and feather pillow in their living room. From my bed I could look into their bedroom. Every night I watched Papa Orr blow out the oil lamp and get down on his knees beside the bed. He crossed his hands on his mattress and laid his head on his hands. He prayed silently, without moving, for what seemed like hours. He prayed feverently for his two sons fighting in Germany and Japan in World War II. I tried to stay awake to see how long he prayed—my prayers never took longer than a minute to finish and I wanted to know how much I was missing the mark—but I always fell asleep before Papa Orr said Amen.

One night I woke up out of a scary dream and saw Papa Orr still on his knees beside the bed. I didn't know how much time had passed but felt as if I had traveled a great distance through the middle of the night. Mama Orr slept softly. The windows were bright with starlight. The ghostly outlines of the leafy, summer trees were sharp against the sky; the rich, country dark rattled with the rhythmic natter of insects.

Papa Orr, I knew, was dead.

I have never been more scared of anything. I was terrified, and didn't know what to do. I had never seen a dead person so close. I wanted to wake up Papa Orr but was afraid to pass by Mama Orr in the dark. I opened my mouth to call out, but the darkness swallowed up whatever small sound I thought about making. I clasped my hands together underneath my chin and prayed, forming the words inside my head but not saying them out loud, "Please God, don't let Papa Orr be dead. Please don't let Mama Orr be dead."

I had prayed no more than a minute when Papa straightened up. He put his hands flat against the mattress and stiffly pushed himself to his feet. He turned and looked into the living room at me. His face glowed faintly in the darkness; it changed and moved as I squinted at it. His mouth and eyes twisted into a smile. I jerked the sheet over my head, terrified by what I had done, by the power I had called down out of the night with a prayer.

Papa Orr was the first preacher I remember clearly, and I remember him fondly as one of the best. I used his table blessing as I was called upon to say the blessing at mealtime. Children bowed their heads, held each other's hands, formed a circle around our table, and I said:

"Lord, we thank you for all our blessings and graces. Bless this food to the nourishment of our bodies and bless the hands that prepared it. In Christ's name we pray, Amen"

His prayers were special to me because he always called my name when he prayed for me. He came to our house for dinner the night before I left home to join the United States Navy and prayed to the Lord, petitioning God to watch over me, forgive me for my sins and bring me safely back home.

God did that for me and much more. He was with me in my loneliness as I sailed two and a half times around the world aboard the USS Coral Sea and the USS Midway, two aircraft carriers that I served on during my enlistment in the Navy. His prayers helped me remember to pray, and God was the difference in my getting home safely for my twenty-first birthday.

Papa Orr, taught to read by his devoted wife, Hester Ann, "Het," as he affectionately called her, had a strong impact upon religious life in Graham County and upon my life growing up. When he began preaching, he had to support his wife and children by farming on his small rocky hillside farm on Cochran Creek. He rigged a book support between the handles of his plow so he could read his Bible when he gave Nip and Tip, his favorite team of horses, a rest under a shade tree at the end of the furrows. He read Psalms extensively and normally opened his homily with a verse or two from Psalms. His homilies came across with all the poetry and force that the King James Version of the Bible could give them. He preached with such vigor and zeal that everyone who heard his messages liked his preaching.

For many years, the offering was all the pastor received, and sometimes it was only a few dollars. There was always a collection plate at the church, but never much in it. At the end of the church year, members of the Board of Stewards visited everyone in the community who went to church only during revivals, or for all-day singing and dinner on the ground, or not at all. Members of the Board made their case that it was good for a community to have a church. Some money was collected that way.

It was recognized that the pastor might have to take a hand in raising his own pay. Papa Orr was not a paid pastor until several years after he started preaching, but he served as pastor of churches in Graham County and elsewhere continuously for little or no pay through all those years.

One of my favorite things to do when I was growing up was to spend time with Papa Orr. He kept peppermint sticks, orange slices, and circus peanuts in an old work coat pocket for us to eat when we were working in the field.

My journal entry on March 6, 1945, only twelve days before my tenth birthday, reflected that today, "A cold wind cuts like a knife and whistles and tiny round blue balls of snow flies." Papa Orr and I geared up Nip and Tip, put the flip-wing turning plow on the farm wagon, and went to one of his acres that had to be plowed that day.

After we plowed a few rounds, Lazarus Seller, a small, gaunt man who lived up the hollow above Papa Orr's house came up holding his broken plow point. His bib overalls were worn thin; his old shirt was ripped and tattered. Shivering and almost in tears, he said, "Now I have no plow to finish plowing my garden, no transportation to go get it welded, and no money to buy another plow point."

Immediately, Papa Orr handed Lazarus his coat, unhitched his team, loaded his plow on his wagon and gave the lines to Lazarus and said, "Here take my team and plow your garden." Papa Orr's act of generosity and kindness impressed me and was used in his eulogy. Lazarus told me later that he would never forget the act of kindness as long as he lived. I never forgot it.

I helped Mama Orr with chores around the house. I always got into uncomfortable situations as I worked, and some of the situations were dangerous! I respected her and the time she took to help me learn. She could have saved time by doing many of the chores herself that she let me help her with and going on with her busy work day.

I learned to milk Bessie, one of the six Guernsey cows on the farm. Mama Orr asked me to milk Bessie because of her quiet and gentle nature while she milked other cows that were not as well-behaved. One evening at milking time, I found myself sitting on the milking stool with legs spread out and my bare feet extended under Bessie's hind quarters. I washed her utter, and, with my gallon milk pail ready, began filling it with milk. Bessie was her same gentle self, eating her bran food and munching hay. I almost had the pail full. Suddenly, Bessie turned her head, and licked my toes. I wiggled my toes, and p-o-w! Bessie kicked the pail so hard the pail went upside down, milk poured out on my head, and ran to the soles of my feet. Mama Orr saved a little milk as she caught the pail. As she gathered up the pail and me, she said, in a calm voice, "Bessie thought your toes were a snake when she licked them."

The Maytag washing machine had the swing out roller wringers with a forward and reverse gear. One day when I was helping Mama Orr wash clothes on her new Maytag, I came close to losing my arm. As I fed the wet clothes between the wringers, I held on to them so long that my hand continued, with a lot of pressure and pain, through the wringers.

I screamed!

Mama Orr panicked. She didn't know how the release on the rollers worked, and my arm ran up to the shoulder and kept grinding as the rollers continued to roll. I was wet with sweat and faint from pain and exhaustion. I continued to weakly scream! Instead of releasing the wringer rollers, Mama Orr reversed it and my already black and blue arm was further crushed before it finally rolled out.

I fainted. Papa Orr ran from the tobacco field, doused me with rubbing alcohol and used water to bring me back to consciousness. He smiled at Mama

Orr and me and said, "Just release the infernal rollers the next time it happens."

Mama Orr simply said, "Yes," but continued cutely, "...the clothes are washed and ready to dry."

Mama Orr put on her old straw hat, grabbed a basket from the kitchen and in an inviting tone, said to me, "It's time to make lunch, and you and I need to go to the garden and gather vegetables for lunch."

I went a few rows over and began to pull carrots, pick bell peppers, and pull up green onions. She asked me to also gather several small yellow squash, little white cucumbers, crinkly lettuce, and tommy-toe tomatoes to make a salad. I was having fun gathering the vegetables!

Mama Orr was squatted down, picking bunch beans at the lower end of the garden. Suddenly she sprang up, twisted her dress into a small sack and ran to the end of the garden where rocks were piled. She quickly squatted down and frantically grabbed a rock, placed the small sack she had made with her dress tail on another rock, and began pounding it until a big hole appeared and blood showed through her dress. By the time I got to her, she was pale and exhausted. The long-tail silver and blue dragon lizard, which normally ran the wood-panels around the garden, ran up the wrong dress tail and was now pulp. Laughing, I said, "Mama Orr, you got 'em that time, didn't you?"

Just at dusk one summer evening, Papa Orr fed his hound dogs all of the leftover cornbread, along with their other food, without telling Mama Orr. She asked him on several occasions not to feed his dogs leftovers, especially the leftover cornbread. "Family or friends may come to visit us," she told him. She looked out the living-room window that evening and pointed to people making their way to their house.

"Oliver, who is that coming to our house this late?" she inquired, with a concerned expression.

Knowing the truth, that he had fed all the leftovers and cornbread to his dogs, he dejectedly said, "Why, Het, that looks like my brother, John, and his family." He realized they would be ready for a meal and Het would work hard to put a meal with cornbread on the table for them that late at night. He felt guilty for the thing he had done to cause her the extra work.

The Great War had just started. Men were being drafted by the thousands. Gardner Williams and Papa Orr had grown up together and were the best of friends. Gardner did not believe in war. "Killing people is not the right thing to do," he said. He was a conscientious objector and asked Papa Orr for a place to hide. For months and months when I visited Papa and Mama Orr, I was not permitted to go into their attic. Gardner lived upstairs in a dim little room and came down only for meals. Gardner was never caught, and after the Great War was over, I knew the reason I could not go upstairs at Papa Orr's house. The Federal Agents who searched for Gardner never found him, and Papa Orr was always afraid he would serve time for harboring a fugitive.

Front row: Roger, Tony; Second row: Gayle, Kay, Marie
Third Row: Ruby, Shirley, Jonnie, Charlotte, Leonard, Ray
Standing: Rilla Carpenter, Henry Carpenter

Henry Carpenter at homeplace

Oliver Orr—"Papa Orr"
Hester (Het) "Mama Orr"

Eller Carpenter—"Ma"
Authur Carpenter—"Pa"

Henry Carpenter
as a young man

Ray Carpenter with dad
Henry Carpenter

A Scarlet Rose

Today I plucked a scarlet rose
From the moist springtime sod
I saw the beauty of the flower
And knew it came from God

I saw His sculpture in the stem
As I'd never seen it before
I saw fine art in every thorn
In every leaf it bore

I saw every
soft red petal
And then I began
to recall

Each was painted by
the Master of Art
The Maker of flowers
...and all

I Had Very Little

I had very little when I was growing up, but I never felt poor. I was never hungry, cold, or without clothes. I had the opportunity to finish high school and work my way through college, for which I am grateful.

My lunch in elementary school was two biscuits: one was a peanut butter and jelly and the other one was side meat or, sometimes, country ham. Mama packed it in a Dixie Crystal Sugar bag and soon greasy spots showed through. I was embarrassed and went behind the coat closet to eat my lunch so no one saw the greasy spots. I folded the bag, put it in my pocket and carried it back home so Mama had a bag to pack my lunch for school the next day.

I had good clothes to wear to church and work clothes. I put on work clothes and hung my good clothes up for Sunday. Both wore thin over time, and I wore bib overalls with a patch sewed on a patch and another patch sewed on that patch.

At Christmastime, as I grew up, we made popcorn strings and cut paper rings to hang on our Christmas tree, the top of a pine tree that I brought in the house and nailed a wooden stand to the bottom so it would stand up. We received no play pretties or toys. Maybe, if we were fortunate, we received an apple or orange. Ms. Boyd brought a handmade rag doll or two and gave them to my sisters. One Christmas, Dad played Santa Claus for us and wore Mama's old straw hat as part of his Santa suit. I was pleased when he brought me a pair of Dee Cee trousers, but I recognized Mama's old straw hat, and after that Christmas, I didn't believe in Santa Claus any more. Not believing in Santa Claus was good for me. I didn't want grown-ups laughing at me because I was afraid of Santa Claus and wet my pants sometimes. Grown-ups never understand anything by themselves, and it was exhausting for me, as a little boy, to provide explanations about Santa Claus over and over again for their entertainment. Perhaps, as time moves forward, grown-ups will become more enlightened and find creative ways, rather than scaring children, to find laughter.

Another Christmas, money was scarce. The wind blew hard as Dad walked up Mill Creek Road to our house that day. He was moving his last five-dollar bill from one pocket to another, along with some change, when the bill blew out of his hand and was gone. He never saw the money again. He had no more money to buy anything for Christmas that year. He cried when he told Mama; then they both cried together. I cried when I received nothing for Christmas that year.

Uncle Clay Carpenter made me a whistle out of corn shucks and taught me how to blow a tune on a corn blade. I adored my Uncle Clay, with his warm smile and funny stories. He came to kill our fattened hogs, when frost walked down from high peaks. He asked Mama to cook fresh tenderloin and hot biscuits for lunch. He drank his coffee black, scalding hot. He wanted rice pudding for dessert. He took fresh ground sausage and ham home with him as payment for his work.

Uncle Clay smoked a lot. It was always a mystery to me how he rolled his cigarette, with one hand, from a small drawstring tobacco pouch from which he shook Old Gold smoking tobacco into a thin cigarette paper with his forefinger, rolled and licked the cigarette, and put it in his mouth to light, all in a single motion. He handed me one of his quirely (cigarettes). I was around fourteen years old, and this was the first time I smoked a cigarette. Cigarette experimentation was as much a part of a 1940s boy's life as Western movies. I didn't like to smoke and never took up the habit after trying Uncle Clay's quirely cigarette.

My parents were neither rich nor famous as the world or Hollywood judges, but their lives were rich and full. Their beginnings were primitive and humble but their spirit never faltered. They accepted the responsibility of daily living with integrity and courage. The true values they taught me and my eleven siblings helped us to grow up with a sense of responsibility. During many years of their marriage, they worked hard and had few of life's luxuries. But even in the most difficult years, they found time enough to bring a richer spirit to me and my brothers and sisters. I appreciated what I had because Dad and Mama sacrificed to give it to me. As I grew older, I worked hard and bought things for myself. I bought my first car, a 1952 blue Custom Ford, my junior year in high school and paid for it with money I earned.

I immortalized my blue Ford in a scribble for my English teacher, Mrs. F.S. Hooper, that year. She read it aloud to the class. I was pleased but felt awkward because of its quality.

Run, Blue Ford, Run...

Where roads unwind,
Like a twist of twine,
Streams swell banks,
Fall flowers fringe,
Village water tanks.
Run blue Ford run,
Leave time behind,
Sunshine and shadow,
Clear rill,
Brown bough,
Nothing is real,
But the here and now.

70

My scribble hasn't sold, but then I haven't submitted it to a publisher. Neither did I give it to any of my girlfriends. Dad maintained the Ford for me during my hitch in the Navy, and I used it during my years in college.

One true sacrifice Mama made for me was to sell eggs to buy my college class ring. I still have the ring and it is a fond memory of Mama that I cherish. I wear the ring on days when she and I enjoyed special moments shared together. During one of the special moments, she laughed and told me that she always wanted me to finish college so I would have a better way to reach my goals in life than she had. My ring, she said, was proof that I had accomplished what she wanted for me most.

I was the paddling-end of fear when I was growing up. Dad used fear to discipline me. His favorite expression was, "I'll jerk a knot in your tail." Many times he did jerk a knot in my tail! He didn't spare the rod. Sometimes he spanked me with his open hand, sometimes he used a paddle. Other times, he sent me outside to cut and bring in a hickory switch, which he used when I made too much noise or neglected a chore. He always gave me another whipping when I got one at school.

Ultimate humility occurred when Dad "thumped" me on the head with his thumb and said, "Be quiet or I will jerk a knot in your tail." I shivered and became quiet. About all he had to do was look askance at me with a frown on his face. The whipping-to-end-all-whippings I got was when I used my pocket knife to cut the bark on Pa Carpenter's sweet apple tree and skinned it down to the roots causing it to rot and die. That whipping I will never forget.

One day I decided to use Dad's straight razor,

the bone-handle one he liked the best of the three that he kept above the washpan with his shaving mug, to whittle a pop gun I was making. When he started to shave the next day, he knew who dulled his razor and I got a few lashings with the leather strap that he used to hone his razors.

Mama used a different method of discipline. To keep me out of trouble, she rewarded me with a twist of taffy she made from white Karo syrup or gave me jelly and bread when I minded her. Her favorite expression was, "Son, you mind me now." I minded her.

I was notorious when I got hungry...and I got hungry often! I pulled at Mama's dresstail when I was a little boy growing up, jumped up and down, kicked, cried, and screamed, shouting for milk and bread. Mama always stopped what she was doing and got me some. It was almost like she rewarded bad behavior but she called it a tradeoff and it worked for me, her blond-haired boy.

As I grew up, she taught me to believe in myself and to understand that real growth comes from within. She continued her philosophizing strain enthusiastically, "Of all the simple motivations, inspirational motivation is often the most difficult but gets the longest-lasting results because it comes from within you." She continued, "Fear is effective as long as the source of the fear is present, but as soon as it is removed, so is the desired improvement," she gestured with her slim finger. Mama smiled as she said, "Reward is effective as long as the reward lasts. Everyone likes a payincrease for a job well done, a pat on the back or a stick of taffy, but when the reward is gone, so is the better result. Everyone is different, just as each of my twelve children are different. What works for one doesn't necessarily work for the other. Sometimes a combination of fear, reward, and inspirational motivation works best. One of my children wanted gravy and biscuits, another one of them wouldn't eat it. One drank buttermilk, another one wouldn't touch it. I learned quickly that I had to use different combinations to get the desired results I wanted from each child," she said, as she continued smiling her sweet smile.

One of the things I learned early in life from Mama was to do things right the first time and in the least amount of time. "Get everything ready before you try to complete a task," she insisted. "Do the task. When you are not satisfied with your work, do it over, don't wait. Finally," she concluded, "put away the things you use to complete the task. Putting things back in their proper places is most important for the next task. When things are put away properly, it saves time that can be applied to the Do step," she mused. Make Ready, Do, and Put Away are the "task busters" I learned from Mama. I kept my room neat and orderly using the task busters when I was growing up. I still use them today.

Mom

Dad was a natural shooter. I've seen him shoot his twenty-two rifle and knock bumble bees out of the air while they were standing still near the top of an old clay-daubed chimney. I saw him make dimes, nickels, and quarters disappear when I flipped them up for him to shoot. He was a gifted shooter! I saw him kill a grey squirrel in midair with the same twenty-two rifle- when it jumped from a high hickory tree.

On Thanksgiving Day one year, I saw him win

the target shoot with the rifle six times. I was pleased when he gave the turkeys to needy families, except for two. He was a skilled pistol shot and won many competitions shooting targets over the years. Normally, he used a six-inch barrel twenty-two pistol to shoot targets, but I have seen him shoot from his hip and hit a target with a .38 special Smith and Wesson.

Dad

Early one Saturday morning, Dad told me that a slow drizzle made for good pheasant hunting. The leaves were already coming down and were a little damp. He promised to take me pheasant hunting that evening. A narrow arroyo at the head of Mill Creek was loaded with wild blue grapes that fall and the "ring necks" liked to fly in late in the evening to feed on them.

Dad and I were there hidden behind some ivy and mountain laurel when the grouse began to fly in to eat the grapes. We waited patiently until the grouse were busy eating. I threw a large piece of wood into the grape ravine to get them to rise. He opened up with his Browning Automatic sixteen-gauge shotgun and shot dead six grouse on the wing. He quickly reloaded and killed four more as they were rising, without missing a shot. He stuffed them all in his duck-back hunting coat and said, "Good hunting, son," as we left the grouse blind to go home. He dressed the grouse and gave Uncle Claude Eisenhower five and kept six for himself. I missed three times with my twenty-gauge shotgun but killed one grouse on the wing.

One afternoon as Dad was coming home from work up Highway 129 from Tapoco, dogs had a

Russian boar backed into a corner of the old rock quarry. Dad jumped out of his pickup truck, grabbed a claw hammer from the truck, and hissed the dogs to catch the boar. He grabbed it by the ear and killed it with the hammer. I was watching out the old pickup truck window and was scared stiff the boar would take his hand off! Gardner Birchfield, a local preacher and a friend, stopped to watch Dad kill the boar and, with his warm and friendly smile said, "Henry, I was praying for you just now."

Dad liked to make money in strange ways. In the spring, when fish hawks were plentiful along the Cheoah River, he got into the back of his pickup truck with his automatic shotgun and asked me to drive slowly down the river road. Some hawks he killed on the wing and others he shot out of trees. They plummeted into the woods and into the water, but wherever they fell, he got them. He cut off their beaks with his pocket knife, put them in a bag and sold them to the Wildlife Association in Robbinsville for the going price that year.

Another way he liked to make money was to dig ginseng he found growing wild in the mountains. He dried and sold it for a few dollars per pound. He was pleased there would always be a market for the forked roots of this plant believed to have medicinal properties. He grinned and said, "Some people think that ginseng is an aphrodisiac that arouses and increases sexual de-sire. If it does that, the market for it will last longer than I will last," he shrugged. Sometimes I went with Dad to hunt and dig ginseng but never learned to recognize it among all the other wild plants. Dad could spot it at a great distance, and that won him the nickname Ole Gin-seng. Ralph Zingline, a German engineer who worked at Tapoco with Dad, was fascinated by the plant and ac-companied Dad many times when he went on ginseng digs. He finally learned to recognize the plant when it got red berries in the fall of the year. Ralph also had a degree in botany and made meticulous drawings of hundreds of the wild plants growing in the mountains, including ginseng.

A unique way Dad got paid for loads of tan bark he peeled from oak and hemlock trees and hauled on a truck to Andrews Tanning Mills to sell was doogaloo tokens. He was rarely paid in real currency for anything then because of a depressed economy. Doogaloo was a substitute for real money with a lower value than green dollars. A 25-cent doogaloo token was worth 18 cents, and it had to be traded at the same store from which it was issued. This method of exchange was used in the 1930s and into the 1940s. Dad worked hard peeling tan bark and was paid very few doogaloo tokens for an entire truck load of it.

A simple way Dad earned extra money was to catch spring lizards and sell them to fishermen for 25 cents per dozen. He got an extra five cents for a red salamander. He put damp moss in the bucket and punched holes in the gallon lard bucket with the green and white clover leaves so the lizards could breathe and stay alive until he sold them. He also collected scrap metal of all kinds and sold it at the junk yard in Murphy to earn extra dollars. Copper brought the highest price, so he always was searching for scrap copper metal.

The thing Dad liked to do best was to trade guns and knives. He was good at it and was the richer man at the end of a deal most of the time. For my fourteenth birthday, he brought me a new western carbine twenty-two special pump action Winchester rifle with a hammer. It was a beautiful gun. I became a marksman with it. It was part of my soul! He suddenly sold it. A special gun and my favorite gift from him gone at a whim! I was angry at him for selling my gun without letting me know. I'll say that again, "I was very angry because he traded my gun and didn't bother to tell me!" I never forgave him for that.

One morning Dad bolted into Mama's hospital room during her long illness and said, "Rilla, I sold the fatten hog today."

Mama, in a sad voice asked him, "Why in the world did you do a thing like that?" Her voice was weak, but she continued, "I grew the hog to share with my children."

Family members were angry with him. They didn't understand his behavior. "He didn't need the money for the hog," they mumbled.

His behavior always puzzled me, but I never disowned him. After all, he was a special person, a dad who loved me. He never bought me a bicycle I wanted or tennis shoes that I needed to play basketball. He said those were foolish things. I got to play football in high school because Mama insisted. Dad was afraid I would get hurt. He never came to any of my games. He never read the scriptures to me or said goodnight prayers for me or taught me to swim. He never put me to bed, read me stories, hugged me, or changed my diaper. He never offered to let me use his car. Mama saw to it that I got to use the car. She asked him to let me use it when I got old enough to drive and go courting. He listened to Mama and sought her advice and intuition.

I could never repay him for the many things he taught me and did for me and for the places he took me. He was special to me in so many ways. A great dad in his own way. He did let me use his pocket knife, which he kept razor sharp, to whittle. I still have a scar on my right thumb that I put there with his pocket knife. It reminds me daily of my love for him. He took me to the movies on Friday nights at Tapoco. Many of the movies were westerns. I saw *High Noon* there starring Gary Cooper and Grace Kelly. It made such an impression on me that I watch repeats of it periodically, even now. He made sure that I always had food to eat, shoes to wear and a warm bed to sleep in. He joked with me and said, "I've got to keep a roof over your head."

Dad was a simple, guileless, childlike man, content to live in Graham County where his life began. He was strong living there on his native grounds, his world of sight and sound. He told me about the bear and deer he shot and about the trout and pheasant eggs he got. Little things he did for me helped shape my life. Many times as I was growing up, he said, "Son, you are a good boy, you never give me any trouble." Confidence and self-worth were important to him and me. He helped me build both.

When I was a baby, he took me to Donald Orr, a seventh son. Donald had the power to heal. He blew in my mouth to heal the thrush! It worked! He took me to Dr. Dick Parrette's office in Robbinsville often so he could clean an aching ear and stop the infection of an eardrum perforated from birth. My dreams were dashed when Dr. Parrette told me that my loss of hearing would prevent me from becoming a naval aviator and flying a jet from an aircraft carrier.

One of the folk medicines that Dad used for my asthma was asafetida. I wore it around my neck. It smelled so bad that Mama kept me out of school for the first year of my eligibility so other children couldn't make fun of me. My asthma attacks were so intense Mama let me sleep with her and Dad for an extra year so she could doctor my wheezing and choking. She was afraid that I would die in the night. I finally grew out of the asthma attacks and took off the asafetida. Everyone at my house was pleased that I smelled better.

With his pocket knife, Dad cut a small stick, fit it inside my shoe, and measured my foot so he could buy me the proper size of shoes. He practiced his simple way of doing things as long as he lived, and it served him well. I was happy with my new shoes that fit. How he measured my foot for them was less important.

I was pleased when he took me with him to Andrews to buy new denim bib overalls and shirts for school. He parked his truck on the main street of Andrews and got out; I followed him a block into a dry cleaner. I was curious! I knew we never used a dry cleaner, even in Robbinsville. I remained silent. He told the owner that he was looking for a coat to fit a little girl ten years old and noticed there were many coats hanging there. The owner smiled and said, "We clean coats here but don't sell them." Turning on his heel to leave, Dad said in a bewildered voice, "Well, skin it back," and quickly walked out. Since then, I have walked in and out of a few wrong doors myself but I never said, "Well, skin it back." I wasn't sure what it meant and didn't want to say the wrong thing.

Later, I knew why Dad always stopped at the Bloody Bucket, a honky-tonk near Topton, on our way back to Robbinsville and always had a brown paper bag in his old coat pocket as he returned to his truck. He liked beer and enjoyed a drink now and then. He kept a few bottles of beer under the cold water at the spring-house branch below our house. To cover his breath, he chewed Sen-Sen, a breath freshener that melted in his mouth. He always brought me stick candy in a small paper bag as he returned to the truck, so I didn't bother to ask him what he had in the brown paper bag in his old coat pocket. Mama never let him bring beer into the house or drink it in front of his family. When he slept, he made a puffing sound, like a purring with his lips. He dipped snuff, chewed tobacco, and smoked an occasional cigar. One day I saw him dipping, chewing, and smoking at the same time. When I asked him why he was doing all three at the same time, he said, in an annoyed voice, "I've got to keep the price up of the damn stuff some way."

I had fun when Dad dropped me off at streams and lakes so I could go fishing. I grew up poor, and my equipment was simple. I never had much, but I was grateful I had some. In my old fishing hat band, I stuck different sizes of hooks. I had no fly rod, fly hooks, or flashing spinner baits to use from a fancy tackle box when I was fishing in trout streams. I had no spinning reel or fiberglass rod for lake fishing. Instead I used a cane pole and a plain hook baited with spring lizards, night crawlers, or grubs from a wasp or hornet nest. Fish, as it is well known, don't know the difference in a cane pole or a fancy pole. They bite anyway. Most of the time, I caught my limit. I used whatever I had to catch fish, but I wanted to give the fish a fair chance and never used low charges of dynamite to stun fish enough to reach into the water and get them. I didn't use trot lines or floating jugs. Again, I wanted to give the fish a fair chance to get away.

"Boy, you laid them out today," Dad said excitedly, as I got into his truck with my string of trout and bass. Dad was pleased when I did well at anything and encouraged me with positive remarks. Dad and I always agreed to meet after my fishing outings at a particular place and time so I didn't get lost on trout streams far in the mountains. He was always there on time at the place agreed upon. We relied on each other's word since cell phones were not invented yet.

One summer when I was about fifteen years old,

Dad and I packed a bag lunch and walked to the Hooper Bald, a mountain peak rising over a mile in elevation in Graham County. He took me there to see the strange writing on a rock that he had seen when his Dad took him there years before. The writing reads, "Perdarms Casada." I still wonder what it means and what tool was used in 1615 to etch the words in solid granite. More writing was written on the rock below ground but we didn't dig away the dirt to see it. Dad and I ate our lunch at the rock and left to return home. A yellow rattlesnake, four and a half feet long with fifteen rattles and a button, lay coiled and ready to strike when I bent over to get a drink of water from a spring along the trail. Before the snake could bite me, Dad shot its eyes out with an automatic pistol he carried on walks in the woods. I pulled the rattlers off and put them in my pocket.

One of the things I wanted to do when I was growing up was to look for the legendary DeLozier Silver Mine in Graham County. Neddy DeLozier was said to have known the actual location of the mine; he died, taking the secret with him. Neddy was born in 1803 and was the son of Jessie DeLozier and Alsey Fields DeLozier. Neddy was the great-grandfather of Homer Constance, who lived on Gladdens Creek and was a distant relative of the late Martin DeLozier, who owned DeLozier's Drug Store in Robbinsville. In 1983, Martin DeLozier presented a DeLozier family history book to Homer which contained references to Neddy and listed Homer as a great-grandson.

Arkie Orr, who lived in the Orr Mountains near the Slick Rock Creek area, told about a man who would spend the night at their cabin on occasion. He would carry sacks of something that resembled rocks on his return trip. No one ever questioned him. Everyone practiced hospitality in those days. As was the custom, he was accepted and welcomed. It is thought that this man was Neddy DeLozier. Neddy was said to have had a silver-dollar mold and would mint silver coins to pay property taxes and buy necessities. He would go to the mine for silver only as needed and would not keep much of it on hand for fear of being robbed.

One story goes that my grandfather, Oliver Orr, and his father, Bart Orr, once cut a tree that had a turtle and snake carved on it. This was supposed to have been a directional tree marking the way to the silver mine. Papa Orr told me that he didn't believe the legend was true and didn't spend time looking for the silver mine.

Homer Constance and his daughter Dorothea also looked for the mine for many years without locating it. One legend says that from the mine entrance, the Little Tennessee River was visible in four places. Another story said seven places.

Neddy DeLozier married Elizabeth Poindexter on May 24, 1834. She is said to be buried in Swain County. Neddy was apparently as elusive and secretive in death as he was in life since no one seems to know for sure where he is buried. Some say he is buried beside his wife in an unmarked grave. Others say he is buried on Tuskegee. Wherever he is buried, the secret of the DeLozier Silver Mine is buried with him. I never got to search for the silver mine.

Hardy Sharp, a barber in Robbinsville, shaved Dad's whiskers and cut his hair each Saturday and dowsed his head with tonic and other good smelling stuff. I watched a Western movie at the old Chic Theater on Main Street while I waited for Dad. Before we left town, he bought me a Coca-Cola and a Moon Pie at Patton Phillips grocery store. These times with Dad were special, and I enjoyed being with him.

When he wasn't working, Dad was always on the go somewhere but stayed only a few minutes before he was ready to leave. He was impatient and never respected the person who was with him who might have wanted to stay longer. Mama always got frustrated when he took her to visit her parents on Cochran Creek. Sometimes he said, "Rilla, it's time to go," even before she had time to sit down.

When he went somewhere, he was up at four a.m. and arrived before the place opened. One Saturday morning in 1942, when World War II was at its peak and times were hard, Dad got me up at an early hour to go to Maryville, Tennessee, with him. We were riding in his old Model A Ford, crossing the mountain from North Carolina into Tennessee on a curvy fifteen-mile stretch of road now known as the Dragon Tail. Hairpin curves prevented our speed exceeding much over twelve miles per hour. Suddenly, out of the dark in a deep curve up over a bank, came three men wearing old ragged coats, sloppy hats, and long whiskers matted in snuff and tobacco spit. They jumped right in front of the car. Dad had to stop. Two men came up on my side of the car carrying short pieces of steel pipe. The one that came up on Dad's side of the car had a long blade knife in hand and a deep scar running down from his ear. I was scared! I thought, "This is the end for Dad and me!"

The man with the knife motioned for Dad to roll down the window. Dad calmly rolled the window down with his left hand. He came closer to Dad's face and said, "Don't I know you?"

"No, you don't," Dad said, in an icy voice, "but you are about to find out who I am." Dad grabbed the man by the back of his neck, jerked his head inside the window of the car, stuck a snub-nose .38 Special pistol in the man's mouth and pulled the hammer back. When he let go, all three men disappeared into the darkness and Dad drove on without saying a word to me.

Such was the tale of my Dad. I thought sometimes he was a loser. Yet, he was a man who was fearless and knew struggle, hard work, and dedication to his family. He was not of the heroic stature, except to me when I was young, when a blizzard blew.

On the morning of March 2, 1942, Dad awoke to go to work at the Alcoa Power House, Calderwood Dam, Calderwood, Tennessee. It was snowing, with about one inch of snow on the ground. It continued to snow throughout the day and by nightfall, sixteen inches of snow had accumulated on the ground. Dad got up the following morning and found thirty inches of snow on the ground. It was still snowing. His foreman at work called and advised him not to come to work, that the snow was too deep. During the night the temperature dipped below freezing and the wind roared continuously. Dad and Clyde Williams, a friend from Meadow Branch, North Carolina who also worked for Alcoa and was a boarder with Dad at Broadus and Mary Orr's house in Calderwood, decided to risk their lives and walk back across the mountain on the dangerous snow-covered and icy fifteen-mile stretch of road from Calderwood to Deals Gap. They reasoned that their families at home were out of everything to eat and wood to keep them warm.

In many of the curves, the snow blew and drifted so deep that Dad and Clyde had to pull each other a step at a time to go forward. In some places above the curves, banks were swept clean of snow and their footing was better there. Their spit froze into ice particles and dropped into the snow. Every creek, rill, and branch was frozen and covered deep with snow. They ate snow to quench their thirst. Food that Mary Orr had prepared and given them to carry in their pockets was gone at the beginning of the second day. Hunger now was a concern as they continued to battle the snow and ice. It continued to snow, and every curve filled deeper and deeper. Trees broke from the weight of snow and ice and fell into the curves with crashes that rumbled like explosions. Snow drifted in places to more than fifteen feet deep.

On Mill Creek, Mama was anxious for Dad to get home. She was worried about him and the safety of her children. I was crying with my brothers and sisters. I was scared and wanted Dad to get home. I kept watching for him but saw nothing in the whirl-dance of the blinding storm except darkness and hoary flakes. No footprints in the snow led to our door and no knock came. I was frightened I would never see Dad again.

Hours turned into days, and time raged on with deafening roars of trees slapping together and breaking on Mill Creek. The snow on Mill Creek was over sixty inches, and it was still snowing. The white drifts were as high as the window frames, and when I looked through the top window glass, the clothesline posts looked like tall, sheeted ghosts. A fenceless drift was once the old dirt road; a brush pile off to the right of the house was a smooth white mound; a strange tower rose up where the corn- crib stood. Icy twigs sounded like castanets, grass blades bowed, ditches leveled, and the old dirt road was only a white crystal trail to nowhere. When I brought in the wood from outdoors, I heard only muffled sounds, a hushed footfall in a long forgotten snow, an eerie sound that still haunts me.

Mama and I were outside in the bitter cold and hoary flakes trying to saw wood. We placed a dead tree limb in an old sawhorse to hold it so we could pull the crosscut saw across to cut off the block for kindling wood. I got frustrated because the limb kept moving. I kicked the block; it broke loose and hit Mama and cut her lip through to her teeth. She screamed, blood flew and I never regretted anything more. Mama carried the scar of that incident to her grave.

Mama asked me to bring the shovel into the house so we could tunnel out through the snow, which was now higher than the windowsill, to get water from the spring, wood from the rack of wood (now snowed under), and milk from the springhouse. She wanted me to bring the ax into the house so I could cut the house into firewood if we needed it to keep from freezing to death. Water and milk froze in the kitchen. Ice needles fell through the air. Ice crystals hung like sharp daggers from the eave of the house.

After two days, Dad and Clyde made it home. I saw him coming up the road on Mill Creek and ran to give him a hug. He was exhausted, wet, numb with cold and hungry. Before he ate or slept, he cleaned the snow off the roof so it wouldn't collapse. What an act of courage! What an act of love for his family! I will never forget Dad's willingness to sacrifice his life, in a blizzard, so I could eat and stay warm.

My parents are gone now and I am bereft. Never again will I have the same secure and unchanging love they gave me. Never again will I have someone to ask for their car to go courting, for money, for food, or for help. And never will I have someone to buy me Dee Cee trousers and play Santa Claus or to love me just as I am. To love and be loved, I have seen it all my life. And, if I had to make a choice, loving is better than anything else. That is the heritage Dad and Mama left me. They taught me to love.

The Creaking Sounds of a Vanishing Grist Mill

Some old charcoal drawings showed my great-great-great-grandfather's mills. They were different from Charlie's mill. Not knowing how to harness the power of water, he used the two oldest milling systems known: the mortar and pestle and the saddle stone. The former consisted of a stone bowl or a hollowed-out mortar in a rock into which corn was placed and pounded with a club-like stone pestle. Years later, in a field on Yellow Creek, I plowed up large pestles which I looked at and wondered what they were before throwing them away.

The saddle-stone mill included a large stone with a saucer-like depression into which the corn was placed and rubbed with a back and forth motion using a po- tato-shaped stone to produce about one- day's bread for the family. Eventually, he abandoned his stone mills and began to pound his corn into meal by placing it on a large, rounded rock and pounding it with a pole pestle so heavy that it was lifted with two hands.

As soon as my fourth-generation grandfather got his land grant and developed his farm, he built a pounding or Lazy Jim mill and let waterpower do the work for him. The most elemental of water mills, though none are in existence today, every pioneer farm had one. They were easy to build and needed only a flowing stream to do the work.

A bucket at one end of a long seesaw pole alternately filled with water and emptied itself as it became overbalanced. The pestle on the other end did the work through the up-and-down motion inherent in this system. These primitive mills made about three cycles per minute, producing three gallons of corn meal per day, with about one-half of the meal suitable for corn bread and the other half for chicken feed.

The value of the pounding mill was that it required no attention at all. My fourth-generation grandfather could pour corn into the mortar, turn water into the bucket, and go about a day's work else-where. They were noisy. Long ago, an old-timer who lived on my grandfather's farm where my kinfolk set-tled, said there were so many of these pounding mills when he was a boy that they awakened him many mornings with the constant thumping.

I have sketchy information that at least one of my fourth generation uncles had a quern to grind his corn. One of the oldest and most primitive grist mills known, the quern mill consists of a bot-tom-fixed stone and a top stone that revolved by hand or animal power, rather than waterpower, to grind grain. The quern grist mill was the kind of mill that Samson (in the old Testiment) was forced to operate until his hair grew back. My explanation of the grist mill was praised by my fourth-grade teacher, Amanda Blankenship. Jessie and Charlie Dehart owned the mill, but Charlie, my men-tor, taught me well about grinding grain and grist mills.

At a higher elevation, Gladdens Creek ran be-tween mountain laurel, ivy, and rhododendron. Currents of fast-moving, clear water slapped, sucked and smacked with a gurgling sound as the cold water

spilled over
moss-covered
rocks and rotting
tree trunks cov-
ered with gray-
spotted mush-
rooms and
lichens.

Other trees
that had fallen
into the stream
during past
windstorms
caused it to
backup and cut
at an odd angle
and flow to a
wood sluice, a
part of an old
grist mill. The
stream rushed

Jessie Dehart

on past a general store west into the valley of the quiet
foothills, then on into the Cheoah River in central Graham County. The grist mill and general store are gone
now, but memories of them wrap around me like an
old knitted blanket.

I remember Charlie's grist mill clearly. It was
dark inside and full of cobwebs and throwaway things
like worn out hand-scythes, broken plows, and old
pitchforks with a prong or two missing. All over everything was a coating of fine white dust from years of
grain being ground. Shreds of pipe tobacco, cigar, and
cigarette butts that missed the ashtray lay scattered
about the floor. The smell inside the mill never
changed. It was musty and always smelled of stale

sweat and tobacco smoke. I didn't know how the mill worked except that Charlie pushed a lever that started the big waterwheel outside turning with a lot of creaking. That caused belts, pulleys, and gears to start moving and the millstone to start turning. "The raceway or sluice, wheel, and grinding stones are the three major parts of the mill," Charlie began. "The raceway channels the flowing water to the  wheel; water forces the wheel to turn. The turning wheel powers the grinding stones by a series of shafts and gears and the grinding action of the stones breaks the grain into small, usable pieces like cornmeal and flour."

He stopped to spit tobacco juice. Pointing to the various parts of the mill, he continued, "The fixed stone is cemented in place, and the runner stone is fastened to the shaft that drives the mill. Grain is fed from the hopper through the center by a simple auger that is part of the shaft. The grain is ground as it runs down toward the inside of the stones and pours out into the mill box."

Moving toward the stones and still pointing, Charlie said, "The gap between the surface of the stones gets smaller as it get closer to the rim. The coarseness of the meal is adjusted by changing the gap."

I could feel the grime and dirt as I wrote in the

dust with my index finger in large letters, "Clean me!" Charlie quickly brushed away my instruction with a wiping cloth and made facial expressions that frightened me. He yelled over the noise, "You stop that. Stop writing now!" in a voice that made the hair on the back of my neck stand up! Charlie had been a bare-knuckle boxer in his earlier days, and I could almost feel jabs to my nose and eyes. I didn't write anymore in the dust inside the mill house.

I liked the scent of the chestnut boards and oak beams mixed with the smell of fresh-ground cornmeal unlike the burnt smell from commercial mill grinding done today. The smell of warm cornmeal coming out of the mill box made my mouth water. It smelled like cornbread baking.

In the valley, the stream's rushing water slowed to a gentle, almost noiseless, flow, lapping against the rocky banks. Small brown salamanders, in a quiet tip-toe motion, slipped sideways to hide under old leaves and scraps of debris. Grayish crawfish, on small islands of sand at the side of the stream, pointed their open pincher-claws upward in mock defense, and then shot backward into the water. The noiseless lapping of the water I will never forget because of its forlorn sound. Farther down the stream, at a break-back eddy, green worms fell with a plop from sourwood

trees over-hanging the stream, causing cascading splashes and widening circles. Fish flashed to the surface and ate the worms. I thought about Darwin's writings on the natural food chain and his theory of evolution as I watched a fish hawk buckle its wings and drop like a bullet from a great height, gliding into the creek to catch a fish in its steely talons. Blood from the fish spread in a widening arc as the predator settled on a dead limb across the creek to ravish the fish.

The beauty of the valley and sounds around the creek never left my memory even after I finished high school and no longer drove the school bus up and down the creek on the winding dirt road.

On cold mornings, I saved the front seat next to the heater on the bus for a beautiful girl with a penchant for boys, a blond beauty with smoky eyes, a sensuous, throaty voice and a smile so pleasing to me that it seemed divine rather than human. I was youthful, had boundless energy, read novels, smoked cigarettes now and then with an air of dissipation and made verses. That age, we all pass through. The challenge was before me, my time had come, and the world was

Forgotten

Let it be forgotten,
as a flower is forgotten,
forgotten as a fire,
that once was singing gold,
let it be forgotten
forever and ever,

Time is a kind friend
letting it grow old,
If anyone asks,
say it was forgotten,
Long and long ago,
as a flower,
as a fire,
as a hushed footfall
in a long
forgotten
snow.

mine! Going after girls was a fun time in my life! But
the beautiful girl's poetic summary in my copy of the
1953 Robin, the school annual, said it best: "Be good,
Think of me sometime, Lots of love, and Best Wishes,
from your gal." That's it. Youthful love whispers end in
a whimper! Later, she thanked me for saving her the
warm seat.

At that young age, I always answered with scribbles love whispers that ended in whimpers. I never gave
her any of my verses because of the quality but rather
because of the beauty. Many of my friends lived there
in the dark wrinkle of these hills where the peaks
touch the sky, where the country is high and peaceful
and the wind blows fresh and damp, where the ax and
chopping block and the woodpile fed the heating and
cooking stoves, and where the water supply came from
a spring out back of the house.

Sitting on the porch, leaning back in a straight
chair, was a whiskered old man with a wooden leg.
The file in his hand made a long, rasping noise as he
filed the blade of his hand-scythe. Chickens scratched
in the yard, and a hound dog lay stretched out in the
sun at the foot of the steps. The old man paused, took
his eyes off his work for a moment, and looked out
across the creek where a boy in overalls walked
behind a plow pulled by a mule. An oil lantern hung
from a nail in the porch wall above the old man's
head, and he turned to light it. The front door stood
open. There was a fire on the hearth. A wick-burning
lamp with a smoked-up chimney sat on the mantel.
Out back was a log barn. An old sled leaned against
one of the walls. Nearby was a can house with many
mason jars filled for the winter.

Next day, a skiff of snow that fell the night before, plus the cold wind, brought the temperature down to a little below freezing. Icy flakes still fell, and twigs encased in ice sounded like castanets in the wind gusts.

The old man wore an old, ragged, unbuttoned, green army overcoat, without a hat or gloves, and was huddled with the school children under a large oak tree where I turned the bus around. All the children hurried to get on the warm bus and left him standing there in the freezing cold, his breath a white wisp around his face. Speaking to me through the open bus door when the last child got on the bus, he said, "I'm going to Robbinsville to get some prescriptions filled. Can you give me a ride?"

"No," I sadly said to him. "Liability insurance written for the bus doesn't cover other passengers, only school children."

He seemed to understand, as he stood there shivering with downcast eyes and rubbing his cold hands together.

"Oh well," I said, "I'll give you a lift down to the main road and there you can catch a ride."

"You're a good'n, son! Somebody will be along," he said, still shaking from the cold. The old man slid in beside a bright-eyed boy on the front seat. He pulled a red bandana handkerchief from his pocket and wiped his nose. The boy scooted over, and stammered, "You still freezing mister? Are you? Are you mister? Are you? Are your feet cold?"

"Yes," the old man said grinning, "One is." The other children sitting close by laughed.

She was only a wisp of a woman. The years had etched her face into a wrinkled mask. Her hair was not yet quite white. The sleeves of her calico dress were bunched above her elbows. A faded checkered apron was tied to her tiny waist. She stood there, her well-arranged tubs sitting on a bench before her. On the ground, at her side, bright flames leapt upward around a large black pot suspended on a pole cradled in the forks of two posts. A cloud of white steam rose from the pot; a curl of faint blue smoke spiraled up from the fire. There was a murmur of running water, the song of the creek. She stooped to stir the clothes boiling in the pot. She was the wife of the old man sitting on the porch.

The wisp of a woman and the old man and the things about them spoke to me of a vanishing way of life, just as many other places in the mountains are proof that the past dies slowly here.

One of the most pleasant memories I have from my childhood was going to Charlie Dehart's grist mill, opposite Arthur Millsaps' grocery store. I went there sometimes to take a bushel of corn to get it ground into cornmeal but, most of the time, I stopped off to listen to stories. I got to tell one of my stories now and then. As a young boy, I couldn't wait to hear the old-timers spin their stories.

"Storytelling at the mill isn't in the curriculum at the University of North Carolina and other schools down east, but someone needs to include them and give credits," Charlie joked. "They are powerful and need to be given to the next generation."

I laughed, and answered, "I agree." Most of the stories were masterpieces and the old-timers telling them were wise, knowing how to wring every ounce of truth, wit and humor from them. "Like Viviane, an enchantress who seduces and casts a spell over Merlin, the old-timer storytellers were proof that nothing is more vivid than the human imagination, right Charlie?" I asked.

Charlie just smiled and shook his head.

I liked to listen to the tales being spun. I could actually see them come to life. What could have just been myth became legend. Much of the past is all but gone, though memories do linger on. That is why I would like to share these folk tales and lore, that they may be enjoyed by everyone, cherished by family, re-membered by mountain folks, and preserved for gen-erations to come.

Storytellers coming to the mill, while waiting for their corn to be ground, sat on the wooden bench and smoked, dipped snuff, chewed tobacco, and told sto-ries that were mesmerizing. Some were mysterious and others were baffling. I hung on every word when they spun plots about the most-feared subject of all to a small boy: death and what happens to a person after death.

A moment of silence and sadness swept over the ten or twelve people around the storytelling bench at the mill that Saturday morning as I listened to Coil Sawyer, my neighbor, finish his story.

"Yes," he began. "It was one hell of a fight. True and Smokey were my two-year-old black-and-tan hunting dogs which I raised and trained from puppies to hunt only wild boar. I was offered two thousand dol-lars for the pair but refused to sell them just before the hunt. I led the hunting party from Patton's Cabin on a cold, frosty morning in and around Big Santeet-lah. True and Smokey were well ahead of the dog pack. I knew they had the wild boar at bay when I heard their loud snarls as the other pack dogs caught up and joined the attack on the boar less than a hun-dred yards away from me."

He continued, "Two hemlock trees over ten feet around had fallen and formed a V across a rushing stream. Seeking protection from True, Smokey, and the dog pack, the boar had backed itself into the V to make a stand. It slung its sweaty head, with flashing white rows of three-inch, razor-sharp tusks on each side of its long snout, at the dogs. Slobber and foam dripped from the mouth. The boar's small, dark deep-set, beady eyes glowed like fiery coals in the dark. The fight was vicious. Blood and hair were flying. Each hair on the boar's back and shoulder splits stood straight up after it got hot and mad from running. It looked like a porcupine with the hair standing straight up and his tail flattened against his hams. I saw one dog split from head to tail lying about six feet away. The boar's tusks had gutted him. Three other pack dogs were gored and bleeding badly. One black dog with a white comma under his left eye lay in a pool of blood, dead. The rest of the pack dogs were circled around the boar, snarling and barking, but were at a safe distance, except for Smokey. He was locked on the boar's throat with his teeth tightly clinched. Blood covered Smokey's face and dripped down his ears. He looked like a red, wet dishcloth as the boar slung him from side to side straight out in front of him. Smokey was tenacious. He never gave an inch. Sinew and blood began to spray in an arc-fan motion, and I knew Smokey had cut the jugular vein in the boar's throat. Blood now spurted in a steady stream at each beat of the boar's weakening heart and pooled on the ground at its front feet. I had to get a shot in and not hit a dog.

"I crawled through thick ivy and vines to within ten or twenty yards so I could get a clean shot. To steady my .30-30 Winchester rifle, I laid it in the fork of a small sapling, pushed the safety off, took aim just behind the boar's shoulders to hit the heart and lungs, then pulled the trigger. The boar sagged and was dead at the report of the shot. Smokey's jaws were still locked on the boar's throat. Unknown to me, True was lying behind the boar's other side with his jaws gripped like a vice on the boar's neck. When I called his name there was no response or movement. My heart fluttered and sank. The mushroom bullet had passed through the boar, killing it, and then passed through True's skull and killed him too. The bullet hit a rock then fell to the ground. I picked it up and put it in my pocket and pushed the safety on the Winchester back on.

"I unsnapped True's leather collar with the brass name plate showing identification and wiped off the blood on leaves on the ground. I put it in my pocket, lit another Pall-Mall cigarette off the end of the one I was smoking, and with tears streaming from my eyes, left to go back to camp. I asked members of the hunting party to get the four-hundred-pound boar, bring it back to camp, and bury True where he died. They did."

His tales were tall, the language risqué. Often they were suspect. Most of them were one-liners. "Folks had a way with words back then," he recalled. "They had a way of expressing themselves on any subject under the heavenly bodies." At twenty-four, his mind was sharp as a wildcat's claws and his memory was as bright as a scrubbed penny. He came to the mill each day as soon as the waterwheel began to turn and left sharply at noon. His only purpose was to spin stories. I knew him only as Blue. He was a huge man, as strong as an ox. I liked him, but people on the creek were afraid of him. He played harmonica and carried a Hohner when he came to the mill. He played it beautifully. One day, as he was warming up to play, I asked him how he learned to play so beautifully. Without hesitation, he said, "To cure my asthmatic chest, I disciplined myself to practice every day for a half hour. It's beneficial for all respiratory problems."

"'Here Stands a Glass, Fill It up to the Brim,'" Webb Pierce's old song, was one of his favorites. I liked to see him tap dance and, now and then, he played rockabilly on his guitar and sang many of the country and western songs popular at that time.

Blue was no professional, but I knew he came from a thespian background because he quoted Shakespeare, the Romantic poets, and many American poets, including Emily Dickinson. I'm grateful he wandered into the valley and I got to know him. Maybe he came from a farm or some poor family or some remote district. Only Zigler knew.

Everyone in the valley called him Zig. He remembered once when the woods were full of game and the rivers and creeks were full of fish. "When I was a boy," he said, "folks who carried rifles to get their living from the limb, never came home a-sucking hind teat."

Yet, when I came in the mill today, I saw the small wicker basket of the best trout fisherman who lives on the creek sitting in his old station wagon with only one little old trout in it. I ask him if the trout were biting today, and he sharply answered, "Hell, yes, trout were biting, but just not swallowing."

A man wearing a fancy blazer jacket, dark sunglasses and driving a long black Cadillac whipped in at the local county grocery store that had one gas pump and asked for a fill up. The owner of the store was patiently pumping his gas when the man asked him, "How in the hell do people around here make a living?" He continued in a ranting voice, "I've crossed the crookedest damn road with no gas pumps, saw only shacks for houses for miles and no businesses."

The owner of the store pulled the nozzle out of the man's Cadillac and said in an icy voice, "Mister, some people are teachers, some people live off the land, some make moonshine and sell it, and others, like me, sell gas to sons-of-bitches like you." The man jumped in his car, leaving black marks on the pavement that are still there today.

Zig referred to his uncle as "smart as a whip," and one of his distant relatives as "rough as a cob and twice as corny."

A local pastor of the community church was after one of his extremely wealthy members to give more tithes to the church. The pastor told him that when he died, he couldn't take it with him. "No," snapped the wealthy member, "I can't take it with me, but my wife can bring it when she comes."

Then there was a woman jangler on the creek who had a passion for spreading news. "One could hear the news prattling," Zig continued, "before she comes within gunshot."

"Zig," I asked, "Why didn't you just say that you killed five hundred hackling blackbirds with one shot from your sixteen-gage shotgun as they skimmed across the field instead of four hundred ninety-nine?" He chuckled and quickly answered, "I wouldn't tell a lie for one damn little old black bird."

Another old-timer had the reputation for "lying at the drop of a word."

Around the mill, there was a saying that "his mouth isn't any prayerbook, if it does open and shut."

Another time when an absent neighbor was

being accused unjustly during a bench session at the mill, one of the men there said, "I am not a judge and there isn't enough of me for a jury."

One woman was described as being "born tired and raised lazy," and another was said to be "so weak she couldn't pull a thimble off her finger." One easy-going lad, whose wife up and left him, was asked how he was faring. "Don't miss her," he answered, "no more than a cold wind after the door's shut."

A dangerous old-timer who was angered by a neighbor's high-handed ways said, "He makes the trigger of my rifle itch."

God only knows where this one came from but he moved into the valley and stayed alone, all alone, by himself. One of the loafers at the mill remarked that "he's as queer as a bitty hatched in a thunder storm."

Charlie was a feisty old man. His swearing came in low tones. Instead of cursing with a big, loud oath, he spelled out the curse words, like d-a-m for damn and h-e-l-l for hell. He always said Judas Priest instead of God damn because he didn't want to take the Lord's name in vain. When I questioned his reason for this he said, "My final judgment, I hope, will not be as severe because I've not sinned as much."

I never understood the degrees of sin, but at least Charlie's reason for swearing the way he did slowed me down from cursing. He continued, "I take people in the order which I receive their grain, and take the original toll of ten percent of a bushel, the legal toll. My measure is accurate because I use the same grain bucket, which holds exactly one tenth of a bushel for everyone." He explained, "Other people earn wages for their work, I earn a toll for mine. And there is another difference," he reckoned. "They get paid after their work, I get paid before my work. I take the toll before I grind one grain." Then, almost in a whisper, he mused, "The Scriptures, especially in the Old Testament, warn about dishonesty of people who used weights and measures to their advantage. I want to avoid God's punishment." He spoke somberly now, "I'm an honest miller."

All memories about Charlie's grist mill were not pleasant. Early one summer day, Mama sent me to the mill to get a bushel of corn ground. I was barefoot, walking on a rocky road, carrying the corn on my back. Suddenly, I stubbed my big toe on a rock so hard it took off the nail and skin tissue that clung to the nail. Both were lying on the ground, Blood oozed from my toe. I felt dizzy. Sweat popped out on my forehead and tears ran down my cheeks. I sat under a large shade tree by the roadside, bandaged my toe with a strip I tore from my white tee shirt, and continued on to the mill carrying my corn. My walk back home, carrying the meal on my shoulder, was tiresome but uneventful, except that I stopped to rest under the same shade tree I sat under going to the mill. Looking up from where I sat, I saw hordes of black ants frantically pulling the toe nail and clinging tissue toward their anthill.

The creaking paddle wheel attached to the outside of the mill house propelled the flowing water from Gladden's Creek across the blades of the wheel, and vapor-like mist from the turning wheel created a rainbow against a pink sunset before dusk when I was there.

Stop the Dawn

Beyond the barn
And through the branches
A cold roseate sky
    was spreading

The rusty seeders
    outside the field
Glittered with
    frosty diamonds
Red, blue and topaz
    in the sun

In the fields
    with knees locked
The cows stood sleeping
    Puffing steam

I Never Started a Fight But Never Ran From One

I was never influenced by the color of someone's skin or the cut of their clothes or the length of their hair. Discrimination is something I've never had to overcome because I've never experienced it. I grew up on Mill Creek in Graham County, where racial prejudice in the 1950s was strong but I was unaffected.

One of the best-liked residents who lived at Tapoco was a one-armed black man named Eli Williams, nicknamed Trixie. He came with other blacks during the construction of the Cheoah Dam and never left. Sometimes he brought back homemade rag dolls from his native Shelby, North Carolina, and gave them to the girls who worked at Tapoco Lodge.

His bed was in the basement of the lodge behind the coal chute. At mealtime, he came silently to a side door of the dining room to get his silverware passed to him then disappeared to eat alone. No one ever knew the truth about how he lost his arm because he told different stories about how he lost it.

When my junior year of high school ended, I worked at the lodge that summer and became good friends with Trixie. We drank glasses of lemonade together and exchanged dozens of funny stories.

We were having fun one day when Trixie said, "I'z likes you. It would not be right for me to dislike you because you are white."

I smiled and said pensively, "It would not be right for me to dislike you because you are black. I was never victimized by discrimination. I thank the Lord for that. I can still hear Mama saying, 'The truth will stand when the world is burning down.'"

I find it is much wiser to listen to people, even if I suspect they are lying, and let them play out their verbal hand. I find if I call their hand too soon, I cut off valuable information that may help me come to the truth. Truth is always elusive. It's hard to find in this life, but the quest is almost always worth it.

Truth for me was self-evident during the crop growing season of 1952 when I worked hard to grow and market one tenth of an acre of burley tobacco. My neighbor, Coil Sawyer, sold it at the tobacco auction in Knoxville, Tennessee, for me and brought me $360 in twenty-dollar bills, all rolled in the white paper wrapper from the bank with a rubber band around it.

He handed it to me standing in my yard where I lived on Yellow Creek. Rain came down in torrents and the wind blew hard as I rushed into my house. Somewhere between the yard and house, my roll of money came out of my pocket. Bob Battle ducked into my house just behind me to get out of the rain. The rain stopped suddenly. I discovered that I had lost my roll of money and immediately began my search for it. I asked Bob if he saw it as he came in the house. He replied, "No." Everyone at my house, including Bob, helped me look for the money. An old walnut tree stood at the edge of the yard. I raked through the debris under the tree to look for the money but to no avail. I was broken-hearted.

Time waged on. Three days after my money went missing, Bob came to my house and offered to look for the money again. He looked again under the walnut tree and excitedly said, "I found it!" He handed me a dry roll of eighteen twenty dollar bills, without the paper bank wrapper but with the rubber band still around the roll of money. Stealing money is easy ,but living with one's conscience is hard and grates on the mind.

I almost never involve myself in direct confrontations. I dislike and distrust arguments. They rob me of both time and dignity. I was never a person who was easily frightened or intimidated by people, danger, or pain. I never went looking for trouble but never ran away from it either. But sometimes I had to stand up for myself and defend my honor so I would not be called the coward of the county.

I was leaving church service at Rock Springs Baptist Church with my friends one Sunday when I was a junior in high school. A stranger elbowed his way through the crowd and found me. He asked me to meet him to fight. My friends heard the conversation. I was puzzled! I had never done anything to him or said anything about him. He called me a coward, pushed me, and asked me to meet him next Saturday at one o'clock. The meeting would be at the bridge crossing the river where the road continues on to Joyce Kilmer Memorial Forest the next Saturday at one o'clock. When he turned and walked away, I was totally baffled.

When I got home, I told Dad about the strange meeting with the stranger and that I had agreed to meet him at the bridge at one o'clock. Dad was pensive but accepted the fact that I had no choice but to defend my dignity and ensure that I wasn't a coward. I didn't know what was ahead for me! Usually, when someone picks a fight with an innocent person, he has a hidden gun or knife in his possession to give him the advantage, I thought.

On Saturday, I got into Dad's old Ford pickup truck with him and we drove to the bridge, getting there a little before one o'clock. The stranger got out of a car driven by a man who operated the grocery store located at the intersection of Cochran Creek and Highway 129. The stranger and I looked at each other. To get out of the traffic pattern, we walked slowly across the bridge without speaking. We stopped walking. I caught him with a hard left hook in the nose, and it exploded in blood. He closed with a right to my stomach but missed with a left to my face. We exchanged fast and furious punches. Blood and sweat flowed.

The scuffle carried us to the edge of the bridge and we continued to rain blows on each other's head and stomach. He spun me around with a hard blow that missed my eye but caught me in the right jaw. I knocked him down into the dirt and gravel. He came up fighting, a more determined fighter than before. I hit him under the chin. He crumpled into the dust. I waited for him to get up again. He was stronger each time he came back to fight. He rushed me and knocked me back several feet while still throwing punches at my face. A tough fighter! His upper cuts were vicious, with many of them landing in my face. The store owner cheered his hero on, yelling, "Kill the son-of-bitch."

By that time, a crowd had gathered. Uncle Clyde, Paul, Ralph, and Arnold Orr jumped out of their vehicles but remained silent. Other people from the community stopped to watch the melee.

The muddle spilled back across the road and a furious exchange of blows continued. His face was cut and swollen. Cuts had opened up under his black and puffy eyes. His long black hair was covered with dried blood and sweat. Dirt flew about his head and made him an ugly sight. He grabbed a fistful of my shirt, tearing it from top to bottom. I turned him around in that scuffle and hit him with a smashing blow to his battered mouth. Blood dripped from a large cut on his lip. I landed another hard left punch to his battered face and knocked him down. This time, as he slowly got to his feet, he pulled a pair of handmade babbitt knuckles from his pocket and had them on his right hand, ready to destroy me. Someone in the crowd yelled, "He has knuckles." Another person next to him jerked them off of his hand and threw them below the bridge. Someone in the crowd retrieved the knuckles from below the bridge.

My next punch to his head sent him over the rocky abutment at the end of the bridge. He fell into rocks and landed on his back with his neck between two saplings. I kicked him in the ribs, and the man moved no more to fight. I stood above him to be sure no more fight was in him.

The store owner slid his hand inside his pocket. Before he could draw his gun and fire, Uncle Clyde Orr walked up to him and slowly said, "It's best that you don't try to shoot anyone here. I've seen many men die. One more will not make a difference to me."

A hush fell over the crowd. Someone handed Dad the babbitt knuckles. The store owner struggled to get his fighter's limp body free of the saplings and up over the rocky bridge abutment. I walked up to him as he struggled to walk across the bridge and said, "Be ready to fight before you ask me again."

Dad and I got back into his truck and turned it around to go home. I was surprised as Dad laid the babbitt knuckles on the seat and reached inside his coat pocket, pulled out his 32.20 automatic pistol, laid it beside the knuckles, looked in the rear view mirror and softly said, "The store owner's attempt to shoot you would have failed. I would have put a bullet between his eyes."

We drove on home in silence. The babbit knuckles hung on a nail in our garage for years. I learned later that the store owner sold moonshine likker and his fighter helped him. He liked to watch fights and had set the stage for the stranger to whip me.

My School Album

Cliff Carpenter with ball

Ray Carpenter and Max McMonigle

Robbinsville Blue Devils Football Team
Ray Carpenter #38

Cliff Carpenter
Under 18 National Soccer Team, Granatkin Tournament USSR

Cliff Carpenter

Ray Carpenter with
Eloise Phillips
and Anna Sue Deyton

Robbinsville High School

Robbinsville · North Carolina

This Certifies That

Ray Douglas Carpenter

Has satisfactorily completed the Course of Study prescribed by the Board of Education for the High School Department and is therefore entitled to this

Diploma

Given this twenty-first day of May, nineteen hundred and fifty-four.

_____
Superintendent

_____
Principal

CLASS OF
1954

114

Ray Carpenter with Avis Ann Shuler

A Swish of the Tail

I looked out the window
And what did I see
A red cardinal
In a leafless oak tree
It was a white winter day
The wind blowing strong
The beautiful bird didn't linger long
With a swish of the tail
It was on its way
But it was a bright spot of my day

An Odyssey of Change

Mama kept saying, "Son, I want more than anything for you to go to college, but Henry and I still have six children in school and a household to maintain. We just don't have the money to send you to college now. You have to make something special of your life, and a college education is the best place to start. We've got to find a way for you to stop picking blackberries and plowing fields on a dirt farm on Yellow Creek for little or nothing," she laughed. "The only thing Dorothy wanted was to get back home in the well-known story, *The Wizard of Oz*. The thing you want most is a way to get out of the low-economic level you were born into. You need to earn money so you can go to college and get an education to help you make a better life for yourself. You'll never amount to a hill of beans unless we find a way for you to make the money to go to college," she mused, with an encouraging voice.

Her voice trailed off as she said, "Jonnie worked hard to earn money to go to college. I'm proud of her. Yes, she wanted to earn her way. She was the first female to hold the position as Branch Office Manager for ASCS, Federal Government, after starting her career in Washington, D.C. She earned her manager's job in New Orleans through determination to have a better life than the one she was born into."

"I'm pleased about her success." I said, and Mama kept smiling.

Dad signed papers for me to volunteer for the United States Navy at the Naval Recruiter office in Robbinsville, North Carolina. I was sworn into the Navy in Asheville at the Naval Office on January 7, 1955, and assigned to the USN Training Center, Great Lakes, Illinois for training from January 14 until March 18, 1955.

My flight from Asheville to O'Hare Airport, Chicago, didn't leave until 9:00 a.m. on January 8, 1955, and the Navy Recruiter dropped me off at the old YMCA in Asheville to spend the night. He agreed to pick me up and take me to the Asheville Airport the next morning to catch my flight.

Even though I was nineteen years old, I was lonely at the YMCA that night. The sun disappeared before it set as dark clouds closed in about the hills around the Biltmore House and downtown Asheville. The temperature dropped to below zero. Freezing cold weather kept me in my room that night. I thought about the sad faces of my family when I left home and the tears running from their eyes as we hugged and said our good-byes. Mama gave me the last hug. In an emotional voice she said, "Don't get a tattoo or learn to smoke or drink. Instead, go to church on the ship, read your scriptures and say your prayers. Take advantage of the opportunity to learn from your travels and save some of your money to go to college. Son, I love you and I'll miss you." Her voice saddened and she began to cry as I left for the Navy.

The land of tears is a lonely place. When I was alone in the room that night, it was different from being alone in my room at home where I felt secure. Never in my life had I been in a place as lonely.

A forty-watt bulb swinging from a flyspecked drop cord in the center of the room gave little light, rust streaked the old enamel sink from a faucet drip, a water hammer made strange sounds in the drain pipes, old stale cigarette smoke left a noisome odor, and a fluttering over my bed was annoying. A slapping noise at my window scared me but turned out to be a loose board blowing and banging into the wall outside. Mice ran back and forth across the rough wooden floor at the foot of my bed. I felt so alone that night.

A thousand furies and nightmare shapes walked through my mind before dawn. I had never before felt that no one cared for me. My sleep that night, all but about three hours of it, was riddled with restless visions.

I dreamed of some old mountain preacher I couldn't make out, seeing the deep lines around his eyes, his callous hand with broken fingernails clasping the King James Bible, a small scar on his right cheek, more clearly in dream than I could in memory. But when he opened his mouth to welcome the congregation, he wasn't the pastor at all but the devil, with a bag full of sin in his hand, sowing his evil across the world to sinners and believers.

And then I was in a forest. I thought it was dedicated as a living monument to the memory of soldier and poet Joyce Kilmer, who was killed in action in World War One and was buried in Oise-Aisne American Cemetery near the hamlet of Seringes–et–Nesles, France. I wasn't sure. I saw dimly a bronze plaque mounted on a large rock in the forest that told his story. Somehow, the plaque was upside down and difficult for me to read.

My dreams waved and floated in front of me like a diaphanous tapestry, out of my reach. It appeared to come from an enchanted desert far away. I saw a scroll rolled up by a fallen tree but couldn't read it. Momentarily, I saw orchards, thousands upon thousands, so tiny and delicate, so fragile I couldn't touch them. Suddenly, they began to walk backward up the trail in front of me and stopped when I stooped to reach for them, but I couldn't pick them. They faded from my sight. My knees weakened and I couldn't walk the many acres of the primitive and natural forest. I sat down near a creek and looked up at the huge trees, many of them hundreds of years old, as much as twenty feet around the base and more than a hundred feet high. Leaves shut out the sunlight, except for a radiant beam shining through the mist at dawn that gave the forest a glorious splendor. Mosses and ferns of many kinds in different shades of green grew seamlessly and interlaced to make a green carpet sprinkled with tiny white flowers on the ground of the forest. The roaring sound of rushing water was somewhere in the distance but came closer long enough for me to see a swirling band of water droplets with many colors.

Deep in the night, my vision changed. A strange utterance I could barely hear startled me. Something spoke to me saying,"That crystal clear creek you sit by is the Master's stream. It is neither a vision nor a dream. Sing then, with all your heart and soul, about it! Proclaim all its beauties and rugged grandeur to all generations. Surmise that you are a sculptor and have the power to chisel your thoughts on marble. Search all the quarries of this beautiful earth for the purest, white stone, the fine white marble; and somewhere in this enchanted land, where the skies are the bluest, the water the purest, and the birds sing the sweetest, far into the soft moonlit night, begin a work of art, of love, and of duty there.

"Bid the cold, white marble to speak to you. Ply the chisel to its side until the surface takes the shape you wish and at last a creek stands, revealed in all its beauty, ready to give of the pure cold water of its many springs to bless a thirsty drinker. Make a base on which the spirit of your dreams will stand and, around its rim, carve the figures of many dear faces with their hands raised to beckon all people to come and see. For of all the streams, Little Santeetlah Creek in Graham County is the purest."

My dreams baffled me! I awoke from my reveries as a golden ray of sunlight burst through the dust streaked window.

Nye Phyz, the Navy Recruiter, knocked on my door at the YMCA at 7:00 a.m. I grabbed my one small piece of luggage, he paid for my room, and we left for his car. We stopped at the K&W Cafeteria on Patton Avenue, where he bought my breakfast. As we left, I looked across the street at old wooden benches where people smoked, chewed tobacco and spat on the ground; where babies in dirty clothes sucked their mama's teat; and where beggars in ragged clothes held out their empty hands for money. I looked up Patton Avenue toward the square and the water fountain. I felt lonely and sad to leave Asheville and the beautiful mountains I loved.

At the Asheville Airport, Nye Phyz helped me verify my ticket and check in for the flight. He waved goodbye at the gate as I boarded the plane, Delta flight twenty-eight, for Chicago. I never saw that recruiter again. The flight to Chicago was uneventful except for wind drafts that caused the aircraft to dip and rise. I still felt lonely as the plane banked slowly to the left to get into the landing pattern. It landed safely at O'Hare Airport in Chicago, Illinois, in a skiff of snow and rolled down the tarmac to the canopy where I got off the plane. Before I got to gate three, a large man waved me over. I was frightened in this place I had never been before and by someone so large until I remembered Ney Phyz clipping my name on the front of my shirt before I boarded the plane in Asheville. I grabbed my luggage and jumped in a Navy van waiting for me at the end of the loading area with the engine already running. By then, most of my loneliness was gone, but I was still uneasy for some reason. Things happened so fast my head was spinning. Eleven seats were occupied by other recruits, and I had to sit in the front seat by the driver, who was the large man who met me at the gate. I was nervous and kept my eyes straight ahead. The only thing I said on the way to the USN Training Center was my name and hometown when the driver asked for it.

I became number 469 19 81 when I entered the gate at the USN Training Center. Chief Bosun's Mate Andy Farr handed me my dog tags, an identification number needed for my laundry and death. Once a week my laundry was thrown into a pile and washed. Each piece of my clothes was stenciled with my name and service number so it could be returned to me.

On my first leave home, Mama's face saddened and she cried when I told her the small notch at the end of my metal dog tags fit between my teeth if I got killed or died.

My sea bag was the first thing I was issued. I was weighed and measured wearing only my skivvies so my uniforms and other things to wear would be the right size. Every item went into the sea bag in a first-in, last-out order so it could be removed quickly and put in its proper place in my locker in Barracks II, where I lived during boot training. Inspections were held daily by F.J. Faye and his staff. My locker had to be shipshape with all items in their proper place. I couldn't hang pictures in my locker. The inspecting team missed nothing as they moved from locker to locker through the barracks.

Shipmate Quick open his locker at the end of a tiring day and found its contents scattered throughout the barracks. Inside the empty locker was a note signed by F.J. Faye that read, "Hanging a nude woman's picture in your locker is not permitted by me or this command. This is not a bordello; there is no bidet here for you to straddle and wash your crotch Pervert Quick. You damn knucklehead. God gave you two ends: one to sit on and one to think with. Getting through your training and staying in the Navy depends on which end you use most; heads you win, tails you lose. Now you are losing, you damn loser."

Quick began searching for his scattered belongings, knowing that every one of the items had to be accounted for at the next day's inspection or he would be written up and demerits assigned to him. He felt worthless, mumbling, "I don't know if I'll make it through boot camp. This place is hell." Quick sat down on the bench at the table.

Before I could wear my bellbottoms, I had to get a regulation haircut. Snip, whack! Snip, whack! My hair was gone. For the next forty-six months, my hair was cut according to a regulation found on page 21 of the bluejacket manual, but I did use Max Factor wax to train it to stand up in a crew cut.

Our company marched over to a building where ten hospital corpsmen were seated behind their own chairs. Sailors were hurting! They were screaming from pain. Six recruits queued up behind a corpsman for medical examinations and shots. Each corpsman gave me a different shot and examined me for a differ-ent reason. I looked down at my arms as I proceeded through the line and saw needles hanging in bloody

splotches from each arm where the automatic vacci-
nating machine misfired and left them. Men don't cry
and I didn't. I got back in line and the corpsman gave
me the shots I missed because of the misfires.

As I left for my barracks that day, I picked up a
shipping box already labeled with my mailing address
and sent my civilian clothes home. Mama was
anxiously awaiting news from me but had heard nothing until Roxie's mail car stopped at her mailbox on
Yellow Creek and dropped off a neatly wrapped box
with my address on it. Mama was excited as she
ripped the cover off the box but found only my civilian
clothes. Sadly, she looked through the box again to
assure herself there was no card or letter. Tears welled
up in her blue eyes as she held a shirt to her face she
had bought for my birthday and gathered the rest of
her family around in the living room, bowed her head,
and said a prayer for me. Shirley, my sweet sister,
said she prayed, "O Lord, he may never get back home
and we may never get to see him again. I pray
Father, for you to keep him safe and bring him back
home to us."

"She had us all in tears," Shirley smiled. "We
were scared that you wouldn't make it back home."

I learned in boot camp that training for war is a
grim business. Here I was stripped of my civilian ways
and taught military ways. I found myself adjusting to
a different way of life. Boot camp, for me, was interesting and frustrating at times but a learning and growing time in my life that I still value.

I can still hear Ellis Brent singing cadence as I
marched. My favorite cadence was "You had a good
home but you left, give me your left, right, your left."
Then, he trailed off with,"You had a good home but
you left. Sound off, one, two, three, four; one, two,

three, four." When the sound of his cadence rose higher, the degree marker on the thermometer went lower as the biting wind and bitter cold were ever-present on the concrete drill fields where I mustered each day, at five in the morning, to begin marching. Leggings kept my legs warm. My skull cap, wool pants, wool turtleneck sweater, heavy Pea coat, and mittens kept me from freezing stiff on the drill field.

The first day I marched, I was out of rhythm with the cadence call. I disrupted the smooth flow of boots with my broken rhythm and kept kicking my shipmate's heels in front of me with my longer strides in the long blue column. Soon, F.J. Faye, company commander, was beside me. He called the sixty-man company to a halt. Immediately, he was in my face. "You worthless piece of shit, you long-legged pecker," he shouted. "One of your damn legs is shorter than the other, you can't walk straight, your marching is the worst, you damn scum. You're lower than a crab scuttling across the ocean floor. Now, fall out and give me fifty push-ups, Carpenter, you North Carolina hillbilly, you hayseed, you woods colt," he ranted. "Why don't you go back go the damn hills and make hooch the rest of your life?" My name and service number were covered up by the heavy clothes I wore on the marching field. I wondered how he remembered my name and that I was from North Carolina. I finished doing the push-ups and returned to the blue column to continue my marching.

One night my bellbottoms, blue denim shirt, T-shirt, and skivvies got soaked while I was doing my duty washing pots and pans in the mess hall. The temperature was ten degrees below zero, accompanied by a brisk wind, and, as I walked back to my living quarters, my clothes froze stiff on my body. I was a block of ice when I came in the front door of the barracks. My shipmates grabbed a broom handle and broke the ice, causing it to hit the deck in great chunks. They all laughed at me as I stood there shivering. Butler, a buddy of mine, took a picture of me and the ice. F.J. Faye permitted it to be posted on the barracks bulletin board. Underneath my picture was printed, "The Iceman from North Carolina." It was still posted the day I finished boot camp and left for duty in the fleet.

Butler told me, "I'm in trouble with my swimming. I've not passed the one-, three-, six-, or ten-minute basic swim skill tests," he continued, in a depressed voice. "Now, staying afloat for fifteen minutes is the minimum requirement to continue a career in the Navy," he said, with downcast eyes. "I never learned to swim growing up in Liddell, Louisiana. I was afraid of water. The only future I have left is a career in the Navy. I'm from the poorest family you can imagine. I've never had anything in my life. I am fortunate I got in the Navy in the first place. My scores were low and my acceptance was borderline. I must pass the swimming requirement or I'm history. I will never have an opportunity like this again to improve and have a better life. I want something better," he said, with more enthusiasm. "I'm strong and want to learn how to swim. I'm nervous when the swim instructor yells at me. I have a hard time listening to him. He has a vulgar and loud mouth, and I shake from fear when he calls my name."

Tears puddled in his eyes when he asked me to help him learn to swim. Time, for me as well as everyone in the company, was our most valuable asset, and every minute was scheduled. No one could stay up past Taps at ten o'clock. Classes and marching drills were mandatory, and being on time for them was every recruit's responsibility. Each recruit had to pass tests on the material presented in the different classes and make at least a 2.5 on a 4.0 grading system for each class. Study time was important. Time management was more important. On Saturday mornings, everyone in the company had free time from 7:00 a.m. to 9:00 a.m. to write letters, press uniforms, sew buttons on, shine shoes, get haircuts and take care of things required to make a recruit a shipshape sailor.

Four more Saturdays were left in boot camp. I agreed to help Butler learn to swim. I told the swim instructor my plan to help him. He met Butler and me at the pool a few minutes before eight o'clock on Saturday morning to show me where the key to the pool was hidden. He was not there to help a lowly recruit learn to swim. "It's your damn asses if you get caught." he sneered sarcastically. Pool hours did not include Saturdays and the pool was not only restricted but off limits to enlisted sailors on Saturdays. We ignored the fear of being caught off limits, facing captain's mast and time in the brig with suspended pay. We went on to the pool anyway. "Lose your fear of the water, find your float point, relax, fill your lungs with air, and tread water," I instructed him. Butler trusted me in the water. He did exactly what I asked him to do and worked harder and smarter, with greater determination. He wanted to stay in the Navy; I wanted money to go to college when I got out. We both were poor. We shared common needs but for different reasons. We were determined to reach our goals in spite of the consequences of being caught.

Before the hour ended, he mastered staying afloat for three minutes. He was elated! When swim call came on Tuesday of the next week, he passed the one- and three-minute requirements. The befuddled swim instructor shook his head and said, "Good, Butler, you rat, you damn Louisiana swamp rat! Why in the hell did you join the damn Navy anyway when you can't swim?" he spewed. "Go back to Liddell and earn your living noodling."

In two more Saturdays, Butler had mastered staying afloat for fifteen minutes. At our final swim call, the pool was set ablaze simulating a burning ship on the sea. The swim instructor barked, "You damn knuckleheads, swim the length of the pool, then swim carefully under the burning oil the last ten yards. Gently part the oil and fire with your hands from underneath, stick your nose and mouth in the damn hole, breath, go down under the fire and swim out. You pussies," he bellowed. "Save your damn life, you knuckleheads!" pointing his finger at us. "You bunch of Os," he smirked.

Butler finished the swim call in high spirits. He said, "Carpenter, you executed the maneuver under the fire in the pool better than anyone." As we left swim call, he shook my hand and said, "I am most grateful to you for your help. Thank you for that. Thank you for teaching me to swim!"

The last week of my training, F.J. Faye called me into his office at the end of the barracks on Saturday morning during free time. I walked down the hall shaking with fear, knocked on his door, entered and saluted him saying, "Carpenter, 469 19 81, reporting to you as requested, sir."

He motioned for me to sit down in the black leather chair that I had heard about from other shipmates brought into his office for disciplinary action. I was anxious about what was coming down. He gave me a cup of coffee and in a quiet voice said, "At ease,

Tar Heel! Your marching now passes my inspection and your marks total 3.9. Not bad for a fellow North Carolinian! I'm from Denver, North Carolina. Robbinsville, Denver, small towns, some of the best come from there," he went on.

I'm thinking, "Now I know how he remembered my name and that I was from North Carolina on the cold drill field."

"It's my responsibility to see that each recruit under my command passes all tests in training. By taking your free time to help Butler pass basic swimming, you were a team player and, indirectly, you helped me. Thank you." With authority he said, "Dismissed."

I snapped to attention, saluted him, did an about-face, and left his office feeling better about what I had done.

During my training I learned basic seamanship including survival techniques of swimming; and received instructions on atomic, biological and chemical warfare defense. I learned how to don, wear, and care for the Navy Mark IV Mask and how to avoid becoming a victim of an attack using biological agents in food or water. I leaned how to help my shipmates from many types of dangers, including saving them from drowning and from the ever-present danger of suffocating or burning in a shipboard fire. I learned how to tie knots and to tie up the ship when it came into port to dock.

One interesting technique I learned to save myself from drowning was to pull off my bellbottoms, tie the bottoms of the legs in a knot, jerk them quickly over my head to inflate the legs with air as I jumped from a ship, and use them like a life jacket around my neck to float. As long as I kept the inflated legs of the bellbottoms wet, they would hold air and float me. My white hat would float me when I jerked it over my head, filled it with air and kept it wet. The difference was, I had to place the inflated white hat under my navel button and float on my stomach. Air escaped faster from the white hat, and this technique was difficult but would save my life as a last resort.

The next day, Yeoman First Class Sid Pauli sent me a special note with my last pay check from the USN Training Center command. It said, "Congratulations Seaman Carpenter on your promotion and pay increase. F.J. Faye recommended you for the promotion and pay raise with a memorandum placed in your permanent file for taking your time to help a shipmate learn to swim. He also recommended a billet for you to study inventory control and cost accounting for all general supplies for shipboard use except fuel for jets and airplane spare parts. You are going to Prudence Island, Narragansett Bay, Newport, Rhode Island to learn your future work in the Navy. You'll have a good teacher and school there. I wish you the best of everything."

Yeoman Pauli handed me a large manila military envelope with my orders enclosed. Butler, with his orders in hand, came to the end of the long line to tell me he was going aboard the USS Forrestal CVA-59 and to say good-bye. With tears glistening in his eyes, he said, "I hope to see you again someday." I never saw him again but felt good about his future. I left him a happy sailor and a better man.

After a thirty-day furlough in Robbinsville and a chance to go courting again in my blue Ford, I reported to the United States Naval Base at Melville, Rhode Island on a Friday afternoon and had the weekend free. The dress code at my new command included wearing civilian clothes when I was on liberty and off-base. I rented a locker just outside the base to hang my civilian clothes. I showered, shaved, and changed into civilian clothes there. It was a good place to relax and read, which I did often. It had a small desk, and I kept my journals current and did a lot of scribbles there.

I dressed casual and went to Newport on liberty to find the Round Tower, which Henry Wadsworth Longfellow made reference to in his poem "The Skeleton in Armor" (line 134). Longfellow's response was to the debated theories that an ancient Stone Tower in Newport and an armored skeleton unearthed at Fall River, Massachusetts, were relics of a prehistoric Scandinavian settlement. I found the Round Tower but no evidence of a Scandinavian settlement.

A beautiful seaside city was before me. Aquidneck Island never looked so romantic. Beaches, rocky cliffs, old mansions that were architectural masterpieces in themselves, and many bars too numerous to count. Several white sailboats silhouetted against a blue sky and cracking watery ways slapping the sailboats' sides on the open sea gave Newport a beauty all its own in a bursting sunset at twilight.

One moment in my life was the biggest surprise of all. It was endowed with yet another lady, I thought a lady of the night, but she was indeed a lady luminary with a pronounced penchant for men, an auburn-haired beauty, a poised sophisticate with a sensuous throaty voice. She walked energetically with grace and charm. She stopped suddenly and smiled, swinging her body around to face me. The beautiful young woman strolled toward my table at Flo's Clam Shack in Newport. Her two jostling, light tan breasts, pushed up and secured by the lace-edged bodice turned my head. Their large size was accented by a small, diamond-set silver whale suspended on a delicate chain hovering just above her cleavage. Her matching earrings hung freely and the diamonds on them sparkled.

What a dish! Never in my life had I seen a woman with such beauty! I gave a silent chuff and moved my eyes to look slowly across the girl's delicately chiseled face, her dark brown eyes and her long legs, which, even covered by her white print dress, were beautiful. She smiled again, revealing her dimple and her white teeth and softly said, "Hello, I'm Bice Andre."

I pushed a chair in front of her carefully and said in my best southern accent, "Hi, I'm Ray Carpenter. I'm pleased to meet you, Bice. I'm happy that you joined me. What would you like to drink?"

"A Singapore Sling," she said, just above a whisper, pointing to mine. "It's my favorite drink in this place." I ordered it for her and we finished our drinks together. She asked me to dance as The Nelson Riddle Orchestra played an instrumental version of "Lisbon Antigua." Her dance steps and spins were light and beautiful. People were elbow to elbow at Flo's Clam Shack that evening enjoying the music and dancing but the air was stuffy in spite of the air-conditioning and large ceiling fans.

Bice and I fast-danced to Chuck Berry's jump-blues current hit, "Maybelline"; Bill Haley and his Comets' rock 'n' roll craze hit, "We're Gonna Rock Around The Clock"; and The Cadillacs' "Speedo," about sweet-talking women. Bice whispered to me that she loved to dance to this slice of up-tempo doo-wop. The orchestra was still on break and the disc jockey at Flo's continued to spin the current dance hits on forty-five singles. Bice was an excellent slow-dance partner and we danced to The Platters' "The Great Pretender," with its great harmonies, and to "Only You," one of their classics hits. She laced her fingers around my neck and laid her head on my shoulder like a baby scarcely moving except for the gentle swaying of her hips where my hands rested. I drew her closer, and pressed my lips to hers. She responded, opening her mouth for me, meeting my tongue with her own as she continued to keep her laced fingers around my neck. I could feel her breasts against my chest. She kissed me often when we danced that way. After a time, I held her away from me. The smell of fresh apricots wafted around her. Bice's natural body odor and slight perspiration gave her a distinctive woman's scent that I liked. "Bice, your fragrance smells wonderful. What kind are you wearing?' I asked, in a subtle voice.

"None," she answered quickly. "I never use any. I like gifts from Victoria's Secrets. Go there and look for camisoles and teddies for me. I like black negligees, silk and satin ones, and French-laced underwear," she laughed. "Gifts make me happy! There you have it!"

I was pleasantly surprised when Bice answered the disc jockey's challenge to dance for the patrons at Flo's. He grabbed the music for buck-and-wing, a solo tap dance. Her many leg flings and leaps were graceful and beautiful to watch. She was sensational and completed the tap dance perfectly. The patrons loved her tap dancing and screamed, "Mais, Bonito! Mais, Bonito!" She entertained everyone to their delight! She took a bow and asked the disc jockey to play music so she could dance the cancan. Responding to the lively French music and her audience, she held her skirt up in front and did the high kick throughout the dance.

As we sat down, she opened her legs to pull over

the chair, and her French lace underwear shifted slightly. She crossed her legs beneath her skirt, brushing her calf against one of my legs. When she let her smoky gaze flicker across the table, holding my eyes for a second, I knew a lovely thing happened. And the stifling air in Flo's grew hotter.

Over the noise, she asked me to take a walk with her. I paid my bar bill and we walked out of Flo's. After we left the upscale downtown shops and art galleries along the water front, manicured lawn at the Naval War College, the cobblestone streets, and brick sidewalks and began walking along the cliff walk, the scenery was spectacular. Delphinine, tulips, irises, poppies, and shamrocks dotted the landscape, rocky cliffs met the ocean's wind swells and crashing surf, sea gulls and swallows soared overhead. Bice and I felt the energy between us, lying together on the sitting bench on the cliff walk, and at that moment became a part of each other. As the tide ebbed, she was in my arms. We kissed passionately. Time passed quickly. We walked on the cliff walk back to her white MG convertible parked on the street at Flo's. She handed me the car keys and in her soft New England accent said, "I live in New Bedford, Massachusetts, the world's most famous whaling-era seaport." She dimpled, holding up the silver whale at the top of her freckled cleavage. She laughed as she slid into the passenger seat of her MG and said, "You now know my favorite drink, songs I like, and that I like to tap dance, kick high and hold the front of my skirt up when I do the cancan." She hiked her shoulder and whispered softly, "You know, too, that I wear French-laced panties and no slip when I'm dancing."

Young love is beautiful and powerful!

Bice Andre
Ray Carpenter

I met Bice's interesting Portuguese family that day and dated her the rest of the time I was stationed in Rhode Island. Bice owned a dance studio in Boston and worked there as a professional dance instructor. As we walked through her studio one Saturday, she said, "Many Portuguese are born into low economic situations and never get out. I was fortunate that my grandmother from Lisbon, Portugal, left me a Trotten trust with a considerable amount of money and I was able to buy my dance studio and my sports car. There were no claims against the trust when grandmother died, and I was the only beneficiary. Thankfully, I wound up with a lot of money. Dad invested it for me when I was three and now it gives me spending money eighteen years later. Your love note and scribble were adorable this week," she said excitedly, as she handed me the car keys. "Your scribble describes your financial status, without emphasis on money, and lets me know your love and dream for me," she continued. "I don't care if you are a sailor without money. You're my man! You're dependable, smart, honest, hard-working, and the best kisser and lover." She smiled sweetly and said, "Mama and Dad also value your sincere qualities even though they have only kissed you on the cheek! Besides, you have creative ideas and scribble well. Your wit and humor keep me laughing, and your dancing is improving," she spoke softly.

"Sounds to me like you want me to kiss you again. Did someone pay you to say all those things about me?" I teased her.

"No" she insisted. "Its true." She looked particularly beautiful in her white shorts and lavender halter against her tanned body. I adjusted the hair clasp in her wind-blown, auburn hair and told her, "Your are beautiful, just beautiful." I hit the starter and the MG roared to life.

"Go through Hyannis Port and stop at the drug store on our way to the beach, please. I need to buy some sunscreen," she nodded. "When we get to the beach at Cape Cod this afternoon, I want you to hold me and read to me your scribble, "Letter to a Sweetheart." She put her arms around me and kissed me passionately as we drove on to the beach. "We're having dinner tonight in Martha's Vineyard at Lambert's

Cove in Vineyard Haven. I wanted to take you to one of the best restaurants around." She smiled.

We spread our blanket on the sand and rubbed each other with the sunscreen. She handed me the folded piece of paper with my scribble, and I read...

Letter to a Sweetheart

Why wait and worry, what is wrong,
have you not coin to put in phone,
why not sit and write a line,
to let her know she has time,
her picture you touch is not real,
the lips, the eyes you can not feel,
those words you write are concealed,
but to her your love reveal,
love is made by stars at night,
love is made under neon lights,
that love is best which is the feel,
and not the love that is revealed,
the rhythm of the heart will tell,
when you make love by mail,
expression is best in the heart,
how can I express whenever apart."

Bice was silent for a minute then stood up and with her big toe, drew a heart in the sand with an arrow through it. She said, "Not as professional as your quality scribble but this is my scribble to you" as she pointed to her art work in the sand! "I love you."

She taught me to dance. I sent her flowers and love notes through the week, and I couldn't wait until she came for me at 7:00 p.m. on Saturdays outside the gate at my locker. She always planned interesting things for us to do and picked up the tab when we did them.

The Navy boat coxswain reversed the propeller, gunned the inboard engine to kick the boat smoothly into the slip for the tie-up at the pier in Melville at 7:00 a.m. on Monday. Lieutenant Kleck boarded the boat, and I saluted him. Pharmacist Mate First Class Oscar Osby, whom sailors called "Doc," boarded next, and I helped him get his medical bags safely stored under the seat along with my sea bag. A White Star Taxi pulled up to the pier, and three more sailors got out and boarded the boat.

Before the coxswain started the boat engine, he directed everyone on board to put on a Mae West life jacket and sit in an even number on each side of the boat for better balance during the thirty-minute ride. He cautioned everyone to remain seated while underway. Wind swells were running almost three feet high. Narragansett Bay was white-capping and rough that Monday morning. The boat coxswain turned the gray twenty-one, foot navy boat into the wind and choppy sea and brought the boat safety to the pier for tie-up at Prudence Island, which was called The Rock by all sailors. The Rock described Prudence Island, the third largest island in the bay, well. Accessible only by boat, it was a prefect location for the ammunition depot the United States Navy established on four hundred acres and used before, during, and after World War II. Navy ships of all kinds docked at the large, deep pier and took on ammunition brought to the pier by navy trucks driven by sailors from the magazines and underground bunkers built into the sand dunes years ago.

Lieutenant Kleck had taken command of Naval operations on The Rock two week before I reported for duty. My job was to cut the chits and account for each piece of ammunition that went aboard ships as they were loaded and give the gunner's mate of the appropriate ship one copy for his records. I studied at the same time, learning the classifications for all shipboard materials, how to order them, and how to account for them.

One of the three sailors who got out of the taxi and boarded the boat to The Rock would have been just another sailor among hundreds of sailors, except that he was about seven feet tall, and two-hundred-thirty pounds of solid muscle with a long arm-reach. He had blue penetrating eyes and no tattoos that I could see. He wore his white hat at a slight angle, and the rest of his uniform was clean and pressed. His Navy shoes were shined and the laces were tied in rich double knots with no loose ends. He wore a Rolex on his right wrist and checked the time as he extended his hand to me and said in a soft voice for a big man, "I'm Gilmore, other sailors call me Gilly." I looked up at him and said, "Hi Gilly. When we play basketball, I want to be on your team!"

The next time I saw Gilly was when he came to

my office on payday, almost a month later, and asked to borrow money.

"Carpenter, someone told me that you carried several Ben Franklins in your wallet at all times. I need to borrow five. I'll pay you back Monday morning when I return from liberty." I eyed him reluctantly but handed him the five one-hundred-dollar bills. He thanked me and left as quickly as he had appeared in my office. I had my doubts that Gilly would ever pay me back, but it was too late now to worry about that. After muster on Monday, Gilly handed me a white envelope with my name written on it and thanked me again. All my money was there, along with two additional twenty-dollar bills. I slipped them into Gilly's ditty bag that night after he went to sleep so I didn't get caught for usury.

Time waged on. Entertainment on The Rock was limited to ping-pong and touch football; however, there were many interesting people. My work was demanding, but I worked patiently to perform at the highest level I could and studied continually. Navy ships of every kind came to the pier, loaded ammunition, and sailed back to sea.

My immediate supervisor, Chief Gunner's Mate Alex D'Bas was the best! I liked to work for him. He was enthusiastic, competent, and highly qualified in ordnance, ammunition, and procedures of the Navy. He shared his experience and knowledge freely with me. He and I played ping-pong when the ships were not loading and our workload was light. I beat D'Bas playing ping-pong, and when we returned to work in the office, he threw paper clips at me, first one at a time, then a handful. He asked me to call him D'Bas and not to say sir but to have a piping hot cup of Joe with cream and sugar on his desk each morning. I did.

We were the only two sailors working in the office, and it was good duty. He was the best mentor I had in the Navy, and I will always remember him as a professional sailor and friend.

One Thursday at dusk that week, Doc Osby ran over to my office and excitedly called me to come with him. As we ran across the lawn to his office, he jerkily said, "Carpenter, call the boat coxswain on duty in Newport and tell him to haul ass with the Captain's Gig to the pier at The Rock. Tell him to have the ambulance waiting for us on the Melville side of the bay at the pier, hurry! We need a more comfortable boat than the open liberty boat. An emergency is in the making here! Damn it, damn it all, Carpenter, I have never delivered a baby. I know little about bringing a baby into the world."

"Doc, I'm no doula myself, but I'm sure birthing a baby isn't as much fun as helping make one. Why in the hell did you ask me to help you?"

"You have patience, long fingers with clean nails—unlike the sailors who load ammunition—a clean mind, and you say prayers in times like these," Doc stammered.

"Who's having a baby?" I asked curiously.

" Dee Dee, Lieutenant Kleck's wife. You and I are responsible to get her across the bay to the ambulance or deliver the baby, whichever comes first."

Doc continued to talk in broken and nervous sentences. "Both of them finished college two years ago at Brown University and got married right out of college. They are both young and don't know diddle about babies! It's their first baby and he's scared to death! Shit, Carpenter, I don't feel so good my own damn self," Doc frowned.

"Grab two pails from the galley for hot and cold

water, four clean sheets from the linen closet, an arm full of clean towels and wash cloths, a mild bar of soap from your locker, and two clean pillows. Put them in the Navy van parked outside your office. Find the bottle of Jack Daniels whiskey in my locker. Bring it, we'll use it as an anesthetic for pain if we need it."

Sweat was popping out all over Doc as he meticulously went through his checklist of things to put in his black medical bag: a bottle of Lysol, bandages for a belly band, a small pair of scissors, and a cotton cord tape for tying off the umbilical cord. He zipped the medical bag and said in a whining voice, "Drive down to their house and pick up the Lieutenant and his wife so we can meet the Captain's Gig at the pier by The Rock. Damn, I hope the medics will have the ambulance waiting for us at the Melville pier with a Navy pediatrician and nurse with them when we get over there," Doc said in a concerned voice as I drove! "I expect a bloody damn mess on the Captain's Gig," Doc muttered. "How are we going to handle things if Narragansett Bay is rough and white-capping and pitching the boat around?" Doc asked with a sense of urgency as we stopped at the Lieutenant's house.

Dee Dee waddled to the van carrying her pillow with Lieutenant Kleck supporting her heavy steps. Her breasts were big as melons and her belly stuck so far out that she couldn't see her feet. She wedged herself into the van seat with Kleck's help. She leaned over the seat, hugging her pillow. Each contraction was fairly mild at that point, yet she had a difficult time telling her husband exactly when each one came and went. It just took too much energy and concentration from her.

Even though the bay was choppy, the Captain's Gig made it through the rough water from Newport and, with its running lights still on, was tied up at the pier. I parked the van close to the pier and the Captain's Gig. Quickly, Lieutenant Kleck, the boat coxswain, Doc, and I carried Dee Dee from the van into the boat and stretched her out on the long padded seat. A seaman from the crew of the Captain's Gig cast off the lines, the boat coxswain powered the twin inboard engines, and the boat was underway for the pier at Melville. Just as the boat turned into the frothy sea, Dee Dee advised Doc that she noticed a popping sensation down below and knew her water broke. He checked her and said anxiously, "She's completely dilated, Carpenter! Hell, we've got to hurry!"

Contractions took on a new level of intensity! Doc took over the procedures for birthing Dee Dee's baby. Lieutenant Kleck was sweaty, tired, anxious, and speechless as he sat at the other end of the long-padded bench with his head leaning on the side of the boat and his eyes closed. Doc ripped the sheets, hung them like a curtain to make a triage room for delivery. He was unsuccessful getting Dee Dee into the gown she brought to preserve whatever modesty she had left. She couldn't have cared less about being naked in front of Doc and me. Doc observed every move she made and kept his finger on her pulse. There were no machines on the boat to measure her heartbeats, time her contractions, or monitor the heartbeats and rhythm of the baby's heart before it was born. The wallowing of the boat in the wind swells made it difficult for Dee Dee to push at the proper moment. Doc kept urging her to push at the right time and to push harder.

I made masks from a strip of the sheet for Doc and me so we didn't breath germs on the new baby and mama. I was so busy heating water in the galley of the boat, wetting towels, and handing them to Doc that I wasn't aware of how rough the sea was and how the boat yawed and pitched in the wind swells crossing the bay. Doc's tools rolled and slid from the padded seat and hit the deck with banging noises. I picked them up, quickly sterilized them, and handed them to Doc so he could continue his work. Dee Dee kept pushing and moaning louder after each contraction.

Doc mopped sweat from her face with clean towels and moved her into a different position on the padded seat so she could push more effectively. As her labor progressed and her endorphins kicked in, her face became smoother and she began to sway her hips. She became calm and quiet. It was beautiful, somehow, to watch her labor progress undisturbed. With Doc holding her legs apart, she pushed with all her might when he told her to push. She was more than ready to push the baby out. Her one final push got the baby out. Their baby was here! A perfect being, all theirs. It took a minute or two just being in awe before any of us thought about the baby's sex. Then cheers go around as we look and see that it's a girl! Doc snipped and tied the cord and cleaned the baby with a warm towel that I handed him, then he cleaned Dee Dee and the padded seat on the Captain's Gig. Lieutenant Kleck kissed her and held the slippery baby. He stepped closer to Doc and me, put his arm around both of us and thanked us, saying, with a voice filled with emotion, "A job well done to the both of you sailors! Thanks again for taking care of Dee Dee and bringing our baby into the world safely on a wind-swept night aboard a rocky boat."

The boat coxswain slowed the boat, reversed the engines and kicked it smoothly to the pier for tie-up.

The flashing of the ambulance lights was a welcome sight! A doctor and registered nurse, along with other doulas, swarmed aboard the Captain's Gig and quickly checked mama and baby. The baby and mama were removed to the ambulance, and Lieutenant Kleck waved bye to us from where he sat in the front seat. The wailing sound of the siren and flashing lights of the ambulance faded into the night toward the nursery at the hospital. The boat coxswain opened the throttle, kicked the Captain's Gig away from the pier at Melville, and turned it into a calmer sea toward The Rock.

"Carpenter, you're a damn good doula, whatever the hell that is! And, after tonight, you say I'm a midwife, whatever the hell that is, who catches babies better." Doc smiled. "I was damn proud of Dee Dee for having the baby nature's way with no twilight sleep! I asked her to name the Scotch-Irish redhead with blue eyes, Molly Brown. You know, the unsinkable one! I was tickled when she said yes. And the Lieutenant liked the name. Get the bottle of whiskey, I need a drink," Doc continued in a tired voice as he stretched out on the padded bench where he had delivered the baby.

My shipmate from The Rock gave me a ride to Boston on a Friday afternoon and dropped me off about four blocks from Scully's Square. Three of my other shipmates got off the bus and were waiting with me for the light to change across the street from the bus station. Suddenly, four motorcycles roared around the corner and parked at the curb. The men all wore black leather riding jackets with the words Hell's Angels printed in white letters beneath skull and crossbones. All of them had beards and all of them had tattoos on their arms and necks. They were in my face quickly. One of them mumbled something. I answered him saying, "I'm sorry, I don't have a light."

"Damn you swabbies, we want to fight, not a damn light, you sons-of-bitches. You damn dogs. We don't like sailors or dogs and we're going to kick your damn asses. You clumsy, loutish queers."

One of them was now swirling a cudgel stick. My three shipmates stepped over to the side and began removing their white hats. I told the big bastard with the long beard and the ugly tattoos, "I don't start fights but I never ran from a fight," as I removed my white hat and stepped closer to the scarface who was swirling the cudgel stick between the other two Hell's Angels. Gilly suddenly appeared from somewhere, as he had in my office on the The Rock!

"Carpenter, what in the hell is going on? Looks like the asses want something."

"These four Hell's Angels want to fight," I said in a loud voice. "They rode in here on their motorcycles, parked them, and immediately began taunting us. They want to fight is all I know."

Gilly sized them up with his blue penetrating eyes and said, "Now, the louts you call us are one more lout than you four riders. You lowlife, worthless bastards, do you still want to fight? Be sure you want to fight before you answer," Gilly said in an icy voice. "Fighting is what I do. I grew up fighting to survive on the South Side of Chicago. I live to fight. Street fighting is what I like to do best."

The four Hells Angels looked at each other and nodded, "Yes, we want to fight."

Gilly did the unusual. He asked me to hold his white hat and told my three shipmates to standby but not to enter the fray. Under his breath Gilly muttered,

146

"I owe one of my shipmates a payback just to break even." No one present knew what Gilly was talking about except me!

"It's best, most of the time, not to charge usury when you make a loan to a broke sailor," I'm thinking.

Gilly turned to the four Angels and said, "Now you have the advantage, four against one lout, you yellow teeth, dirty, sons-of-bitches. Rumble, you fucking freaks!" Gilly screamed at the Angels.

With that, he broke the arm of the Angel with the cudgel stick, grabbed the stick and stuck the rounded part of the stick in that Angel's mouth with such force it shattered his teeth and left his face a bloody pulp. That Angel fell and Gilly shoved his motorcycle on top of the unconscious man. Blood ran from his mouth and ears into the street gutter. Gilly waded into the other three Hell's Angels so fast they didn't know what hit them!

"Judoka! Judoka! Judoka!!" the Hell's Angels chanted.

They recognized Gilly was a practitioner of the martial arts, and he was now using jiujitsu and karate in the fray. Two Angels ran at Gilly. He did a spin and hit the nearest Angel with a kick that broke his nose and cut a gash so deep over his eyes that bone was visible. He used that Angel as a battering ram and plunged him into the other Angel's gut. Both Angels crumpled to the ground. With powerful karate kicks, Gilly broke the ribs of the two crumpled Angels and rib bones stuck through their skin. Blood was running from their rib wounds and making red puddles in the dirt where they lay. Gilly picked up both their motorcycles and threw them on top of the broken Angels.

The big Angel with the long beard and ugly tattoos brought up a long arm and hand filled with a switch blade knife, its long blade gleaming, toward Gilly's throat. Gilly sidestepped the arcing arm, did a spin move, and kicked the knife away. Gilly's karate-chop to the back of the big man's head staggered him. He drove the heel of his hand into the man's nose and broke it. His face exploded in blood and sweat. The beaten man continued to fight. Gilly wrapped his hand in the long beard and pulled him over to a parking meter where he drove his head, face down, four or five times, into the top of the meter. Limp, the big Angel smeared blood on the meter as he slid down.

"Die, bastard swabby," the big Angel grunted, as he pulled an automatic pistol from the inside of his bloody riding jacket and pointed it at Gilly's back.

I yelled, "He's aiming a gun at you, Gilly!"

Whirling, Gilly did an outside, inside, spin move and broke the bloody Angel's ribs with a thunderous kick. The big man tried to lift the automatic again, but Gilly wrung it loose and used the gun like a hammer to break all his fingers on both hands. With all the power in his muscular body, Gilly slammed the barrel of the automatic into the skull of the Hell's Angel with the long beard and ugly tattoos. He gathered the man in his hands and pitched him in the bloody mess on top of the other Angels and their tangled motorcycles and calmly said, "Carpenter, call that pile of shit over there with flies beginning to buzz around it Motorcycle Hell, where Angels don't rest. Hand me my white hat, please. Lay the gun, knife, and brass knuckles beside the big Angel so the cops will understand. Leave the cudgel stick in the Angel's mouth." He smacked his lips, as some Swedes do when they finish a brawl.

He brushed a little dirt off his white bellbottoms and adjusted the money belt around his waist before he left the scene to go downtown in Boston for a high-

148

stakes poker game,

I asked Gilly, "What belts do you hold?"

He answered with a wink, "I have first-degree black belts in six martial arts but use only two arts when I rumble with four Angels."

My three shipmates put their white hats on and walked across the street to Zoniz, their favorite bar, and I walked toward Bice's dance studio. Curious on-lookers who had gathered to watch justice done faded into the side streets before the cops arrived.

My Life at Sea

Too often the act of creation brings its own disenchantment. It was easy at times to be cynical or casual about what I had seen or what I had experienced. However, a moment's thought still serves to bring back the wonders of my life at sea. Visiting lands whose very names create a magic of their own was sufficient to rekindle my excitement. The Mediterranean and her surrounding countries are the birthplace of Western culture and philosophy—our heritage. The sea, the sky, the sun...from Gibraltar to Istanbul, from Arabia to Tangiers: heat, rock, dust. Red-brown land as old as time and the sea, even older. Around the Mediterranean Sea, people carved cities, cultures, and civilizations out of eternity. The places are timeless—men die, stones do not. There are many cities, and most of us have forgotten why they are there.

The Mediterranean is rich in history. More than 3,000 years of historical process, initiated in the same countries I was privileged to visit, have gone into making us as we are. Democracy and philosophy from Greece, Roman law, Italian art, Judaism and Christianity...we have inherited all this from the Mediterranean. It is important for you to know that I joined the United States Navy at an early age and served proudly to defend our freedom and heritage.

My life at sea began when I was assigned to an aircraft carrier home-based at Norfolk, Virginia. Sixth Fleet operations, and the wonders of my Mediterranean cruise unfolded for the next eight months aboard a magnificent ship, the aircraft carrier USS *Coral Sea CVA-43*.

I sat on my sea bag on the pier at Mayport, Florida watching for the ship to come over the horizon and tie up at the pier where I was to board. I had never been aboard an aircraft carrier and was excited about my new duties aboard ship.

Suddenly I saw a swirl of blue smoke as the *Coral Sea* came over the horizon into view. I was astonished at the size of the ship. Sailors scurrying on the flight deck looked as small as ants; fighter jets looked like toy planes. Four million meals were served on the ship each year. If stood on end, she would be only 150 feet shorter than the Empire State Building. Capable of staying at sea for months at a time, the ship provided every necessity and many luxuries, from laundries to newspapers, haircuts to a ship's band, and a foreign-goods store. Even after I went aboard, the size of the ship amazed me. She was 968 feet long; her flight deck 932 feet; breadth at the widest point was 136 feet; depth from her center-line flight deck amidships was eighty-four feet; full-load displacement 60,000 tons; draft 35 feet; shaft horsepower 200,000; speed in knots 33; number of aircraft carried 125; number of crew 3,500 sailors and marines; with a monthly payroll 1,650,000. I had read these statistics and now knew the truth behind the numbers. She was my dream ship.

I walked quickly up the gang plank of the ship for the first time, saluted the officer of the deck, held my orders and dog tags for him and said, "Carpenter reporting aboard for duty, Sir."

The lieutenant returned my salute sharply and said, "Welcome aboard for duty, Carpenter. Your battle station is the 5"/38 anti-aircraft gun mount number five on the starboard side of the ship all the way forward, in the event general quarters sounds or we have a drill before you get your official assignment from your division officer."

"Yes, Sir," I replied. I knew the first duty of any sailor was to defend and save the ship. I was pleased to know where my battle station was located so I didn't get confused if general quarter sounded.

Security was priority on the ship. The lieutenant handed my paperwork to the Marine Sentry standing watch with him and asked the orderly to make an entry into the ship's log book of the time I reported aboard and record information data from my transcript since I was an expected sailor coming aboard the ship for the first time.

The junior officer of the deck asked a second Marine Sentry standing watch to escort me to the ship's personnel office for processing and assignment to S-1 Supply Division of the ship. First Class Yeomen Yates processed my paperwork, issued me an S-1 liberty pass and a ship's identification card for access to all facilities provided aboard the ship, including the chow line and barber shop.

Third Class Yeomen Shaw grabbed my sea bag and led me down a long passageway on the starboard side of the ship to S-1 Division, located on the third deck down beneath the elevator. I entered the compartment with Yeoman Shaw leading the way, using the six steel folding steps running from the second deck to the third deck through the four-feet-by-six-feet hatch that served as the only entrance and exit to the compartment.

My rack was a four-feet wide by six-feet long white piece of canvas stretched and tiedoff by small nylon lines on aluminum poles attached to the ship. It had a thin mattress, a small pillow, two sheets, and two blue navy blankets that were folded up on my bed. There were sixty racks tiered four high in the compartment. Mine was on top of the tier on the starboard side, facing aft.

My small metal locker attached to the ship's bulkhead next to my rack was the last one in the compartment. The compartment had a long metal table attached to the deck with benches that ran fore and aft. It was used by sailors in S-1 Division for mail call, playing poker, and many other things. The sleeping quarters were clean and neat; everyone's area was shipshape. I threw my sea bag on my rack, picked up a copy of my orders, and left the compartment.

Yeoman Shaw showed me the way down to my work station and supply office to meet my new boss. He said, "Your division officer is well liked by other officers and by sailors and marines who know him. He knows his stuff and treats people right. You will like to work for him."

I was excited to meet my new boss and shipmates and begin working.

Lieutenant Commander D.L. Lake, a graduate of the United States Naval Academy and a handsome man in his early thirties, extended his hand with a warm smile and friendly handshake and introduced himself as the S-1 Supply Division Officer. With a wide grin he said, "This is your desk beside mine. Your name is on the desk and it has work material in the drawers to get you started. Welcome to S-1 Supply Division. I look forward to working and laughing with you. A lot of each goes on here. I saw in your transcript that you're from Robbinsville, North Carolina, in the Smoky Mountains. Thomas Wolfe, the author of *Look Homeward Angel* was from Asheville, I know, and looking on the map, Robbinsville is even more west in the state," the Commander continued.

"Yes," I said. "Moonshiners and bootleggers still make corn liquor and haul it on Thunder Road to cities around there. Robbinsville is ninety-two miles West of Asheville. Ronnie Milsap, the country singer and songwriter, lived on Meadow Branch near Robbinsville. I was privileged to hear him sing and play at a young age. When he hit the highest notes on the Christmas carol "O Holy Night," I got goose pimples."

"Higgins, Worrell, Dominick, and I want you to tell us one of your mountain stories now," he went on.

"Sir, thank you for your valuable time to tell a story. I'll be brief. I had to hitchhike from Yellow Creek where I lived, to Robbinsville to go to the old Chic Theater to watch Roy Rogers bring all outlaws in the West to swift justice. I had to hurry to make the movie on time. An old gentleman stopped and said, "Get in." I saw a long line of people behind his car blowing their horns and getting more frustrated. I recognized his old green Plymouth coupe and the slowest driver in the

United States immediately and said, in a casual tone, "I'm in a hurry, go on." Another car picked me up in about fifteen minutes, and I waved to the old gentleman as we passed the jalopy about two miles from Robbinsville. I made the movie with time to spare."

They all laughed and agreed that stories and laughter were some of the best ways to get to know each other and form good relationships quickly.

"Carpenter, Higgins is our Chief Petty Officer; Worrell and Dominick, First Class Petty Officers; Blazer and Bishop, Second Class Petty Officers; and Jerez and Kans, Third Class Petty Officers. Many of the other fifty-two non-rated sailors in the division are studying for advancement. I encourage each one of them to better themselves and advance in their job and pay. All of them are good men and sailors.

"From your transcript I received last week, I was pleased to see you have already taken the examination for Third Class Petty Officer, and your marks from the past year in the Navy are excellent. Our education officer is Lieutenant Nali; I encourage you to set up an appointment with him and begin work on your college degree. I'll introduce you to him tomorrow. I am proud of you. I wish you well on passing the examination for Third Class Petty Officer. I want to pin your promotion crow on you soon."

"Thank you, Sir."

The things that struck me most about Mayport were the quiet things. The pelicans diving into the water of the basin, the fishing boats that sailed out to sea every morning at dawn, and the clothing drying in the sun on the fantail of a tug. There was even a soothing monotony in the endless approaches and takeoffs of the jets and the rhythmic swing of the crane as the next squadron was hoisted

aboard. All of the F9F-8 and the squadron of AD-6 planes were hoisted aboard the big ship.

Making the ship ready for deployment was much like producing a new play. It was hard work, from start to finish. Sets must be built, roles learned, and jobs done. Personnel must be coached and drilled repeatedly until they become an efficient team. All of these activities must be organized and controlled by the director. Then, after endless rehearsals and an extensive road tour, the play is brought before the critics. It is ready for the big time.

It was the same with the *Coral Sea*. The raw material was there: a huge, complex, gray steel ship; a crew of 35,000 officers and men; and 125 aircraft. The responsibility of putting the three quantities together rested in the hands of the Captain. The crew chipped and painted, drilled and sweated. The planes flew all day and even at night. All the while the big ship moved: Norfolk, New York, Cuba, and Florida. Mayport was still a constant whirlpool of activity loading the ship. During this period, the crew gained proficiency in the split-second timing necessary for conducting efficient and safe flight operations. Over and over the lessons were repeated, the drills rerun.

There came a time, though, when the big ship did not move. Unexpected repairs were needed to the main reduction gears, and a trip to the naval shipyard at Portsmouth, Virginia, became necessary. But in less time than expected, she was out of the yard and ready once more for the big time—Mediterranean deployment with the Sixth Fleet.

Shakedown training; operational readiness in Guantanamo Bay, Cuba; fleet training for battle problems; carrier pilots qualifications; and the operational readiness inspection were all completed. Working parties had completed their loading of the ship.

Dominick said, "Carpenter, take this bill-of-lading of all the general supplies we've loaded here over to the Naval Supply Depot Office and get it signed by the Navy Commander in charge there. Bring one copy back for records so you can account for each item and post it to the inventory control cards in the pullout metal drawers here in the supply office. Have him date the document and sign his name in front of a notary. You may witness his signature and date your signing of the document," Dominick continued. "It's an important official record of over $3,000,000 of general supplies."

"Wow!" I thought, "I've never signed any paper before that represented that amount of money."

A Plan of the Day was posted in my compartment each day. It gave information on the day's activities and anything special that might be occurring that day. It was an unclassified document but was not to be sent or carried off the ship. Information such as duty section, working division, water score, and if the ship was at sea or in port was shown. The officer of the deck and the junior officer of the deck were shown with the hours of the watch they were standing. The rescue and assistance boat officer was shown, and the work and dress uniforms of the day were shown. Each sailor on the ship was responsible for knowing the information and carrying out the directive for that day. I always read the Plan of the Day so I would know the proper uniform to wear and keep from being out of uniform and put on report for captain's mast.

Mama, in one of her letters, asked me to write to her what my day at sea was like. In my next letter to her I wrote, "Each morning, reveille is piped over the intercom at 0600, morning devotions start at 0715, breakfast follows. Muster is held on the flight deck to determine if all are present or accounted for at 0745 and turn-to announced over the intercom at 0800. I go to my work station in the supply office, and the other fifty-two non-rated shipmates in my division go to man the twenty-five storerooms for general supplies at various locations throughout the ship. Stub requisition, afloat signed by a particular department officer, are presented to me at the window of the supply office. I check the inventory control card to be sure I have the stock or part requested. I subtract the quantity requested on the control card, initial and date the requisition, and send the sailor to the proper storeroom where the stock or part is located. The storekeeper manning that particular storeroom issues the material and turns in a copy of the stub requisition to the supply office to let me know the material went to the proper department."

I concluded the letter, "Before the day is done, I read my scriptures and say my prayers. I rest safer from the perils of the sea and war. Mama, tell Dad that I'm behaving in the Navy. Uncle Sam sees to it. Yes, Uncle Sam will jerk a knot in my tail every time I misbehave, just like he did. I miss all of you every day. That's it Mama, for now, love and kisses to you."

Supply is, to the crew, the most important department on the ship, providing many of the more civilized touches: ice cream stands, the laundry, the ship's store. I could buy anything from typewriters to perfume and cameras to watches in the ship's store. More importantly, Supply fills the sailor's belly three times a day and his pocket twice a month. And who can deny, after buying three Hershey bars for only a dime, that life is good.

Many tears where shed, kisses and hugs went on and on the day the ship left. Leave-taking was difficult for those who had found sweethearts, who had families and who had struck up friendships in Mayport.

On deployment day, the Plan of the Day showed underway at sea. The *Bosnian* Mate's pipe sounded,and a tug boat pushed the *Coral Sea* away from the pier.

The Navigation Officer's voice came over the ship's intercom loud and clear, "Now hear this. Secure everything on deck, set the special sea and anchor detail, and carry out the normal daily routine shown in the Plan of the Day."

Commander Lake said, "We're underway. Carpenter, bring me a cup of tea, please, and let's get to work while this big ship brings us to the Mediterranean and to all ports-of-call, including Naples, Toronto, and Genoa, Italy; Palermo and Augusta, Sicily; Athens, Greece; Istanbul, Turkey; Alexandria, Egypt ;and Cannes, France."

He continued, "Some of the most interesting

places in Europe to visit have been arranged by Lieutenant Nali, the education officer, including Capri, Pompeii, Amalfi, Italian and French Riviera, Monte Carlo, Monaco, Grasse, Cannes, Eze, Rome, Florence, Pisa, Collodi, and Venice. I've never been to any of these ports or places; have you?"

"No, Sir. I'm looking forward to the next eight months," I told the Commander, as I handed him another cup of Earl Grey tea and an updated schedule of all the places where we would pick up supplies on this cruise.

Even though the ship was sailing at about thirty knots and the shaft horsepower was 200,000 for the twin screws, noise pollution was minimal in my office, and the work environment was surprisingly comfortable. From my work space, I couldn't hear the planes landing and taking off on the flight deck. The inside temperature was controlled at seventy-two degrees and working conditions were pleasant.

In eleven days, the big ship passed through the Straits of Gibraltar, and three days later it arrived at the Golfo de Palmas to relieve the USS *Intrepid*. In a few hours, the anchor was lifted and the ship was

underway again.

My special place after working hours was the fantail of the ship. I stayed there until Taps most evenings during favorable weather. For hours, I sat on the bench there and read books and poetry and watched the furrow, the white wake of the ship churn and roll; sunsets that quickly sank into the sea; and the moon and stars came out to work their magic of shadows beyond the ship. Sunrises and sunsets at sea were astounding. The sea claimed the sun rising in the east or setting in the west. It appeared to fall off the sea when it went down with a sudden fiery flare and to shoot straight up from the depths of the sea with a fiery halo when it came up.

Most interesting were the quick flashes of dolphins swimming and frolicking alongside the ship, and the tiny birds that sat on the ship's antennas and chirped. I wondered with awe about the fires that

burned green, blue, and white at night as the prow of the big ship cut through the water. The smell was always salty and there were smacking, sucking and liquid sounds that caught my interest in the relatively quiet sailing of the ship. I wondered how the rows of tiny birds sitting on the antennas could survive thousands of miles from shore and about the eerie lights in the water that the ship sliced through.

Two days later the ship rode anchor less than a quarter mile from the pier at Naples, Italy, where the harbor was deep enough to accommodate the ship. The Bosum's Mate's pipe sounded liberty call for my division, and that created a flurry of excitement for me and my shipmates—especially those, like me, who had never set foot on foreign soil.

I was pleased to be in the first liberty call. My white uniform was freshly pressed, my shoes shined, my white hat clean, and my tie neatly tied with a single passthrough knot. I was one sharp sailor with my German Retina CIII 35mm camera and my money belt full of Italian lira. I was ready to go ashore. But not yet.

Before I saluted the officer of the deck and requested permission to go ashore, I had to make a mandatory stop at the Pull It On Before You Squirt Off station on the ship to pick up three packages of protection, all free. I held up my liberty card and protection, and the officer of the deck gave me a snappy salute and said, "Permission granted for liberty, Carpenter."

I walked down the gangplank quickly and boarded *Coral Sea 1*, the first of four liberty boats plying the harbor between the ship and the pier at Naples, Italy. The boat coxswain feathered the propellers and trimmed the inboard engine, reversed the gear, and kicked the boat smoothly into the pier for tie-up. Thirty young, excited sailors from the boat swarmed the streets of Naples.

Naples exhales a smog that is peculiarly its own. As I strolled down its narrow alleyways, poverty stuck out from all sides. All my senses were aroused: smell, sight, and sound. The Neapolitan is a gregarious, vociferous fellow offering his services as a guide, his homemade pens and jewelry.

Beautiful Italian women lined the streets and brothels, selling themselves and the use of their beds to the sailor willing to pay the most lire. Unfortunately, for many sailors this was the first and lasting impression of Naples. However, to appreciate Naples, I had to regain my perspective. Along the Via Partenope, I found interesting art and artists and discovered an excellent opera company, which I enjoyed for two hours. The Bay of Naples was magnificent; the surrounding area was historic and colorful. Naples was a city of many aspects—difficult to know, but with intimacy grew fondness. Distance and darkness, I found, lend changes to Naples.

At night, the city swarms with characters intent upon relieving me of my *lira*. Some of the brassiest, bawdiest night clubs and women in the world are there in this teeming city. I didn't understand a lot about women then. My limited experience and young age left me ignorant. In this harbor town, beautiful girls in night clubs were dancing nude and selling their bodies. I had never experienced anything like it before. One girl was not pretty but she smelled nice. Her perfume was strong enough that it made my eyes water. How she managed to put up with the stink of it trapped inside her frilly bodice, I couldn't understand. Italian women, without perfume, had a particular scent all their own. It was like their country, like the sea: not salty but fresh like a sea breeze, unlike smog, pungent and strong, slightly acid like dried sweat, like the smell of a ripe lemon.

For more *lira*, there were different kinks available other than normal intercourse. At my young age,

I knew nothing about a futatrix, a female who practices tribalism, a relationship in which women attempt to imitate heterosexual intercourse with each other by rubbing; or scopophilia, the gratification of sexual desire through gazing. This kink was the cleanest and safest of all kinks. The scopophiliac is safe from flesh contact and all the sexual-related diseases.

In the brothels women were provocative in every way: naked; sheer see-through clothes, when they wore any, with visible cleavage; lustful kisses; sizzling dances with their legs spread apart and breasts jiggling like a flivver. One special brothel featured voyeurism, for sailors seeking sexual gratification from seeing sexual acts. The sordid or the scandalous didn't appeal to me, but it was there in the brothels. Yet, what I first saw was a historic old castle set in a large square constantly swept by street cleaners. The open friendliness of the Neapolitan was often expressed. "I'm your friend, Joe."

There was the beautiful bay, the slums, the hodgepodge of houses rising up onto the hill. In the distance, Mount Vesuvius brooded silently, dreaming

of the days when it was young and strong, as does, perhaps, Naples herself. A few half-naked children swam while the old men mended their boats and basked in the warm Italian sunshine. At night, colored lights and snatches of songs from outdoor restaurants created an atmosphere on the island for which Santa Lucia and its inhabitants are famous.

One of the most interesting places on the Neapolitan waterfront was the small rocky island of Capri, about two hours by ferry from Naples. It is as fragile as a work of art: small villages carved out of reddish stone, fields of wildflowers, and casinos. Capri has been a fashionable resort since A.D. 200.

Blue Grotto may refer to a cave on the coast of the Italian island of Sicily, a cave on the coast of Malta, a cave on the Greek island of Kastelorizo, a cave on the coast of the Croatian island of Bisevo, or it may refer to a cave on the coast of the Italian island of Capri. Capri's Blue Grotto is known throughout the world for its size, the intense blue tones of its interior, and the magical silvery light that emanates from the objects immersed in the waters.

I took a boat from Marina Grande to the cave entrance. In order to enter the Grotto Azzurra, I climbed aboard a small rowboat with a capacity for two passengers, and, lying on the bottom of the boat, the coxswain paddled to near the entrance, where we rode like a bobbing cork until the tricky wind swells, tides, and crosswinds calmed and it was safe to enter the low and narrow mouth of the cave.

The lucky coincidence of geological and speleological conditions had created a double enchantment. The interior was effused with magnificent blue tones created by the daylight, which enters by way of an underwater opening located immediately below the entrance to the cave. The light is filtered by the water, which absorbs the red tones, leaving only the blue ones to pass into the cave.

A second phenomenon created the silver appearance of the objects immersed in the water: given that the index of refraction of the bubbles of air that adhere to the surface of the objects is different from that of the water, the light is allowed to egress. The boatman set down his oars and maneuvered the boat inside with the aid of a chain attached to the vault of the entrance. The ceiling is rounded, and from its entire surface it distills fresh water, which fell on me like the first drops of a rainstorm.

On the ferry back to reality, some thoughts kept occurring to me. The gaming industry and casinos were real, and Capri was truly a playground of millionaires and sailors alike. The coxswain said, "Your lover will never forsake you, and both of you will be immortal when you dip your finger in the blue water inside the cave and kiss your lover under the silver lights of Capri's Blue Grotto."

These words continue to inspire me to this day.

I didn't get to kiss my lover under the silver lights of Capri's Blue Grotto, but I did get to dip my fingers in the blue waters of the Blue Grotto.

Pompeii is the mummy of a once great city, a unique ruin because it never had the time to decline; there were no scars of transition by conquering cultures. Vesuvius erupted in A.D. 79, burying the fashionable Roman resort at the height of its glory. It lay that way, protected by volcanic ash, for nearly 1800 years. Now the old stones endure endless streams of sailors and the hot sun with equal unconcern. I could imagine beautiful Roman women, with their long flowing dresses, stepping on the raised stepping stones to keep their dresses from dragging in the mud in the narrow stone streets left rutted by chariot wheels and the fading sounds of horses' hoofbeats. Sitting in one of the amphitheaters that had been unearthed, I caught myself thinking, "The audience is long dead, but the applause still echoes."

A small village couched on a rocky hillside, sleeping in the sun, with faded pastel villas, the bright sea, and a people as old as Western civilization, Amalfi, I still see as one of the most interesting and beautiful places in Italy. It is a town in the province of Salerno less than thirty-five miles southwest of Naples. Situated at the bottom of a deep ravine at the foot of Mount Cerrito, Amalfi is surrounded by dramatic cliffs and coastal scenery. According to myth, the god Hercules built the city on the spot where he buried the nymph whom he loved.

In the center of Amalfi stands a big church for a big God. The sight of this cathedral dedicated to Saint Andrew with its sixty-two wide steep steps and its off-center bell tower is awe-inspiring. Its interior is adorned in late Baroque style with a nave and two aisles divided by twenty columns. The gold caisson ceiling had four large paintings by Andrea d'Aste. They depict the flagellation of Saint Andrew, the miracle of manna, the crucifixion of Saint Andrew and the Saint on the cross. As one of God's mortals, I felt smaller than a grain of sand when I was leaving the cathedral, still looking up at the paintings.

Through its prowess of the seas and dominance in international trade, Amalfi drafted the most effective code of maritime law of the time, the

Tabula Amalfitana, which was adopted by all the maritime powers of the area. The compass was invented by Flavio Giola of Amalfi and first used by ships of Amalfi. Today it is used by all countries.

Palermo, the capital of Sicily, by the Gulf of Palermo in the Tyrrhenian Sea, was founded by the Phoenicians but named by the ancient Greeks as Panoramas, which means all-port, because of its natural harbor.

I walked through one of the thirteen original gateways entering the Old City. I saw a fountain with water spraying from fifty-six spouts, round buildings on the main square, charming old houses surrounded by palm trees; I sensed the smell of horses in the air; I admired some masterpieces of Arab-Norman art, a peculiar fusion of stark Nordic stone and lavish Byzantine mosaic; and I watched a long-eared donkey with smiling children riding on its back. I wondered why the flop-eared old donkey didn't smile. Mondello is a pleasant beach there, and I enjoyed swimming and playing in the surf with many beautiful girls before going to dinner with one of them.

The cloister of St. John of the Hermits is a quiet place, smelling of mint, where delicate flowered vines creep over the weathered gray stone. The church is noted for its brilliant red domes, which show clearly the persistence of Arab influence in Sicily at the time of the reconstruction in the twelfth century.

Palermo Cathedral is the city's main church. One of the things in the cathedral most interesting was the heliometer, a solar observatory dated 1690. The device itself is quite simple: a tiny hole in one of the domes acts as a pinhole camera, projecting an image of the sun onto the floor at solar noon—1200 in winter and 1300 in summer. There was a bronze line on the floor, running precisely north and south. The ends of the lines marked the position of the sun at the summer and winter solstices; signs of the zodiac showed the various other dates throughout the year.

The purpose of the instrument was to standardize the measurement of time and the calendar. The convention in Sicily had been that the twenty-four-hour day was measured from the moment of sunrise, which meant that no two locations had the same time and, more importantly, did not have the same time as in St. Peter's Basilica in Rome. It was also important to know when the vernal equinox occurred to provide the correct date for Easter.

Open-air fruit and vegetable markets in and around Palermo are the eighth wonder of the world. Eating a prickly pear is quite an art. I tried it in Capo, Bullario, Borgo, and Vecchio with little success but got help in Vucciria. Vucciria is located in the center of Palermo. It closely resembles the ancient kasbahs. It is the largest and best known market all over the world. It is separated into food and everything else. The food section was full of lovely sights and scents— except the fish, which didn't smell good. As I walked around in the puddles of fish water at La Vucciria, the local cats followed me about, meowing and rubbing my leg.

A variety of fruits and vegetables gave the over-all market a magnificent color. Melons, spices, peppers, grapes, pears, green beans, Brotzeit bread rolls, yellow peaches, oranges, apricots and red apples were displayed in row after row inside Vucciria. Turk-ish slippers, leather goods, fabrics from India, and art including original paintings and sculptures were avail-able at La Vucciria. Fruits and vegetables displayed as they were in this famous market made true works of art.

Teatro Massimo opera house is the largest theater in Italy and the third largest in Europe. It opened in 1897, and it was closed for renovation from 1974 until 1997. It is now carefully restored and has weekly performances. I paid a shipmate buddy to take my duty so I could attend a performance of Enrico Caruso in *La Giaconda* during the opening season in 1956. Caruso returned for *Rigoletto* at the very end of his career. *La Giaconda* was excellent and one of the most important musical events I have ever attended.

My expectations of Palermo perhaps were colored by its checkered past: violence in the streets, crumbled structures left in the aftermath of World War II, corrupt politicians, and home of the Sicilian Mafia, or the Costa Nostra, as it's called there. However, now it's safe and peaceful; rich in history, culture, art, music, food, and good Mediterranean weather. I'm pleased that I walked through one of the thirteen gates and discovered Palermo's renowned gastronomy, restaurants; its Romanesque, Gothic, and Baroque churches, palaces and buildings; and its nightlife and music, especially its opera.

The Black Plague that swept Genoa, Italy in 1656 killed over half of the inhabitants. Now Genoa, a modern prosperous city of 700,000 people, is proud of its historical heritage. La Superba is a great industrial center as well as the busiest port in the Mediterranean Sea. Always having lived off the sea, Genoa is proud of her most famous son and symbol, Christopher Columbus.

A wilder side of this harbor port is set apart by Zanzibar Bar with many dancing girls and the Via Gramsci, a street similar to Third Avenue in New York or East Main in Norfolk. Bars, cheap night clubs, armed with B-girls and street walkers, are its adornments; their patrons, the transients of the city and sailors.

Genoa is rich in the arts, museums, castles, and monuments, which preserve her long history. Surrounding mountains have forced Genoa to the edge of the sea. She is proud of her sea-going history and soldiers commemorated in a memorial to an Unknown Solider. The Old Harbor, Porto Artico in Italian, is the ancient part of the Port of Genoa. The Genoese architect, Renzo Piano, developed the area, creating space for the world-renowned aquarium, the Bigo and the Bolla, the sphere. A large monument dedicated to Christopher Columbus in the Port Harbor of Genoa and a special flower garden designed with flower beds arranged to form the shapes of his three sailing ships—the Nina, Pinta and Santa Maria—echo the honor and tribute given to the world's most famous explorer, a Genoese who discovered America in 1492. Even though his major goal in life was to become rich and famous, I felt it commendable that he left an endowment of one-tenth of his income from the discovery of America for Spain in an escrow account in the Bank of Saint George in Genoa, the oldest bank in the world, to relieve taxation on food and wine for his fellow Genoese.

Although rich in sculpture from other periods, Staglieno has become particularly associated with Re-

alism. One of the better examples of this truth that I saw was the sensuality in the "widow with a prayer book in her hand coming out of the chapel," sculpted by Giuseppe Benetti. This powerful sculpture adorns the Piaggio Tomb in the Staglieno Cemetery, Genoa,

Italy. Many famous sculptors' works are represented in this gallery of monuments offering an exploration of man's struggle with death, transcendence, salvation and mortality. Nietzsche; Guy de Maupassant; Elizabeth of Austria; and Mark Twain, in his book *Innocents Abroad* all left their impressions of the well-known sculptors and their work, but they considered Staglieno Cemetery an open-air museum, as evidenced by the number and quality of the memorial monuments. I was enthralled with the beauty of the sculptures and the variety of subjects they depicted. I kept thinking Staglieno Cemetery provides deluxe accommodations for those wealthy and famous enough to be buried there.

I learned that during the medieval era, the naked body often stood for temptation and sin. In Christian theology, the emphasis was not upon physical beauty but upon the inevitability of the body's decay and the shame in nakedness that came from eating the fruit of the tree of knowledge.

As I left the gallery of monuments, I thought that the images and their associated symbols explored a collective yearning to understand the human condition, our vulnerability and mortality, renewal, redemption, and terror of the unknown. These are the deep issues seeking transcendence and result in a profound desire to understand the meaning of our existence. Such passion is at the foundation of the heart of the world and the ultimate hope that the universe is not random. Life, then, is short, as is the exquisite beauty of a woman. Cemeteries such as Pere Lachaise, Staglieno, Novodevichy, Montparnasse, Monumental, Forest Hills, and other great cemeteries are sacred places for sculptors to depict female nudity and its beauty even unto death.

Shipboard life would be an unbearably dull and drab routine of watch, sleep, eat, and turn-to if it were not for the humor that abounds in so many unexpected places and the variety of recreational diversions available: gymkhana, mustache contests, smokers, happy hour with comedy and musical talent shows, skeet shoots, flying model airplanes on the flight deck, and card games—any time, any place a greasy old deck of cards was pulled out for a few fast hands—and Sam.

Sam, a stowaway, entertained us all by bringing his master a beer (and tasting it for him), his socks, his shoes. He knew the difference between the dress uniform and work uniform and brought his master the correct uniform of the day. He could go to the bathroom by himself and flush the commode. He knew where to hide and not make a sound when the Captain and his inspecting team came below decks. Sam was special–a plank owner of the ship, a sailor's sailor, a beautiful German dachshund, illegal but one of the favorite entertainers on the big ship.

Sometimes at sea, after working hours, the hanger bays looked remarkably like Stillman's Gym. I trained hard—sweating, groaning, jumping rope, and punching the bag—readying myself for the big go for S-1 Supply Division.

"I'll deck de bum in de foist round," I jeered as I mimicked the Italian sailor I was to fight for my shipmates, much to their delight.

During the smoker on fight night, Commander Lake and my shipmates where seated next to the ring to support me. Commander Lake, a great competitor himself, kept applauding and saying, "Take him now, don't wait another minute."

"Deck the bum." Commander Lake echoed my

jeer. "Carpenter, you are our man," he continued to applaud and yell.

At the bottom of the first round, I scored with a thunderous left hook that sent the Italian boxer to the deck, and was rewarded with a roaring applause from my shipmates. The fighter slowly got up and staggered to a sprawling fall. The referee stopped the fight and held my hand up for the winner. I had won my first and last smoker. My shipmates and Commander slapped me on the back as we left the ring for our office and said, "Good fight, Rocky."

After twenty-eight days at sea with no liberty and tensions running high among the crew, Captain Japp brought the big ship to anchor off the coast of France. Four destroyer escorts and two cruisers, operating with the *Coral Sea*, formed a circle around the ship to make a large swimming pool in the ocean, which was as calm as a mill pond that day. Eight pontoon boats with four Marines in each boat, with their M-1 rifles and megaphones, took their places inside the circle to watch for sharks, pick up tired swimmers, and give instructions to swimmers during swim call.

From the hanger deck to the water it was 125 feet. Cargo nets were secured at the edge of the hanger deck and dropped down to the water. Swimmers used the nets to climb down into the water and climb up to the hanger deck after swimming. Swim call had been going for about two hours when suddenly fins were slicing the water just outside the circle of the swim area, and the Marines called through their megaphones to clear the water. Jellyfish were now stinging swimmers and causing them to swim toward the cargo nets. Marines followed the sharks closely but did not fire. Swimmers swarmed toward the cargo net in near panic.

A smaller swimmer was too tired to climb the nets farther and was hanging like a wilted butterfly about half-way up. Other swimmers were climbing up the nets frantically, and, in their frenzy to get to safety, the ones above the small swimmer were using him like a rung on a stepladder, stomping his face as they went up the nets. Blood flew from the tired swimmer's nose and mouth as he hung on the nets, unable to move.

The officer of the deck was screaming through his megaphone, "You damn knuckleheads, help your shipmate, don't kill him."

I had worked myself across the cargo nets to the tired, bloody swimmer and was reaching for him when a large muscular arm shot under the swimmer's arms and the giant of a man muscled his way up the nets with his other arm carrying the swimmer to the hanger deck.

Two Navy corpsman were there to give the tired exhausted swimmer medical attention, the officer of the deck thanked the large man, and, as he turned to go, I recognized Gunny Toro and said, "Thank you, Marine, for saving a shipmate's life."

The cargo nets were pulled back into the hanger deck, swim call was secured, and the anchor lifted. The big ship was again underway.

Traditionally, a plane forced to land on a carrier other than the one it was assigned to was in for it. It was a chance for the flight-deck crew to demonstrate the partisanship in the fiercely competitive spirit that existed between two carriers operating together.

Mistaking Pisa for Marseille is quite a feat, but one of the pilots from USS *Coral Sea* managed it. He had to land on the USS *Randolph*. How he did it is still a mystery to me, but I saw "flying foolishness" scribbled in large letters with red paint in front of a frightened character sketch of the Leaning Tower of Pisa on the fuselage of the Banshee fighter jet he flew when he returned to the *Coral Sea* the next day. My shipmates and I applauded when he landed aboard the right ship that day.

Every major port in the Mediterranean possesses the common denominators of beauty, merchants, travelers, filth, cosmopolitanism, and poverty. Indeed, as it is true that the sea has always been an avenue for the exchange of ideas, of ways of life, so it is true that the sea is a great equalizer. Despite the difference in language, there is a remarkable similarly between the bars, night clubs, and women of the night in Istanbul, Turkey, and Naples, Italy.

For the sailor, this is especially true. Faced with only a relatively short time in a particular land, he is likely to spend most of his liberty within a small radius of the fleet landing. The only opportunity he really has to become acquainted with the country is through his own initiative and information acquired through the education officer of the ship.

I learned infinitely more by comparing the North Italian countryside to central North Carolina while on my way to Venice than by comparing the Kit Kat Klub in Athens, Greece, to Smoky Joe's bar in Philadelphia.

My desire to learn heightened with every new port of call. After the big ship passed through the Strait of Dardanelles and sailed on to Greece, my thoughts turned to the country that I had waited so long to see and to learn more about.

The sky was the bluest, the air clearer and cleaner in Greece. I watched sponge divers bring up their catch off the Island of Crete. Water in the Aegean

Sea was blue and calm. Athens, Greece, lies in a dried bowel of earth rimmed in bare hills. At the center of this valley rises a small navel of rock, and on it, the remains of a civilization that other countries, including my own, have often tried, unsuccessfully, to emulate. For over 2000 years the Periclean Age has fascinated and baffled.

I thought, "How, at one time, in that small city-state, such a tremendous blossoming of thought could have occurred, is no small wonder. Within a hundred years, Socrates, Plato, and Aristotle all lived and taught, while Aeschylus, Sophocles, and Euripides created tragic dramas that only Shakespeare has ever equaled. In that same century, the Parthenon was built. Western civilization has made the fruits of the Greek mind and soul a fundamental part of its own except, perhaps, for the most important principle of all—moderation."

Athens was a history book for me. A statute of St. Paul, Olympieion, Hadrian's Arch A.D.125 and the fallen pillars of the Acropolis formed chapters in my mind. The altar at Pantanassa Convent in Mistras, and the fat-tailed sheep cared for by native people at Dodecanese on the Island of Rhodes was like a Sunday walk to church back in time. The Epidaurus theater, located at the eastern end of the Peloponnesus south of the Corinthian Canal, is an almost perfectly preserved amphitheater built 2,500 years ago and still hosting Greek dramas. It is a major cultural venue in Greece today. Epidaurus was the birthplace of Asclepius, the god of healing and son of Apollo. It become one of the important centers of healing in the ancient world and by the fourth century B.C., the sick were traveling from far and wide to seek medical and mystical cures at the sanctuary dedicated to Asclepius. The ruins of Epidaurus included the foundations of the Temple of Ascelpius, a sanctuary of Egyptian gods, a sports stadium, odeum and bath complex.

The major attraction was the wonderful theater, with its legendary acoustics, which amazed and delighted me. If one dropped a matchstick in the center of the original beaten earth stage, it could be heard by people sitting on the highest of the fifty-five tiers. The awe-inspiring acoustics were down to the mathematical precision with which the 14,000-seat theater were constructed in the fourth century B.C. Music, poetry contests, and theatrical performances, all ancient entertainment, were held in this theater. I stood on the earthen stage thinking, "How simple the stage sets and props were in ancient times and how much more the Greek audience would have appreciated deus ex machina when the stage manager caused gods to appear and disappear using hidden ropes and pulleys."

Epidaurus is one of the best-preserved structures from Classical Greece, having lain hidden and protected beneath layers of earth for centuries. Excavations began in 1881 and since 1954 ancient Greek dramas have been staged at the theater. I used my imagination to fully appreciate everything else there. Alongside the Temple of Asclepius were the remains of the abaton where patients slept in the hope of receiving a visitation from the healing god, who would weave a diagnosis and a miraculous cure into their dreams. Besides the theater, the other best-preserved structure was the beehive shaped Tholos that once contained a snake-infested labyrinth through which the mentally ill had to crawl in darkness. The treatment was to shock them into good health.

The Temples of Zeus, Eleusis, and Daphne were interesting for different reasons. The latter was famous as one of the earliest of Christian churches, and, architecturally, as the humble origin of the great Islamic mosque. I felt that I had been in an ancient world of faith when I left the entrance of the Temple of Daphne.

The gods of Attic are dead; their marble winding streets were on view for a few drachmas. That, after all these centuries of war, weather, and plunder there should be anything left of the Acropolis is itself a miracle. Sitting on one of the huge fallen pillars at the Acropolis ruins, I thought, "Enough remains of the Parthenon, Erechtheum, and lesser structures for me to appreciate the beauty and nobility of the Greek soul. In the massive grandeur of these temples there was a harmony so perfect that the whole appeared remarkably simple. But the subtleties that produced this effect—the slightly curved surfaces of the columns (indeed there were no straight surfaces on the Parthenon), the pillars that lean inward, that strictly adhere to proportions—were discovered only a few

years ago. Proportion, harmony, and grandeur massive against the blue sky and the Porch of the Caryatids, even though painful for women to hold up the roof on their heads, truly expressed the glory that was Greece."

Another example of classic Greek proportion was the beautiful Greek women. "Ees very pretty," was their favorite expression as they sprayed another fine mist of cologne. At the Ritz Night Club, there were many beautiful Greek women. By their very nature, Greek women are some of the most ardent, passionate, lusty lovers in the world. The one I danced with was curvy, with chestnut hair and green eyes. Her skin was not white, neither was it olive; it was a beautiful color somewhere in between. A Greek woman making love does so with passion from the depths of her soul. Mixed with their own body odors, their scent is sweet and spicy, and one of their favorite perfumes is Byblos. I gave the one I danced with a small bottle, which delighted her. She kept hugging and kissing me, wearing my sailor hat, and saying, "Ees very pretty."

Late in the afternoons, crowds of people flowed back and forth over the Galata Bridge: brightly painted boats standing in brown-green water; fishmongers and an old water seller; men earning a few *lira*—smiling, walking, smoking—and the points of the minarets...dulled by the hanging, dancing dust were the images of an ancient city—Istanbul, Turkey.

History remains for me a rather vague abstraction. A few names and dates and the recollection of musty old textbooks...a city like Istanbul can blow away the dust and destroy the cobwebs for it is historical process, exciting as time crushes an old culture and sweeps it away like an invisible glacier. In this city, the ways of the West are slowly supplementing the way of a once great empire. American taxis, huge mosques, neon signs and spice bazaars, the Hilton and the Golden Horn—all creating a harmony in contrariety that makes Istanbul the most exciting

port in the world.

The Mosque of Sultan Ahmet, the Blue Mosque, is imposing, not beautiful from the outside but magnificent within as the blue and red stained-glass-filtered light created a rich atmosphere in which to worship. The Blue Mosque, the supreme achievement of Islamic art: a shell of stone where people come to pray, I'm thinking.

Belly dancing has roots in the ancient Arab tribal religion as a dance to the goddess of fertility. The Turkish dancers wore a strippersque costume with plunging bras and skirts designed to display both legs up to the hip. The playful, flirty style of the dancers was a Turkish delight as they did their moves of shimmering vibrations of the hips, a staccato movement of the hips out from the body, and the fluid movements of the hips or chest in a circular fashion. The move I liked best was the rotating movements of the chest forward, up, back, and down that created the impression of riding a camel. At a fashionable night club, I watched Tulay Karaca, Nesrin Topkapi, and Birgul Berai, three famous Turkish belly dancers, perform and caught myself thinking the dance is perhaps man's oldest from of expression. Make-believe became my favorite pastime in Istanbul, and being a Sultan for a day was worth it.

The big ship continued its operations. The mission of an aircraft carrier is to put planes in the air. In the movies, everyone flies and is a hero; there are no mess cooks, mid-watches, or cleaning dirty bathrooms. No mention is made of bright-work polish, chipping and painting, memos in triplicate, tons of supplies or cargo nets, refueling, or manning battle stations. Only a sailor knows how much there is to getting planes off the flight deck and recovering them.

I grabbed my camera and found a clear view of the flight deck when the air boss of the ship called flight operations over the ship's intercom and said, "Pilots, man your planes. Secure all wing lines, wheel chocks, fire bottles, and loose gear about the decks. Standby to start engines. Launch jets first, and then the propeller AD-6 aircraft." These were his simple commands.

"Expedite, expedite," the air boss continued.

I was excited to take pictures of the sheer beauty of the launch and recovery of the planes. I never tired of watching the smooth coordination between the sleek, grey forms and the many brightly colored shirts on the flight deck. It was a thrilling moment for me when, with the ship kicking up a thirty knot wake and the signal hoist standing straight out in the wind, the first Cougar and the first Banshee were catapulted out over the water and up into the blue sky.

A formation of Cougars streaking along at 600 miles an hour, the refueling in flight of the versatile Banshee, a fly-by of jets by Stromboli Volcano, and an Italian island in the Mediterranean north of Sicily with an active volcano 3,040 high belching a smoky halo were some of my best pictures.

Plane in the water...port side—these words

throw into play a dozen or more coordinated acts. This is the instant that everyone has trained for so exhaustively yet hoped would never come. It is only a matter of moments before the plane sinks and with it go the lives of the men flying it.

Only seconds after the crash, two helicopters hover over the area. The ship's crew stands in tense silence as the cold, shaken pilots are helped out of the helicopter and onto the stretchers. A team of hospital corpsmen races onto the scene. It is only a matter of minutes from the time the plane hits the water to the time the men are in sick bay, where they receive the best of medical care. The entire ship's company relaxes as the word is passed, "The pilots are safely aboard."

After their mission, planes return to the carrier. Following the wake of the ship to get into the groove, the plane approaches the flight deck. It is the Landing Signal Officer who has the ultimate responsibility of bringing a plane in. He is a qualified pilot of every type he directs. It is his mature, split-second decision that may be the difference in a wave-off, a crackup, or just another safe landing.

Venice is one of the most beautiful cities in the world. Once the greatest commercial power in Europe, today she is an inhabited museum. Geography has frozen Venice in time: built on a foundation of 117 marshy islands, reinforced by timber, nothing new can be constructed, nothing old destroyed. She is there to be looked at, as magnificent in reality as Titian and Tintoretto once painted her, I thought.

Doge's Palace and St. Mark's Square, two of the most renowned sites in Venice, placed against the deep blue of the Adriatic sky, were alive with activity. Looking across the piazza, I saw other major landmarks: the Basilica, the Campanile and the Clock Tower from the fifteenth century. A city of winding alleyways and canals, there is not much room in Venice for a square. The one exception is St. Mark's piazza: ancient, sophisticated, perfect. The magnificent 1,000-year-old cathedral that is the piazza's focus of attention is rich both historically and artistically. I stood in awe inside St. Mark's Cathedral; however, because of church regulations, I was not allowed to take pictures. The famed Greek horses bronze sculpture on the façade of St. Mark's, how it survived wars and thefts over centuries and finally was brought back to Venice, fascinated me. Biblical stories from the Old and New Testaments, inlaid in mosaics, were beautiful; and in one part of the church, relics brought back from the Crusades were interesting.

After leaving St. Mark's, I went to Doge's Palace, considered by many to be the most exquisite in the world. Built in the thirteenth century, this beautiful building is Venetian Gothic architecture at its finest. Wandering through the palace, I could not believe my eyes when I saw the Golden Staircase, the Great Council Chamber, and the grand paintings of Tintoretto and Veronese.

As I walked through this part of Venice, I stopped at the Bridge of Sighs. Spanning the canal between the palace and the historic prison, the bridge was named for the sighs made by prisoners as they crossed

over to the jail beyond. Long ago, Casanova was sent across the bridge to meet his fate with Spanish Inquisitors. Today this is a favorite spot for romantic lovers, and it is widely held that a kiss under the bridge will bring eternal love.

In his play *The Merchant of Venice*, Shakespeare wrote about a bridge in Venice. Rialto Bridge, a big, white, stone bridge over the Grand Canal is high and humped in the middle because it was built to allow a fully armed galley to go beneath it. On or near the bridge, shopping was excellent. Gold was sold by the ounce in Italy and it was 18K gold. Shop owners had never heard of 14K gold. Music boxes were expensive but they were worth it. Inlaid pieces created beautiful designs in all colors, and the music was, of course, Italian. I bought a gold necklace and had a goldsmith make a small gold whale charm. I sent the music box, necklace, and gold whale charm to Bice Andre in New Bedford, Massachusetts.

Numerous sleek, black gondolas glided over the green-water canals, and I rode one to see the rest of Venice. The wind caught my white hat and blew it into the water. It sank before the gondolier could scoop it up. Now I'm out of uniform and will be written up as I try to go back aboard the ship. The gondolier saw my concern, steered the gondola over to the side of the canal, and motioned for the sailor standing shore-patrol duty to bring me a white hat. They brought me a white hat two sizes too big, but I was pleased that it got me back on the ship and saved me from being out of uniform and placed on report.

After another month at sea, the big ship dropped anchor in the harbor of Naples. Lieutenant Nali handed me my travel package to Rome, including permission to wear civilian clothes after leaving the ship. I quickly changed into civilian clothes in a Roman bath in Naples and boarded a train to Rome, Italy. My first sight of Rome astounded me. Thoughts that man could have built this city amazed me. Rome, the Eternal City, with its broad avenues, magnificent fountains and buildings, and impressive ruins was a sophisticated modern city and, at the same time, a graveyard. If ever a city could be called a projection of its people's personality, it is Rome. Side by side were the remains of a vast, pagan empire and the shrines of an even greater spiritual one.

Because of my limited time, I could spend only a short time in Rome, so I went to St. Peter's Basilica. It is the largest church in Christendom, capable of accommodating an estimated 60,000 people, and represents the heart of Roman Catholicism. It serves as a seminal point of pilgrimage and is crowned by a vast dome designed by Michelangelo. The church owes its site and spiritual legitimacy to Peter the Apostle, who is believed to have been buried here after his crucifixion close by in the Imperial Gardens in either A.D. 64 or 67. Once inside the church, the first breathtaking impressions are its staggering size, although

wandering endlessly amid the cascades of marble, somber tombs, and mountains of baroque décor, I realized that the interior was surprisingly bereft of major works of art. One notable exception was Michelangelo's *Pieta*, completed in 1499.

It was hard to think of any greater museums than those of the Vatican. Other galleries may match the broad span and myriad origins of its artifacts, but none can also offer works of art that include entire rooms painted by Raphael and the ceiling frescoes of the Sistine Chapel. *Apoxyomenos*, literally the Scraper, which shows an athlete scraping the sweat and dust from his body after a wrestling match, impressed me; but my favorite work of art in the Vatican was the ceiling of the Sistine Chapel, where Michelangelo's frescoes tell the story of Genesis and the history of humanity before the coming of Christ.

In the face of collapse and death, each culture immortalizes a bit of its soul in stone: Arch of Constantine, Victor Emmanuel Monument, and the Spanish Steps. I'm thinking, "What do I want to remember most? Gay dance halls on the Tiber River or perhaps, black-frocked priests riding their Vespas past the Coliseum, or the opera at the Baths of Caracalla, or St. Peter's or the Vatican Museums." One thing is for sure, having been to Rome for the first time, I will never be satisfied until I return. As I left Rome, I tossed a coin in Trevi Fountain, frightening pigeons that lifted into the air. The legend goes that one is bound to return to the Eternal City—a hope shared by most sailors, particularly me.

Roman baths, groves of olive trees, red-tile roofs, and sunflowers dot the beautiful countryside of Tuscany, Italy. At San Galgano and Monte Oliveto Abbeys, acres of sunflowers grew with beautiful or-

ange centers surrounded by yellow pedals. Sunflowers do not, as many people think, rotate to face the sun all day; they face just the early morning sun in the East. Montecatinc Alto is the original Montecatini settlement, lying a few hundred meters above the new town of Montecatini. I reached the top of Montecatini Alto by funicular railway. I'm still trying to determine how it worked, but reaching Montecatini Alto was worth it for its splendid views of Tuscany.

Carlo Lorenzini, an Italian writer, selected his pen name, Carlo Collodi, in honor of the small town of Collodi, Italy, and lived there while writing several world-famous stories for children, including *The Adventures of Pinocchio*, about the mischievous adventures of a wooden puppet whose nose grew longer when he told lies. Idle curiosity got Pinocchio into plenty of trouble, but the fairy with turquoise hair saved him in the end by turning him into a real little boy. Values expressed through allegory gave the story a unique literary appeal.

Vinci is famous as the birthplace of Leonardo da Vinci. It is located on the hills of Montalbano in the heart of Tuscany, not far from Florence, Pisa, Lucca, and Siena, which are all important cities of art. The landscape around Vinci, shaped over eons, was typical Tuscan hillside milieu, famous for its beauty and the subject of Leonardo's paintings of haunting land-scapes.

An agricultural economy, based on *mezzadria,* or tenant farming, has remained fundamentally un-changed; and the landscape as a whole still mirrors this type of rapport with nature, traditionally based on the production of Chianti wine and extra virgin olive oil. Grapes continue to be grown near the plain or on some of the terraces on the hills that rise toward Montalbano, while olives dominate the higher zones.

About three kilometers from Vinci, in Anchiano, is located the farmhouse in the open countryside where Leonardo da Vinci was born on April 15, 1452. He was an Italian Renaissance polymath: painter, sculptor, architect, musician, scientist, mathemati-cian, engineer, inventor, anatomist, geologist, cartog-rapher, botanist, and writer. I'm thinking as I stood in his bedroom in the simple farmhouse in Anchiano, "He was the archetype of the Renaissance Man, a man of unquenchable curiosity and feverishly inventive imagination. He is one of the greatest painters of all time and perhaps the most diversely talented person ever to have lived. The scope and depth of his interests were without precedent, and his mind and personality seem to me to be superhuman." Leonardo is renowned primarily as a painter. Among his works, the Mona Lisa is the most famous and most parodied portrait. Standing in front of the famous painting in the Louvre, in Paris, France, I thought, "The fame of the Mona Lisa (or *La Gioconda)* rests, in particular, on the elusive smile on the woman's face, its mysterious quality brought about by the artist's subtly shadowing the corners of the mouth and eyes so that the exact nature of the smile cannot be determined. The shadowy quality for which the work is renowned came to be called 'sfumato,' or Leonardo's smoke. The smile was so pleasing to me that it seemed divine rather than human." His painting of *The Last Supper* is the most reproduced religious painting of all time. His drawing of the Vitruvian Man, the idolized human body shown in perfect proportion, is also regarded as a cultural icon.

In Pisa, Italy, a small train took me from a parking lot to The Square of Miracles: The Leaning Tower of Pisa, the Cathedral of Santa Maria Assunta, and the Camposanta, a burial place. The Tower of Pisa, an architectural mistake, has made the sleepy city of Pisa famous the world over. Designed as a bell tower for the nearby cathedral and baptistery, The Leaning Tower was begun in 1173 and took over 200 years to finish. It is a series of six superimposed pilloried galleries and leans to the southeast and is, at present, twelve feet off the vertical because of soft terrain under one side. A special staircase leads to the top of the 188-foot tower, from which I had a commanding view of the city and the surrounding Tuscan countryside. The Cathedral of Santa Maria Assunta contains the ceiling mosaic Christ in Majesty between the Virgin and St. John the Evangelist. The first of the buildings in the Square of Miracles was financed by rich booty brought back

from a raid on Palermo in 1065. The pulpit in the Baptistery at the Square of Miracles was made from various colors of marble, and the baptismal is adorned by a statue of John the Baptist. Details from the frescos The Triumph of Death, painted in 1350, reflect the horror of The Black Death of 1348. On July 27, 1944, Camposanto was bombed by American war planes. Fire from the roof melted lead panels and molten lead ran down the frescos. Damaged frescos hang in Camposanto built over shiploads of Golgotha dirt brought back during the Crusades.

Seven hundred years ago the cities of northern Italy awoke and, like young giants, destroyed the feudal order that bound them. Florence, a small city on the banks of the muddy Arno River, along with Venice, Genoa and Milan became wealthy and independent. With the genius of the Medici family guiding her fortunes, she grew to be the greatest cultural center of Renaissance Europe. Here the Italian language and Italian literature were created. Today, Florence is no longer a giant but a gallery, hung with memories of a glorious past. Durante degli Alighieri, commonly known as Dante, was a major Italian poet of the Middle Ages. His *Divine Comedy*, originally called *Commedia* and later called *Divina* by Boccaccio, is considered the greatest literary work composed in the Italian language and a masterpiece of world literature. In Italy he is known as "il Poeta." Dante, Petrarch, and Boccaccio are known as the three fountains or three crowns. Dante is also called the father of the Italian language.

Giovanni Boccaccio, an Italian poet, scholar and diplomat, created writing in the Italian language that helped raise Italy's literature to a classic standing. The *Decameron*, his world-renowned book, was completed in 1351 and opens with a description of the Black Death, which leads into an introduction of a group of seven young women and three young men who flee from plague-ridden Florence to a villa in the countryside of Fiesole for two weeks. To pass the time, every night all of the members tell one story each. Although fourteen days pass, two days each week are set aside: one day for chores and one holy day during which no work is done. In this manner, one hundred stories are told by the end of the ten days.

The *Decameron* is an allegorical work best known for its bawdy tales of love, which appears in all its possibilities from the erotic to the tragic. Other topics such as wit and witticism, practical jokes, and worldly initiation also form part of the mosaic. Beyond its entertainment and literary popularity, it remains an important historical document of life in the fourteenth century and has been influential with later authors such as Geoffrey Chaucer.

I felt a sense of awe standing below the 330 foot high Dome of the Santa Maria del Fiore, Florence's most dominant architectural landmark, and the Campanile with its 416 steps to the top.

I'm thinking, "Italy's immense artistic and cultural heritage is its greatest legacy. Over almost 3,000 years, the paintings, sculptures, mosaics, operas, and works of literature of the country's countless artists, composers, and writers have helped shape and define Western civilization. Florence, *Firenze in Italian*, Europe's premier artistic capital, is crammed with paintings, frescos, and sculptures from the richest cultural flowering the world has known. Renaissance treasures fill a host of museums, churches, and galleries, while the roll call of famous names from the city's past—Dante, Machiavelli, Michelangelo, and Galileo among them—are some of the most resonant of the medieval age.

I started my artistic odyssey with the two main squares: Piazza della Signoria and Piazza del Duomo, the latter home of the cathedral, Baptistery, and Campanile. I climbed the cathedral dome for some fabulous views of Florence and its surroundings.

In the Museo dell' Opera del Duomo, my senses were haunted by Donatello's wood sculpture, *Mary Magdalene*. While the Bible never names the sin forgiven this woman, the Roman Catholic Church portrayed her as the penitent whore. She was shown in the sculpture covered by her own hair. Gaunt and weak, she seemed close to death. A tradition puts her in the wilderness of France.

Michelangelo's *David*, in the Galleria dell'Accademia, is the best-known sculpture in the world, a symbol of the art of all time. My first impression was that of a colossal naked body of an ancient athlete or of a classically designed pagan god, perfect in anatomical form and proud of glance. I'm thinking, "David, the young Jewish shepherd, is, for Michelangelo, already a mature man, and the artist depicts him in the moment before the slinging of the stone with which he is to strike the Philistine giant.

    Primavera, or Spring, and *The Birth of Venus*, in the Uffizi, two of Botticelli's most famous paintings, both celebrate female beauty and the joyous rebirth of spring. Each has a mythological element, the same goddess as protagonist, and similar references to love and the rebirth of spring. The two Venuses complement each other—one nude, the other dressed—as if the two paintings side by side represent two contrasting aspects of holy love: yearning for heavenly things, and profane love, earthly, lined to the regeneration of life in nature. Santa Croce, Florence's most compelling church, is not only an artistic shrine with frescoes by Giotto and others but also is the burial place of 270 of the city's most eminent inhabitants, among them Galileo, Michelangelo, and Machiavelli.

    San Lorenzo is Florence's oldest church. It was founded in A.D. 393 and served for many years as the city's cathedral. It was also the Medici's parish church. Sagrestia Nuova was designed by Michelangelo as a riposte to Brunelleschi's Sagrestia Vecchia in San Lorenzo. The sculptor was also responsible for the sacristy's three tombs, one depicting a man of thought. The tomb's two attendant figures represent Dawn and Dusk. One other important church in Florence was the Santa Maria Novella, the mother church of the Dominican order. The columns of the aisles become progressively more narrow with height, a trick designed to confuse one's sense of perspective. Masaccio's fresco of *The Holy Trinity* used the mathematical proportion successfully and kept me wondering where the Holy Spirit was in the famous fresco hanging in the nave of the church.

My train from Florence to Naples was nonstop. I had to make one stop at the Roman bath house in Naples to change into my uniform before I got to fleet landing and *Coral Sea 4*, the liberty boat that took me back to the ship anchored in Naples Bay. Commander Lake and my shipmates were all around my desk to welcome me back. Banners and balloons floated over a large cake that was always given to the sailor being promoted but I didn't know that it was I who had been promoted.

Commander Lake, in an excited voice said, "Carpenter, good news for you" as he handed me my certificates. "The academic work you have been doing, recommended by Lieutenant Nali, to improve your scores to get into college paid off! You passed every course and your profile looks good for officer candidate school or for a university, whichever you choose. Your shipmates and I are pleased for you! Come over here to me." He shook my hand and continued with great enthusiasm. "I brought some scissors to cut off your patch and a needle and thread to sew the new crow on your sleeve which you have earned. I'm proud of you, sailor! I wish you continued success." With tears of joy in my eyes, I thanked the Commander and my shipmates for my party and cake. I knew that now I had a better opportunity to go to college, something I had always dreamed about.

Music, a French girl, the smell of perfume, the sound of feminine voices...ooooh la, la! Cannes, France, was a new port of call and a new and different country for me to explore and learn. A bare, green checkerboard of stone-fenced farms under cultivation for a thousand years was in front of me. As I rode a bike that I rented along a farm road outside of Menton and saw the beautiful farms, I was reminded of my own struggle for existence resolved in a patient marriage of human hands, a plow, a team of horses, hard work, and tired soil.

The Côte d'Azur still retained the characteristics for which it was renowned: wealth, gracious living and natural beauty. Along a relatively short strip of coast, there is town after town, each one world famous as a resort: Cannes, Golfe-Juan, Juan-les-Pins, Nice, Monte Carlo, and Menton. Thousands of sailors went to the Riviera, to the beaches, to the casinos, and to the cabarets, seeking pleasures and spending money with an abandon that one finds nowhere else in the world.

Monaco is a tiny principality actually belonging to France but governed by her own monarch. This microscopic state has become famous through the Casino at Monte Carlo. The government is run on

profits from the gambling, making Monaco a taxless paradise. The problem when I was there was that of obtaining an heir to the throne, continuing the state of bliss. America did contribute its solution to the problem by lend-leasing a homegrown product, Miss Grace Kelly. The Royal Palace, with its mosaic sidewalks, cannon to shoot when babies were born, and flower beds in front of the palace growing in beautiful red and white colors in the design of a roulette wheel will always be Grace's Place, the palace where luck is king.

There are thousands of perfumes made in France, where flowers are grown especially for use in the manufacturing process. The town where many kinds of perfumes were made was Grasse. Shelves were lined with Amarige, Hypnose, Amor Amor, Chanel No. 5, Caleche, L'Air Du Temps, Arpege, Ivoire, Fleurs, Tumulte, and many other brands. I bought Quelques Fleurs, made by Houbigant, the oldest perfume house in France, and sent it home to all my sisters.

A few miles from the coast and some hundreds of years in time from the swank modern resorts, lies Eze. This provincial village is practically stone for stone as it was in the thirteenth century, 700 years ago. It was settled in 600 B.C. by Greeks, and the people, with their own language and culture, continued to live a simple life, untarnished by wealth or fame.

A funny thing happened in Taranto, Italy. The old and new cities of Taranto were built on two fragile arms of land embracing a bowl of sea-green water that is the southern anchorage of the Italian Navy. After several weeks at sea, our big ship dropped anchor so liberty call could go for each division. I was walking up the gangplank, coming back from liberty late at night and a sailor was in front of me with his pea coat buttoned up to keep warm. He held up his arm to salute the officer of the deck and to request permission to board the ship when suddenly a large white duck stuck its head out of his coat and gave a loud "quack, quack, quack" in the officer's face. The Marine orderly standing watch grabbed the drunken sailor and the duck. The officer smiled and said to the drunken sailor, "Why are you bringing the duck aboard?" Slowly the sailor raised his head and answered, "My mama always cooked me a duck with orange sauce for Thanksgiving, Sir, and my shipmate in the galley will cook this one for me tomorrow for Thanksgiving lunch. The only thing I have done wrong was steal the duck." Everyone laughed, and the officer smiled and said to the Marine orderly, "Take this man and duck to the ship's galley and kill the duck for him and destroy the feathers."

I enjoyed Christmas and bringing in the New Year in Cannes, France. The big ship continued fleet exercises until the USS *Forrestal* relieved it at the Rock of Gibraltar and it sailed toward the Continental United States. Cheers went up from the crew as the Rock of Gibraltar faded from view.

Crossing the Line is a tradition that dates back to ancient times when ships first sailed the world. The line is the equator, and when I crossed it and went through the initiation, I became a Trusty Horned Shellback; before I crossed the line, I was a lowly, slimy Pollywog. Exactly how a Pollywog becomes a Shellback differs from ship to ship. It is at the discretion of the Shellbacks as to what the Pollywog goes through on "Wog" day.

My reveille was 4:00 a.m. on the ship, and all I ate that day was spinach. However, there were a few basic steps in the ceremony that were mandatory for me. I reported to my duty station and put my clothes on inside out with my skivvies on the outside. Shellbacks painted a big "p" on my back. I went around to other compartments on the ship where other Shellbacks were waiting to apply various fluids, grease, red lead paint, dirt swept up from the deck and whatever else they could find. They applied it to my hair, on my face, and all over my body. I had to roll in it, beg for more, and like it! I was asked questions and no matter my answer, it was always wrong. Not giving the right answer got me swatted with a piece of wet fire hose and

more substances flung at me. After about an hour or two of this, it was time for me to move up to the flight deck. By this time, I was completely covered in goo and sore from walking like a duck around the entire flight deck, crawling and getting swatted with a piece of two-inch wet shillelagh applied to my wet dungarees so it would sting.

Somehow, I was laughing my ass off at it all but not as much as the Shellbacks. I was paraded out onto the forward elevator of the ship that brought the airplanes topside and told to keep down and not to look up. As the elevator started up, fire hoses from the flight deck were trained on me and the latest pack of "Wogs" to come topside. The pressure from the fire hose and water about washed my eyeballs out. Shellbacks put me in a long waiting line to go through the final hazing at their hands. As I inched along, I was pulled out of the line to do things like blow water out of a pad-eye, lay on my stomach with my arms straight out till they burned, and look for the line. Finally, I was put in a stockade, and the Shellbacks

started their interrogation to see if I was worthy to go before the Royal Majesty, King Neptune. I was not. They charged me with a serious crime: spying on a Shellback meeting. Of course, there wasn't a thing I could say that would prevent me from getting swatted and made to beg the King to let me become a Shellback. He finally agreed but not before I kissed the Royal Baby's belly, the belly of the fattest Shellback on the ship, which was covered in grease, yellow mustard, and mayonnaise. I tried to turn away from the heaving belly and not kiss the navel of the Royal

Baby, but a Horned Shellback saw me and pushed my face deep into the belly and held it there until I almost suffocated.

It wasn't over yet. My pitiful Pollywog body needed to be cleaned of all its slime which can be accomplished only by crawling and swimming in, of all things, slime. First I had to crawl through a garbage chute that was full of two-week-old garbage. Wieners puffed up from decay were hard for me to crawl by in the chute, lettuce was rotten and slimy, and water and flour had been added to the garbage to make it even more slippery for my crawl in

the chute. The stench was almost unbearable. It about got me, but crawling out of the chute, I made the jump into a makeshift tub that was filled with rotten bug juice and other god-awful liquids. I had to dunk my head under and crawl to the other end like a slimy Pollywog. I tried to get out too fast and up from the bottom too early, but a Shellback caught me and made me do it again.

I finally emerged from the tank, and fire hoses at full force sprayed me down, almost washing me overboard. I stripped everything off and threw it into a large container at the end of the flight deck. I took a shower with the best-smelling soap, but the stench was still there.

Happily, I was done. I was sore from being swatted, crawling on the deck, and walking like a duck. I

had been covered in the disgusting garbage from head to toe. I had been humiliated from start to finish on Wog day. Hey, wait a minute! I had made it! I was a Shellback, too, and still carry my Shellback card signed by the captain of the *Coral Sea* to prove it.

The big ship dropped anchor at midnight in the waters of the Mediterranean and the compass on the navigation bridge read 0' – 37' West. My search for the equator ended there.

Immediately after "Wog" day ended, the big ship was in route to the United States. In a few hours, Captain Jaap came on the intercom and said, "A wide-spread storm caused a British merchant ship to floun-der and send out a distress signal. Law of the Sea makes it mandatory that *Coral Sea* search for this ship," he continued. "Launching helicopters or any other type of aircraft is impossible because of the high seas. All planes are below in the hanger decks and condition zebra sealing all hatches has been set for this watch and until further notice."

Coral Sea searched for the British merchant ship for three days without success. The sea was so rough, Captain Jaap called off the search, but the storm was so widespread, it took another day for the ship to sail clear of the rough seas.

Ten days later, at Hampton Roads, Virginia, fly-away day occurred, and all aircraft flew off the ship to mainland United States without an instance. Tug boats pushed the big ship into the pier for tie-up, and

sailors swarmed onto the dock to hug and kiss their loved ones.

I grabbed my small duffel bag and left the ship to fly home for thirty days of fun. While I waited for an open phone booth to call home for Mama and Dad to pick me up at the airport in Knoxville, Tennessee, a little thing caught my attention. I watched a large wharf rat that was searching for food run the five-inch hawser that secured the ship to the pier. It tried to board the ship, but the round metal disc rat guard dumped the unwelcome guest into the sea.

I had time to reflect on my life at sea for the last year. I had sailed 88,000 nautical miles, visited seven countries, received three promotions, passed twelve college level courses, enjoyed my work with my shipmates and division officer, and got a cultural boost from my intellectual and artistic quests across Europe. I got no tattoos or diseases in the dens of iniquity I went to. Now I was ready to visit my loving family and friends at home and tell them about my life at sea.

Delta Flight Nine, which I boarded in Norfolk, Virginia, touched town at the Knoxville airport on schedule and rolled to a stop at the outside gate. Mama and Dad, excited to see me, stood just inside the gate as passengers came down the ladder from the big plane. I was the last sailor behind four other sailors all wearing blue uniforms. In her excitement, Mama ran and threw her arms around the first sailor coming down the ladder, closed her eyes, and kissed him on the cheek. She finally opened her eyes, looked up, and to her surprise recognized she had kissed the wrong sailor. Everyone around saw what happened and began to laugh. The red-headed sailor Mama kissed simply said, "No apology needed, madam. I needed that because my parents aren't here today."

Mama fell into my arms, and she and Dad hugged me as we walked to the car to drive home. As we crossed the Smoky Mountains into North Carolina, I said, "Mama, there is something I want to show you." I pushed the sleeve on my uniform slowly up my arm. Mama stopped talking, gasped for breath and turned to look at my arm as she said, "No, oh no, you didn't get a tattoo, son." I laughed as I pulled my sleeve down and shook my head no. She hugged me, smiled, and said, "Thank goodness, I knew you wouldn't get a tattoo."

The yard, the house, and benches and chairs

under the big walnut tree at the old house on Yellow Creek were all full of people to welcome me home! There was music and so much food. What a welcome-home party my family and friends gave me. Soon I got to drive my blue Ford again and go courting. I had fun and a great time at home, but it ended soon and I said goodbye to everyone at home and returned to the *Coral Sea* still tied up at the pier in Norfolk, Virginia.

Two weeks after I returned to the ship, *Coral Sea* entered dry dock. The crew lived aboard for three months until it was ready to sail to the Naval Ship-yard, Bremerton, Washington. There it would be con-verted to an angled deck carrier with steam catapults so jets could be launched from the side as well as off the front of the ship.

With all planes off the ship and the crew still intact, the big ship began the cruise from Norfolk, Virginia, to Bremerton, Washington. *Coral Sea* was too big to go through the Panama Canal. Two natural sea routes were options for the ship to sail from the Atlantic to the Pacific Ocean. The Strait of Magellan, a navigable sea route south of mainland South America and north of Tierra del Fuego, was the shortest route but difficult to navigate. Unpredictable winds, cross currents, and the narrowness of this passage created dangerous and treacherous hazards for the big ship. Many additional sailing days and about 14,000 nauti-cal miles were added to sailing time to sail around the tip of South America and Cape Horn, but this water-way was safer.

I was pleased I was able to go on liberty in Panama to satisfy my curiosity about how a ship passes through the Panama Canal. I marveled at this engineering feat as I watched a Brazilian Reefer ship go from one lock to another on her way to the Atlantic

Ocean. From Panama, the ship sailed on to the Naval Shipyard, Bremerton, Washington; was decommissioned; and put in dry dock. Work to convert the ship began immediately.

I lived on the ship for a few more weeks. Bremerton was a small town with very little for entertainment and not suitable for liberty so I took the ferry boat to Seattle, Washington. The ticket for the ferry boat cost five dollars, and I had to catch the eleven o'clock ferry to make it back to my ship by midnight so I wouldn't be absent without leave, a captain's mast offense.

I was running as fast as I could down a long walkway with hedge bushes on each side to go aboard the ferry boat before it left the pier. I had no time left. A storm was approaching with a fierce wind blowing, lightning flashing and deep thunder rumbling in the distance. I ran faster, fishing in my money belt for money to buy my ticket. I checked the money belt again—no money. Lord, I looked up and big drops of rain hit me in the face. What am I going to do? I'm about to miss the ferry boat, about to be written up with a possible captain mast, and no money to buy a five-dollar ticket! Lord, help me!

I turned the corner and the wind subsided somewhat. I heard a noise, a fluttering, like a paper hung up in the hedge. I looked again and a faint smile jerked at the corners of my mouth as I grabbed a frantically shaking wet, twenty-dollar bill from the bramble and ran on up the gangplank on the ferry boat. A piece of paper blown randomly by the wind and caught to frantically flutter on a bramble, luck, divine intervention, or maybe the goodness of a foolish sailor's heart to spend his last dollar to buy drinks for a beautiful girl earlier in the evening—the reason things happened as they did I will never know but I was thankful that I heard the fluttering bill.

From the noisy shipyard in Bremerton, I left the *Coral Sea*, which would be in the dry dock there for two years, and went to school at the Naval Base Training Command, San Diego, California for continuing education on many changes that had occurred in cost accounting for all general ship supplies coming aboard the ship. At the Training Command, I sat for my Second Class Petty Officer examination. I finished the eight weeks of training in San Diego and stayed an extra week there awaiting orders for my next duty assignment.

Sailors knew it by its initials T.J. I had heard about Tijuana, Mexico, and Tequila, Mexico's national drink, since I became a sailor. I used Mexican pesos to cross the border into Mexico from San Diego, California and used caution wherever I went. North Zone is a red-light district located in Tijuana. It is known for its brothels, street prostitution, and illicit drug sales. Prostitution is permitted in Tijuana. Legal prostitution within the city required sex workers to obtain a permit and be subjected to monthly health checkups. Brothels in Tijuana, many of them modeled on strip bars and hostess clubs, were also required to conform to certain health regulations of cleanliness and fixed operating hours. There were other prostitutes who worked outside on the *callejones*, or alleys. They were referred to as *paraditas*, Spanish for "the standing girls," for their habits of standing on the streets to advertise their services. *Paraditas* have long been regarded as part of Tijuana's cultural history. These street workers were either illegal prostitutes who didn't have permits or legal prostitutes who prefer the relatively quiet environment of the street to the loud music and smoky atmosphere of the bars. Strip clubs were full-contact, meaning the dancers permitted patrons to fondle them.

I left the sordid entertainment, night life, loud music, and smoky bars behind in Tijuana to make a final stop in a small village to see a Xoloitzcuintle breed. Local Mexicans called it the Mexican Hairless or Tepeizeuintli, breed. I walked to the back of a shanty house and there, to my surprise stood a hairless dog.

A week later, Commander Epps, director of the Naval Base Training Command at San Diego, handed me my orders and, smiling, said, "You are going aboard a magnificent ship, USS *Midway CVA-41*, home port Alameda Naval Air Station, Alameda, California. I wish you the best of everything. Keep up the excellent work you demonstrated while you where here, and I wish you continued success with your studies and promotions."

I had less than eight months left in the Navy when I saluted the officer of the deck and requested permission to come aboard the *Midway* tied up at the pier at Alameda, California. C. Ryder Griswold, Commander of the Supply Division, and my shipmates welcomed me into the division and showed me to my desk. A few weeks after I got aboard the ship, my promotion to Second Class Petty Officer was presented by Commander Griswold and my shipmates. We ate the traditional cake, and I thanked the Commander and my shipmates for the presentation and cake.

The *Midway*, after two years in the Naval Shipyard, Bremerton, Washington, got underway as an angled deck carrier. The complete renovation and new paint made the ship like new. She was a beautiful ship and had already gone through all shakedown and readiness exercises before I boarded her in Alameda.

Many of the crew members from the USS *Coral Sea* was assigned to the *Midway* because they had carrier experience, but the type of planes and pilots were all new.

Carrier Group Two was composed of two supersonic fighter squadrons and three attack squadrons among her complement of 132 jet aircraft and 4,200 sailors and officers. There were no propeller planes aboard *Midway*. She was streamlined with her hurricane bow, new deck elevators, new steam catapults, bridle arresters, and a new primary flight control station.

On the second day after I started working in the Supply Division on *Midway*, Commander Griswold called me into his office to inform me that I was the new supervisor over the fourteen sailors working in the supply office. He said, with his wide smile, "Congratulations, Carpenter, on your promotion to Second Class Petty Officer and your new position. I'm here to help you if you need me. Feel free to come by my office any time," he continued in a friendly tone of voice. "I saw in your profiles that you like to study and that one of your hobbies was creative writing. Are you a published author?" I laughed and said, "No, my writing is only scribbling now, but I do like to try to write."

Aboard *Midway*, the educational officer was Lieutenant Franz Belara. I made an appointment with him to schedule a time to sit for my college board examination. Lieutenant Belara advised me that he gave the college board examinations on Friday of every third month in the Pilots' Ready Room. Testing began at eight a.m. and finished at two p.m. and he would send the test grades by telex machine to the Naval Academic Center in New York. The processing center would grade my examinations and would send the results back to him by telex on the ship. He advised me that he would review the test results with me and send the results with his letter to ten colleges of my choice and to the Naval War College, Newport, Rhode Island for officer candidate consideration.

Lieutenant Belara was most helpful and gave me a loose-leaf binder marked College Board Testing with tabs for each subject on which I would be tested. It included good examples and things I could expect on testing day and advised me to study the testing procedures for each subject. He enrolled me in two more math courses to complete in two weeks and he returned to him for grading. I thanked him, shook his hand, saluted, and returned to my work. I was elated. I felt that my dream of going to college was coming true.

Flight operations and pilots' readiness activities were conducted off the coast of California by *Midway* for several weeks before the ship sailed to Hawaii and tied up at the new pier across Battleship Row, where

the battleship USS *Utah BB-31* sunk by torpedoes from Japanese warplanes on December 7, 1941 during World War II, was still visible. As I approached the island of Oahu and the sunken USS *Arizona BB-39*, I was saddened by the loss of life at Pearl Harbor when the Japanese attacked and deeply saddened by the loss of lives given for my freedom. The Japanese sank many smaller ships, and five battleships, and killed or injured 3,581 military and 103 civilians but missed their prize, the American aircraft carriers. They were operating at sea and were not at Pearl Harbor when the Japanese struck the American fleet.

Midway operated from Hawaii for the next four months, and Lieutenant Belara called me to remind me when my examination for the college board was scheduled. I continued to review the material he had provided me for the rest of that week and was pleased to finally sit in the large, black leather chair in the Pilots' Ready Room for the examination.

Although the ship was at sea and the jets were roaring just above on the flight deck, the room was soundproof and comfortable for the examination. Lieutenant Belara administered the examination from 8:00 a.m. until 2:00 p.m. Timing for each part of the examination was monitored down to the last minute at 2:00 p.m. that Friday. I was happy to finish the examination process. Commander Belara shook my hand as I left and said, "Carpenter, I wish you all the luck in the world on passing all parts of the college board examination. I'll be in touch with you as soon as the results come back from the Naval Academic Center in New York."

Midway returned to the pier in Hawaii for the weekend and a special entry in the Plan of the Day for Saturday caught my eye. Maureen O'Hara would be at

the quarter deck signing autographs at 8:00 a.m. The entertainment committee of the ship had constructed a replica of a supersonic fighter jet complete with a pilot's seat for her to sit in while she signed autographs. When I got to her chair, she handed me a signed black and white photo of herself and I said, "Thank you, welcome aboard *Midway*." She smiled and said," I wanted to come aboard a real aircraft carrier. It is more beautiful and exciting than the sets and props used by Hollywood directors in *The Wings of Eagles*, a recent movie about an aircraft
carrier that John Wayne and I starred in. I wanted to see the real ship and thank you for your service to our country." I had to move along, but I was captivated by her beautiful red hair and flashing blue eyes. She was stunning!

The first firing of a Sparrow III missile was conducted by VF-64 based aboard the *Midway*. During this cruise, she operated off Taiwan in support of the Quemoy Matsu crisis as the flagship of Command Carrier Division Five. I hadn't seen this weapon before and thought about the destruction and death it could bring when it was used.

In the early part of the year, *Midway* returned to Alameda Naval Air Station, and after a one-month turn around period, she redeployed to the Far East. *Midway*'s first stop to replenish supplies was at the U.S. Naval Base Subic Bay, located in Zambales, Philippines, where the ship tied up at the pier. Commander Griswold handed me a checkoff list of all supplies ordered while the ship was in route and said, "Carpenter, take your working party to the far end of the pier and the crane operator will help you get the supplies and materials aboard the ship. Sign and date the bill-of-lading and bring a copy back to the supply office so the supplies can be accounted for and posted to the control cards."

After three days at Subic Bay, taking on fuel and supplies, the *Midway* got underway for Japan, a new country and different ports of call from those in Europe. I eagerly looked forward to learning about a country I had only seen in a movie and read about.

Japan has a total of 6,852 islands extending along the Pacific coast of Asia. The main islands, from north to south, are Hokkaido, Honshu, Shikoku, and Kyushu. The Ryukyu Islands, including Okinawa, are a chain to the south of Kyushu. Together they are called the Japanese Archipelago. Tokyo, Yokohama, Osaka, Nagoya, Sapporo, Kobe, Kyoto, Fukuoka, Kawasaki, and Saitama are the ten largest cities. Fewer than one percent of Japanese are Christian; Buddhism and Shinto are the two major religions, and Taoism and Confucianism from China have also influenced Japanese beliefs and customs. As I walked through the Pagoda of Horyuji, a many-storied Buddhist tower and the oldest wooden building in the world, I thought that this religion, although strange to me, was in its own way beautiful. The temples were different, and the shrines dedicated to venerated shoguns and dynasties were ancient, strange, and a little eerie to me.

The primary staple in Japan is rice. Wet-rice farming framed the countryside where farming could be done. Beautiful manicured flower gardens bordered the rice farms as I walked down a winding path to Ueno Park, in the Ueno section of Taito, Tokyo, Japan to see the cherry blossoms that blanketed the park. The colors and fragrance of the cherry blossoms were breathtaking, but I was sad when I saw all the homeless people living there.

The Land of the Rising Sun was interesting but different from Europe in more ways than being on the opposite sides of the world from each other. I thought, "What better entertainment do I need?" I soaked in an outdoor onsen with beautiful women who were most gracious, sipped sake and ate soba and Kushiyyalic sushi while loose in Tokyo, one of the largest cities in the world. Acres and acres of fish and fish products, mountains of octopus, rows of giant tuna, endless varieties of shellfish, and tank upon tank of live exotic fish fascinated me at Tsukiji Fish market in Tokyo.

From Tokyo, sixty miles southwest of the city, I could see Mount Fuji's exceptionally symmetrical cone formed by deposits of lava and volcanic ashe from continuous eruptions over many years. It is a well-known symbol of Japan and is frequently depicted in art and paintings. Mount Fuji is one of Japan's three holy mountains, along with Mount Tate and Mount Haku. It is the archetype of an active stratovolcano and rivals Vesuvius as best-known volcano in the world.

If I were a toponymist, I would say that Fuji is the word for rainbow and that Mount Fuji is the end of

the rainbow, but I'm not and will turn to my reflections on the sacred peak that floats above and beyond the tea fields, the rice paddies, and the lakes and towns of Japan. While standing there in the shadow of Mount Fuji, I saw its magical, whimsical outline standing tall in the blue sky, wearing a kimono of snow and a drawn-out hem of mist stitched in golden-sunbeams.

Holding an iconic place in Japanese scenery, the beauty of Mount Fuji has for ages been painted by artists and celebrated in prose, poetry, and songs. I celebrated Mount Fuji with love that decorated the mountain with sunrises and wove valleys delicate with the edging rim of sunsets.

When I returned to the ship from liberty, Lieutenant Belara called me into his office, shook my hand and said, "Carpenter, I have good news for you. You scored in the upper eighty-nineth percentile on all parts of your college boards. I'm pleased for you," he continued excitedly. "I am excited to write my letter of recommendation to the deans of ten colleges or universities you choose, and I will send a copy of your profiles along with my letter of recommendation to the Naval War College in Newport, Rhode Island, for officer candidate selection." The next morning I handed Lieutenant Belara a list of ten universities and colleges of my choice, including Western Carolina College.

With a deep feeling of joy, I shook Lieutenant Belara's hand, thanked him for his help and guidance, saluted him, and left his office feeling that I now had the best opportunity for a better life than I ever had.

After three weeks at sea, *Midway* sailed slowly south down Tokyo Bay to Yokohama, a major port. I saluted the officer of the deck and requested permission to go ashore.

From a sleepy fishing village, Yokohama grew into a major foreign trade port with ships from all over the world coming to trade everything in the market place including dolls, tea, and silk from China.

In Japan, every harbor has its class that knows no other house than its boat. Every boat is a boat-house to the Japanese water population. The sampan boatman, in countless thousands, are born, live, and die on the sampan boat. Sampan men, clustered around merchant ships in the harbors, each with his head thrown back and voice raised to its highest pitch, shouted their abilities to work. As soon as the sampan men in a boat were hired by a merchant ship, the other sampan boats disappeared to find another merchant ship to earn their living. The sampan is a boat about sixteen feet in length by four feet in breadth, flat-bottomed, and propelled by sculling instead of rowing. I watched the sampan men heave their weight against the oars and listened to them repeat in unison a guttural sound, "ohuk, ohuk."

Ukiyo-e, literally "pictures of the floating world," is a genre of Japanese woodblock prints and paintings produced between the seventh and the twentieth centuries, featuring motifs of landscapes, and tales from history, the theater, and pleasure quarters. It is the main artistic genre of woodblock painting in Japan.

My art teacher, Mrs. John Howell, maiden name Mary Lackey, at Robbinsville High School introduced me to ukiyo-e and shared with me the paintings she had collected. Her words, "Floating world referred to a concept of an evanescent world; impermanent, fleeting beauty; and a realm of entertainment, kabuki, courtesans, geisha, divorced from the responsibilities of the mundane, everyday world" remained with me. In her art class, years ago, she continued, with her warm smile, "This concept broadens to mean living only for the moment, turning one's full attention to the pleasures of the moon, the snow, the cherry blossoms, and the maple leaves; singing songs, drinking wine, diverting oneself in just floating; refusing to be disheartened, like a feather floating along with the river current. This is what I call the floating world of the Japanese people." Standing in the Yamanashi Prefectural Museum looking at Katsushika Hokusai's *Thirty-Six Views of Mount Fuji* and other ukiyo-e wood prints of beautiful courtesans, pan-pan girls, bulky sumo wrestlers, and popular actors, I found Mrs. Howell's description of the floating world to be true.

With interest, I watched the Japanese martial arts instructors teach judo, karate, and kendo. I saw the sweaty Sumo wrestler's skillful moves, silk worms, and dolls of every kind and rode the bullet train before liberty ended in Yokohama. I felt sad and a little relieved knowing this was my last liberty in Japan.

After two weeks at sea, the *Midway* tied up at the pier in Subic Bay. On Friday morning, Commander Danzi, Personnel Officer, USS *Midway*, advised me that I had passed the examination for First Class Petty Officer, to become effective in thirty days. He extended the opportunity for reenlistment for four more years. I thanked Commander Danzi and said, "I have made a decision to get out of the Navy and go to college," as I saluted him. He handed my papers to First Class Yeoman Pritchard for him to process so I could leave the ship by 2:00 p.m. Yeoman Pritchard asked me to wait by his desk until he finished my papers and paid me the $2,000 I had kept on the books.

In the next few minutes, I checked my papers to be sure they were in order. Pritchard handed me twenty one-hundred-dollar bills and my orders. I thanked him, said goodbye, and went to my compartment to pack my sea bag.

I grabbed my old sock from my locker and took out a silver cigar case, opened it, and took out eleven one-hundred-dollar bills rolled snugly inside that I had saved. I kept one of the bills out for spending money and put ten one-hundred-dollar bills in my money belt.

Buzz Aldin, one of my buddies, said, "I'll take your sea bag to the quarter deck and leave it there in  the luggage room for you to pick up when you leave the ship." In an emotional voice he continued, "I don't want you to wrinkle that dress uniform. Goodbye and best of luck to you. You have been a great shipmate and friend, Carpenter."

When I got back to the supply office to say goodbye, Commander Griswold had mustered all my shipmates.

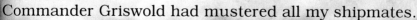

They sang, "For He's is a Jolly Good Fellow," shook my hand, wished me well, and returned to their work stations.

In my hand, I had a small, brown, leather case I bought in Florence, Italy, with my orders inside, a screwdriver, and a small box-end wrench. Commander Griswold shook his head no and said, "It's too fragile to ship or for you to carry off the ship. It will get destroyed. It is too good to be broken. When *Midway* gets back to Alameda, California, I can get it safely home," he continued in a soft tone. I had purchased the mahogany wood and all its fittings in San Francisco, California, and spent endless hours in the ship's hobby shop constructing the perfect Spanish galleon. I handed the screwdriver and small wrench to Commander Griswold and said, "Yes, you are right, I'll never get it off the ship in one piece. It's yours, sir," I said as I saluted him and said good-bye.

At the quarter deck, a Marine sentury carried my sea bag off the ship. I saluted the officer of the deck and requested permission to leave the ship. He returned my salute and said, "Good luck to you, Carpenter." At the top of the gangplank, I stopped and saluted the American flag waving on the fantail of the ship and quickly walked down the gangplank to the pier to catch a ride to the processing  center, U. S. Naval Base, Subic Bay, Zambales, Philippines. I handed the processing officer my orders and a special white envelope that Lieutenant Belara included in my papers from him and marked, "Surprise, please don't open until you are processing out at Subic Bay." Commander Eji Barni, the processing officer, smiled and said, "Carpenter, Lieutenant Belara did a special thing for you. Report to flight line three at 0600 hours in the morning. You have a seat on a military flight leaving for the Naval Air Station, Alameda, California. You may spend the night here in this building, room four on the second floor. Grab the shuttle at the front door at 0530 hours."

He dated and signed my orders. I thanked and saluted him, grabbed my sea bag and went upstairs to my room for some well-deserved sleep.

For the next three days, I was on time for the military hop at flight line three but was bumped off each time by an officer returning to the United States. On the fourth day an orderly knocked on my door at 0900 hours to advise me that a troop transport ship was leaving for the U.S. Naval Receiving Station, Naval Station, Treasure Island, San Francisco, California, in three hours.

I boarded the ship in an hour and left the pier at Subic Bay, Zambales, Philippines, for Treasure Island, San Francisco, California, on schedule. A mixture of Navy, Marine and Army troops made up the complement of 1,200 troops returning to the United States. The ship stopped in Hawaii for three days, and sixteen days later tied up at the pier at Treasure Island.

I grabbed my sea bag and orders, saluted the officer of the deck, and requested permission to leave the ship. I went directly to the Naval Receiving Station. I handed my orders to Captain H.P. McIntire, and he began processing me out of the Navy. Lieutenant J.R. Lee, Medical Officer, gave me my physical the next morning and found me physically qualified for release from active duty in the Navy. Commander H.I. Wells recommended me for reenlistment and extended an invitation to me. I thanked Commander Wells and said, "I have made a decision to go to college. I have passed the college boards and am ready to enter college." He changed my rating from SK2 and advised me that my U.S. Naval Reserve designation would be USNR-R for four years, at which time I would receive my discharge certificate. Ensign Chico Serrata, disbursing officer, handed me $100 and a form advising me that I would receive two hundred dollars in the mail for mustering-out pay. Commander Wells called me back into his office and said, "Carpenter, it is a great pleasure to extend to you the thanks and appreciation of the U.S. Navy for the faithful and honorable service you have rendered our country during your tour of active duty, which ends this date. Congratulations and best wishes for your continued success."

In three hours I boarded Delta Flight Eight at the airport, San Francisco, California, for my flight home.

College Years

My college years were filled with learning, surprises, and a time in my life that I met some of the most interesting people who ever passed through my destiny. I was excited to be standing in the Dean of Men's office at Western Carolina College the next day, after my flight to Asheville from San Francisco, California. My dream of going to college to improve myself so I could have a better opportunity for life had come true! Mama's dream for me to go to college had come true! Now, my world and my destiny would change for the better, the one I envisioned. I was elated! I was out of the Navy and ready to go to college.

The Dean of Men shook my hand and said, "I've been waiting for you."

I'm thinking, "What could I have done?" He showed me to his office and gave me a leather chair to sit in to wait for the answer that wasn't long in coming. He opened his bottom desk drawer and took out a large military envelope as he said in a friendly voice, "I was pleased to receive your college board profiles and your letter of recommendation for college from Lieutenant Belara, the education officer on the USS Midway. Professional and well planned, thank you for selecting this college to attend." He continued, "Classes run on a quarter system here and the winter quarter starts next Monday to run two weeks before the Christmas holidays. Time was running out for you to register to begin the quarter, so I registered you for twelve hours of freshman classes. Come to my office on

Monday and I will show you your classrooms and introduce you to your instructors. You will live in room
twenty-three, second floor, in the freshman dormitory."

The Dean of Men showed me the bursar's
office and I paid my tuition. He shook my hand,
wished me well in my studies, and said, "I wanted to
keep the perfect wax seal of the *Midway* and that is
why you saw the round hole in the middle of the military envelope where I cut it out to remind me of the
happy days I spent aboard her years ago as the Executive Officer. That is why I had been waiting for you to
come: to show you my seal, not to give you demerits,"
he laughed.

The freshman dormitory was a madhouse. Kids
were skylarking constantly, rolling toilet paper up and
down the halls, shooting water guns at each other,
playing grab-ass, and raising hell when the dorm
master was not looking.

Kuddy's antics, at times, were scary when he
came up from the field. He waded through dozens of
bodies lying around the floor in the recreation room
watching "Mission Impossible" on the tube, kicked
bodies out of his way, and flipped the channel to "The
Roadrunner" cartoon, his favorite, without saying a
word. The other kids said nothing and some of them
left their favorite television show when he came.
Kuddy wore ragged old shorts year-round, and he took
his seat on the divan, where moments ago, other
freshmen sat before he shooed them away like chickens. He always held the leg of his old shorts out and
farted on the freshmen who stayed to watch television.
Kuddy had three or four hairs on his nose, no neck
and a head that sat flat on his shoulders. He was five-
feet, six inches tall and weighed 230 pounds, square

like a block of wood, solid muscle, legs slightly bowed; and he waddled when he walked. His old shirt had the number thirty–five on it. His roommate and other freshmen kids complained about his feet stinking from the sweaty old sandals he wore without socks, but they were afraid to report him because he threatened to rub toe jam up their noses. Some said that his intelligence quotient matched the number on his jersey. Kuddy came to college to play. He was highly recruited as the nose guard for the football team. The noise pollution was at such a high decibel that no one could study. Freshmen came to college to play; not to study. I came to study and had to find a way to get out of the freshman dormitory and noise. I was two years older than the average freshman and wanted so much just to leave the dormitory.

Students around campus affectingly called him Doc Dean. He was my freshman English and philosophy teacher. Doc had a beautiful house he built from river rock and called it Rain Rock. His house was in walking distance of the campus overlooking Cullowhee Valley and he and Danny, his brown cocker spaniel dog, walked daily by the cemetery around a mountain trail and used the short cut to the campus. Sometimes Danny stayed in Doc's office while he taught classes, but most days he came into the classroom. Doc would say to him. "Danny, sit in the corner and don't move until the bell rings." Danny would whine, take his seat in the corner, and never distrub the class. Doc gave him a sugar cookie each day.

At the end of class one day Doc asked me how I was doing. I answered, "Not so well. I'm trying to find a place to move out of the dormitory to get away from the noise."

"Do you smoke or drink?" he asked.

I quickly answered, "Neither."

"Come up to my house, the rock one you can see from the coffee shop on campus, and look at a room on the driveway side of the house. That room is unoccupied and I live in the other end of the house. Can you come at 5:00 p.m.?"

I said, "I'll see you then."

Doc showed me the room with a bay window, a private drive, and a private entrance with all the amenities and asked me if I liked the room. I said, "It's perfect Doc but I can't afford it."

He asked, "What are you paying for your room at the dormitory?"

I handed him my receipt from the bursar, which he studied for a minute before he said, "You can have the room for the amount you are paying the college.

The bursar and I can work out this quarter's room payment since you paid your tuition yesterday, and you can pay me direct from here on as long as you want the room." he smiled.

I was so happy with my room and a different living environment. It was a defining moment in my college career. I lived at Doc Dean's house until I finished college.

Classes were most interesting and my professors were among the best. Dr. Mabel Crum, head of the English Department, and my sophomore

English professor, was teaching American literature and gave each of her sixteen freshmen an assignment to either read or write a poem.

A male student sitting next to me in class had the highest intelligence quotient of anyone at this college. He had a photographic memory and made straight A's and the Dean's List without much studying. His background was mathematics and science, and he believed that reading or writing a poem was foolishness and called it "fruity." His nocturnal sojourns ended in heavy drinking, and one morning he wobbled into class with his breath reeking alcohol. Dr. Crum asked him if he had elected to read or write a poem and he mumbled, "I'll read a few lines from 'I Wondered Lonely as a Cloud' by William Wordsworth."

He closed his book and asked Dr. Crum if he could quote the poem. She answered, "Yes."

He quoted the poem in its entirety without missing a word. She thanked the student and asked him to comment on the daffodils metaphor in the poem. He smiled a whiskey smile and in an iterated voice said, "The daffodil image is pure bunk. If I had been the poet, I would have written, "Along the margin of a bay, I saw tens of thousands upon tens of thousands of the sons-of-bitches tossing their heads in sprightly dance."

A hush fell over the room. Dr. Crum dismissed the student from her class and asked him to never return.

My college surroundings were a girl-rich environment. Never had I seen so many beautiful women. They were everywhere I turned. She came to the campus in early spring my sophomore year, in all her beauty, from the University of Mississippi. Every movement was graceful. Her flashing blue eyes, long blond hair, trim body, and long legs gave her an air of elegance. She came that spring to instruct the majorettes of the Pride of the Mountains marching band. She started as a twirler at four years old in a dance school in Wynne, Arkansas, and became the Drum Majorette at the University of Mississippi her freshman year there. She was energetic and full of life, a social butterfly. Students around the parade field and at the student union building loved her. Sometimes introductions are strange. She caught up with me walking to class and said in a beautiful voice, "You are different. Do you know the mountains and streams around here?"

"Yes," I answered.

Before I could introduce myself, she asked, "Can you clog?"

"I'm not the best dancer, but I can clog," I answered.

"Meet me at the coffee shop after your class," she continued.

She walked over to my table at the coffee shop and said, "I'm Neal Foust and you are Ray Carpenter."

It surprised me that she knew my name. I packed a picnic lunch and picked her up at the apartment off campus she had rented for the spring.

"You and I are going swimming in the lake at Little Canada."

What a body! She had no bathing suit and went swimming in her shorts and cotton blouse. After the swim, we ate our sandwiches and walked in the creek, to her delight. She picked small purple flowers along the bank and handed them to me. I asked her to pack her bag because she and I were going to my sister Marie's house at Tapoco. I had a special treat for her. She thought the mountains were beautiful and liked that Marie lived there. I took her to a square dance in Fontana, and someone there gave her a lesson in clogging. Before the night ended, she borrowed a pair of tap shoes and did the jingling tap dancing to perfection. She was so pleased to learn that dance.

She asked me to write her a poem and I scribbled on a scrap piece of paper:

Love

Love like a flower
Fills the air with power
And allures some poor soul
To a mate they will never know
Love like a river ripples along
Eating away with passion
The heart of some lover
Love like a traveler
In and out it goes
In and out
And out forever
Love like a bubble grows and grows
and at the first sign of a hole
it bursts into nothing.

Neal returned the scribble to me many years later and said, "I remember this well after all the years and wanted you to have it."

Dr. Herring, a bohemian, a pedantic icon around campus, was my favorite professor in college. He broke all dress codes and etiquette rules. His dress wasn't sloppy or dirty but different. He was a clean dresser and shaved daily. His ornate and colorful silk ascot fastened with a stick pin gave him a little dignity, but wearing the ascot with an old crumpled shirt and a baggy corduroy sport jacket with leather patches on torn sleeves, together with ancient white sneakers with holes made by long-time wear and old threadbare pants excluded him from receiving any awards for dress.

He walked with a bounce, and when he talked one-on-one he sucked in air and exhaled with soft snorts. To motivate his students, he wrote and lectured sometimes in Latin. He spoke and wrote Italian, German, Spanish, Russian, and Japanese fluently. He ended his lecture one day in English and emphasized that it was easy to get through college since the entire education system for the English-speaking nation was based on twenty-six letters of the alphabet and numbers from zero to nine. "Learn those two things and their variations," he said, "and you will all go home with degrees."

Dr. Herring and the subjects he taught were extremely popular with the students, and it was difficult to get into one of his classes. Jerry Ballard, a twenty-one-year-old Marine just out of the corps, an excellent student, and a good friend, and I got into his class called Basic Logic one summer session. Our study covered all types of logic but focused primarily on syllogistic logic. Jerry and I made up our minds to tear up Dr. Herring logic class and to maximize quality points. We both had A's going into the final. Jerry came over to my room to prepare for the final examination in the logic course. After four hours, we were ready for Dr. Herring's final examination. Dr. Herring always called the roll from memory with his back to the students. He finished that and said, "You have one question for your final examination, and I will write it on the board instead of handing it out on test paper. Quickly he wrote, "What three things do the premises written on the board have in common? Two men carrying a rail on their shoulders, the symbol for pi square 3rd power, and an angel drinking a cool glass of beer?"

I tried to apply all the formulas for logic that I learned in the class: deductive and inductive reasoning, direct and indirect analogies, syllogistic logic, and serendipity. Nothing that I thought of applied to Dr. Herring's three premises written on the board. I looked around the room and everyone in the class was writing furiously. I hadn't written a word and remained dumbfounded and silent, trying to think what my answer should be. Twenty minutes into the first hour, I wrote three things the premises have in common: written by the same professor, by the same piece of chalk, and on the same blackboard. I signed my paper, dated it, handed it to Dr. Herring, and left the room. Jerry wrote the entire two hours. At the beginning of the next quarter, Jerry asked Dr. Herring, in my presence, what he was looking for on the question for the final examination. Dr. Herring snorted slightly and said, "Carpenter had an answer that was close to being correct." I made an A in the course and Jerry made a B. because his final examination was so-so, according to Dr. Herring.

Western Carolina College

To all to whom these presents may come

Be it known that

Ray Douglas Carpenter

having successfully completed the prescribed course of study and having complied with all other requirements established by the College, has, upon recommendation of the Faculty been declared by the Board of Trustees a

Bachelor of Science

In testimony whereof we have hereunto subscribed our names at the Halls of the College, Cullowhee, North Carolina, this the third day of June, one thousand nine hundred and sixty-two.

Chairman Board of Trustees   *President of the College*

Dean of the College   *Secretary of the Faculty*

I met Zella with a question. "You are tearing Dr. Crum's English literature class up. How are you doing that? I'm a pretty good reader myself and never make the scores on the pop quizzes or term examination that you do. Do you use magic?" She laughed and said, "How do you take notes? Let me see your notebook. One of your problems is trying to take down everything the professor is saying. This might be possible if you used shorthand."

"May I see your notebook?" I asked. She handed it to me, and for Dr. Crum's lecture that day she had written four or five sentences. "Listen to the professor and most of the time they give you clues, such as 'this is important;' 'make special note of this'; and 'you may see this again.'"

Dr. Crum's question was "What is the unique thing about the gates of hell from John Milton's *Paradise Lost?*" I wrote the description of the gates of hell word for word as John Milton wrote them. Dr. Crum gave me no points on my answer, and when I asked Zella how she answered the question, she said, "The unique thing about the gates of hell was that once they were opened, they have never been closed."

Dr. Crum wrote on her paper "excellent" and gave her ten points.

Zella and I met my junior year and continued a great relationship. She pulled a small piece of crumpled-up paper from one of her old textbooks years later and handed me the paper on which I had scribbled for her, "Venus herself, the lovely one, was present at your birth, she touched you with her wand and placed you here on earth, for me."

Zella and I were married in St. Mary's Episcopal Church in Asheville. George Mears sang "The Lord's Prayer," and I will never forget the beauty of that moment and the life that she and I had together.

My Career

A fter college, I sold my blue Ford for $800 and used the money for my job search in Atlanta, Georgia. I met E.G. MacNarris, a Greek, in a trout stream with his fishing line badly tangled. I helped him learn to catch rainbow and brook trout with his fancy fly rod in Big Snowbird Creek in Graham County, North Carolina. Helping someone untanglehis fishing line and teaching him to catch trout is the best way to make a friend. Mac and his lovely wife Kathryn invited me to live at their home in Atlanta until I found a job.

Mac set up my first job interview with his friend, Kleg Pipronia, Personnel Manager for Nestle Food Company. Mr. Pipronia offered me a job as a rack jobber distributing Nestle products in businesses in remote areas across the plains of West Texas. The pay offered was excellent but the distance was too much. I didn't take the job.

I went from one job interview to another. Mr. R.L. Klac, Personnel Manager for Glidden's Paint Company, was robust, and red-faced with stubbed fingernails and old sweat around his dirty shirt collar. He never smiled.

"You've finished high school, served in the Navy and finished college but you have no work experience." He drummed on, "You know nothing about the paint industry. I don't want to commit company resources to training you." He frowned and said, "I hire people who have skills and can contribute to bottom-line profits for the company immediately." I thought about kicking his ass but kept my patience and left his office in a snit.

Holes worn in the soles of my wing-tip cordovan slippers got bigger as I walked the streets of Atlanta, going to job interviews and follow-ups while searching for work. Even in this large city, the dirty old side-walks and streets became familiar. Soon I knew where all the public bathrooms were up and down the hot, dry, and dusty streets and where the twenty-cent Krystal Burger restaurants were located where I ate regularly. Many interviews and three weeks later, I still had no job, not even a promise of one.

One day I sat down to think about why I had no job. True, I had no job experience, but I was young with a college degree, an honorable service record, and a desire to work. "Some company out there needs me," I thought. "Sell yourself, don't pay an employment agency a fee for a job." I liked this thought because my $800 was running out.

I remembered these guidelines from a business class:

• Learn from each interview what you did right or wrong and correct the things you did wrong before the next interview.

• Study the company you are about to interview with. Especially study their growth, profit, service, expense control, and people development. Sometimes, companies have no training programs and long-term plans for your future. I'm thinking I am worth a lot, and I deserve an opportunity with the company that offers me a job.

• Know more about the company than anyone. Be ready to sell yourself kept ringing in my ears.

• Know the reasons you want to work for a par-ticular company and be able to tell the interviewer.

• Show the interviewer how your skills and potential can benefit the company and how your work will produce a profitable growth long-term for the company.

• Be open to salary discussions and value other company benefits the company offers.

Dr. Fred F. Wyatt, my business instructor, taught me these basic guidelines for job search, and I appreciated his efforts to teach me. I needed to use them in my next interviews.

After two more unsuccessful job interviews in the business sector, I decided to explore a job with a major newspaper using my writing skills. My interview with the sports editor of the *Atlanta Journal* newspaper was unusual and different.

I walked into a small, dusty office on Peachtree Street in downtown Atlanta on a hot, muggy day and saw a small, college-age, wiry man wearing penny loafers with no socks, dark shades, a plaid shirt with the sleeves pushed up to his elbows and held in place with orange arm bands. His long hair was blowing beneath the visor cap he wore. His quick smile gave me an opening.

"I want to discuss working for the newspaper with you," I stammered, as he turned around in his swivel chair.

"You're at the right place, young man. I'm always looking for good writers." He spoke clearly as he blew smoke rings that floated past me and fumbled in a stack of papers on his desk for my resume. "Oh, yes, Carpenter, here we are," he said as he stood up. "Have a seat at my desk," he said, as he slid a pen and a lined tablet in front of me. "Write one short paragraph using all the prepositions you can and spell all words correctly. I'm going next door to drink a beer.

When you're finished writing, come next door for a beer on me and we'll finish the interview. Bring your paragraph," he said in a quiet voice, as he slammed the office door noisily.

Smiling to myself, I wrote, "Before writing a paragraph using prepositions, a rule review is in order. "But" is very seldom a preposition. When it is used as a preposition, "but" means the same as except as in "Everyone ate caviar but Ivan." "But" usually functions as a coordinating conjunction."

I began to write my paragraph using prepositions:

At dawn during flight operations on the big air-craft carrier, Coral Sea, *Ivan Cici, a jet ace, walked to his instrument of death, a Banshee fighter jet, before the air boss sounded man your plane. Because of semi-darkness, Ivan walked along the lighted markers, on the port side of the ship, past the small signal deck, under the flapping pennants used by the Landing Deck Officer to guide jets in for a safe landing. Before he climbed into the cockpit of the Banshee, as before, Ivan made a final check of all his equipment in spite of the air boss's command to expedite. In addition to the thrust of the powerful jet engines, a steam catapult was used to assist getting the Banshee off the flight deck and into the sky. By means of a refueling snorkel on the nose of the Banshee it was refueled in flight and flew on into the darkness until the mission was com-pleted. Throughout the flight, Ivan flew the jet flaw-lessly and upon returning safely to the ship and a safe landing on the flight deck of the big carrier, he received praise from the air boss.*

I checked my work and went to the bar next

door. When I stepped through the doors of the bar, the wiry writer for the paper motioned me over to his booth.

"The only way a paragraph of prepositions makes any sense to me is when I'm drunk." he laughed, draining his draft beer. He motioned for the bartender to bring me a draft beer and reached for my paragraph. His perusal of my writing was less than a minute. I'm thinking he has no interest in hiring me.

He surprised me by turning my paragraph face down and quoting it verbatim saying, "You are good enough to start. I like what I read. Company benefits with the *Atlanta Journal* are better than most publishing companies. I'll give you a handbook that shows you all the benefits when we get back to my desk. It gives you everything else you will need to know to work for the *Atlanta Journal.* You'll have an opportunity to increase your salary based on job performance. Thirty-two hundred dollars annually is the starting salary for this position. Your work will be to help me as the sports editor of this paper. You will work from my office instead of the corporate office. Specifically, you will take the sports pictures from the staff photographers and lay them out so they can be printed with the story they accompany for the next edition of the paper."

Everything about this interview had gone well, but it was so fast and unusual that it left me without words for a minute. I thanked the young sports editor for his time and the beer but told him the salary was too low. He made no salary counter offer, and I shook his hand and left the bar.

An old man, who limped and carried a cane, was selling the *Atlanta Journal* outside the office. He mumbled something about a twenty-three-year-old

Lewis Grizzard who had done well for himself becoming the sports editor for the *Atlanta Journal* at a young age, loud enough for me to hear above the din of the traffic. As I passed by the old man selling papers and mumbling, I thought maybe I missed the best opportunity I would ever have by not accepting the job the wiry sports editor offered me. Little did I know that the Sports Editor that asked me to work with him at the *Atlanta Journal* would later become a major journalist and well-known writer.

The next day I went to the Atlanta-Fulton Public Library to learn everything I could about a company I wanted to interview with. Two weeks before graduating from college, I completed an application expressing an interest to work for The Hartford, a large Property and Casualty Company, but I had not heard from them concerning my request for an interview. I picked up the phone the next morning at 8:00 a.m. and discussed a job with Homer Willis, Personnel Manager. "I am from Robbinsville, North Carolina, and am in town looking for work." He mumbled, "Do you have a college degree?"

"Yes, sir, I finished college last month after serving my time in the United States Navy," I said with enthusiasm.

"Have you worked, except your military job?" he asked.

"Except for a summer job with Harrison Construction Company my senior year in high school, I have not worked. I filled out a job application for The Hartford two weeks ago and, to date, have heard nothing from them."

He mumbled, "The Hartford uses an employment agency with a $500 fee for new hires."

I answered, "I don't have five hundred for the fee

and besides, I feel more comfortable selling my potential for becoming an employee of a company."

There was a long pause at the other end of the phone, then Mr. Willis said, "I found the job application you completed in my file and want to give you an opportunity to come by my office at 9:00 a.m. tomorrow for a battery of tests and so I can meet you. There will be no employment-agency fee involved. My office is on the fifth floor, first door on the left, in the Trust Company of Georgia Building, Little Five Points, downtown, Atlanta."

I thanked him, said goodbye, and hung up the phone. I was so happy. I was shaking with joy that I sold myself for the job interview and didn't have to pay an employment agency.

At 8:45 a.m. the next morning, I introduced myself to Mr. Willis' secretary and said, "I'm here to see Mr. Willis."

"Welcome to The Hartford," she said, as she offered me a seat. "Mr. Willis will be with you shortly."

Mr. Willis reached to shake my hand and, with a friendly smile, motioned me to a smaller, private room in the back of his office. "When you are finished with one test, hand the answer sheet and copy of the test to the secretary and she will hand you another test. Please follow this process until you have taken the four tests and then come to my office," he continued. "I wish you well on the testing."

The first three tests were the same tests that I graded for Dr. Fred Waytt when I was his lab assistant at college. I scored perfect on all three and missed two on the last test. Mr. Willis complimented me on my scores and asked me why I wanted to work for The Hartford.

"I'm interested in making a career in insurance

and risk management long-term, improving my skills in the insurance industry and management, and self-improvement. I like the consistent underwriting, profitability, productivity, performance and that the company trains its people. The company has been in business since 1810 with its corporate office in Hartford, Connecticut, and Regional Offices located in major cities across the country."

Mr. Willis asked me if I could come back to his office tomorrow at 10:00 a.m. for another part of the interview. I said yes, shook his hand, thanked him, and left his office.

I had one other interview scheduled that day with a paper-shredding and recycling company. The salary was the lowest that I had been offered, and I turned the job down based on the type of work and the low salary.

I'm thinking, "What could this part of the interview with The Hartford be like?" as I got off the elevator next to Mr. Willis's office at 9:45 a.m. the next day. Mr. Willis, in his pinstripped suit and well groomed hair, smiled and asked me to have a seat. "Ray, this part of the interview will be conducted in the Board of Directors Room on the second floor. The attendees will be managers, including the Regional Manager, four of the line managers, and me. Mr. Ralph Skelton, a lawyer for The Hartford, will attend also. They'll all have the opportunity to ask you questions but some of them may not. I'm the moderator to keep things moving."

A long, oval-shaped, teakwood table sat in the center of the Board of Directors Room, with a vase of red roses as the centerpiece, A silver tea and coffee serving set rested on the credenza, carpet that seemed to be four-inches thick matched the drapes, and a large *Monarch of the Glen* painting adorned the wall at one end of the table. A portrait of Nathaniel Terry, first president of the company, hung at the other end of the table. A podium with a speaker's mike stood to the right of table, and a portable chalkboard with chalk was in place close by. Twelve large, black, leather swivel chairs were already occupied with attendees and guests when Mr. Willis and I entered the room.

"Ray, you are our special guest today," he said as he took a chair beside mine at the head of the table. Mr. Willis introduced me and said, "He is here for the final part of his interview. Today, we will conduct the formal part of the interview with a question-and-answer session and wrap up the interview with Mr. Ledbetter, Ms. Berry, Mr. Fulton, and me remaining in the room at the end."

All participants had their pens and note pads in front of them on the table. Mr. Ledbetter asked me, "What do you look for in a company you wish to work for?" I asked to use the chalkboard and he granted my request. I walked to the board and quickly wrote: people development, profit, growth, service, and expense control, returned to my seat and said, "I wrote a term paper on creating a company while attending college and used the five objectives written on the board as corporate objectives for my prototype. I look for a company to have a business plan, definite objectives with long-range goals for underwriting profit and controlled growth. My professor commented on the people development objective and said that out of the five objectives, it was most important to train people for their jobs. Without quality people, the other four objectives can't be reached. Mr. Ledbetter, sir, I look for a company which will give me the opportunity to study and learn the business. The Hartford, with its parent company and seven subsidiary companies, would seem to offer me that opportunity."

Mr. Skelton shuffled slightly, adjusted his small round reading glasses on the bridge of his nose, looked over them, and said, in a slow Southern drawl, "Your resume reflects that you have a degree in engineering and I wish to ask my questions in that discipline." I answered him quickly, "My degrees are in business administration, personnel management, and English and philosophy, not engineering, to clarify, sir."

Mr. Skelton pulled his reading glasses lower on his nose, continued to look over them and said, "Thank you for the clarification. Please define the word philosophy for me." Again, I requested permission to use the chalkboard and Mr. Skelton granted its use. I walked to the chalkboard, buying myself some time to think. I wrote on the board *phil* underlined it; *oso*, underlined it; and *phy* and underlined it. I pointed to the prefix *phil*, explaining that in Latin, it means love; *oso*, the root word from Latin means thinking; and the suffix *phy* in Latin means the science of. Putting them together, the definition for philosophy is love of know- ledge or learn- ing.

Mr. Skelton nodded and said, "Define aplomb for me."

Self-confident and assured, I answered, "Hopefully, I walked to the chalkboard that way this day."

Everyone laughed. With a broad smile, Mr. Skelton picked up his pen from the floor and said, "Define the word *orts* for me." I slowly wrote it on the board, to buy time to think, and said, "The word may be lost in antiquity, but my definition is a scrap of food. It is what I fed pigs as I grew up in the Smoky Mountains west of Asheville."

This response brought a roar of laughter from the group.

Mr. Willis dismissed everyone from the interview except Mr. Ledbetter, Ms. Berry, and Jim Fulton. They concluded the interview by handing Mr. Willis a folded piece of paper, and Mr. Ledbetter extended his hand and offered me a job. I thanked him and held up my wing-tipped cordovan slipper I was wearing with the hole in the center and said, "I needed that." He shook my hand again and wished me the best in my employment with The Hartford.

Mr. Willis advised me that I would be in a management-training program for eighteen months in the Atlanta Office, with periodic visits to the home office for training. At the end of the training program, I would be assigned. "Your beginning salary will be $112.50 weekly with excellent benefits and an opportunity for advancement," he continued. "Before you finalize the paperwork, you need a physical, which I have scheduled for you at 10:00 a.m. tomorrow. The doctor is four buildings down the street. The company pays for your visit with the doctor. Don't eat or drink anything after midnight, and I will see you tomorrow."

I was pleased to have a job. The next morning the doctor declared me fit for employment, and I returned to Mr. Willis's office and gave him the form signed by the doctor. He took me to my office on the second floor. On my desk was a package that outlined all my work activities for the next eighteen months. It advised me that I was enrolled in a risk-management and insurance course at Georgia State college and that classes were held on Fridays for a three-hour period. "You are responsible for carrying out your schedule," he said. "Good luck with your training program and drop by my office to see me soon."

My trainee program was an on-the-job training program filled with all the ways to study insurance, risk management, and public speaking, in addition to the five professional courses I completed at Georgia State College. Mr. Skelton's office was two doors down from my office, and each day when I got off the elevator, I had to go by his office to bring him a new word. I made good friends with Mr. Skelton, and he sometimes rode home in the evening with me after work.

Just before I finished my training program, I was selected to attend a creative seminar to bring back to The Hartford some creative sales and management ideas. It was to be held in Henna, New Hampshire. Sixteen attendees, including a botanist, archaeologist, alchemist, philatelist, numismatist, geographer, artist, insurance instructor, minister, philosopher, farmer, sociologist, physicist, writer, philologist, and an architect gathered on a snowy day in late November there. I looked over those gathered and thought, "A motley bunch but a cross-section of several disciplines ready to create something." Participants were broken into teams of four and instructed to work on their projects using direct and indirect analogies, syllogistic logic, and serendipity. Each team had to create something, but each team's project had to be different.

My team, made up of the farmer, the artist and the writer, was assigned to create something using a direct analogy from nature. We were to make a final presentation for twelve minutes, before all other team members, instructors, staff members, and ten chief executive officers of large companies from New York who would be our guests on Friday. Materials were provided, including access to a petting farm with butterflies, fish, birds, and animals of all kinds to stimulate thinking. A pottery wheel was also provided so the idea could be formed, shaped, fired and polished.

Flowers were out of season, but many books about flowers and plants, with pictures and information summaries, were available for our use.

My team appointed me spokesperson. In our trial-and-error and brainstorming sessions, it was my responsibility to pull ideas from the other team members as well as contribute ideas of my own, then organize them in a workable order. The writer was helpful, writing the summaries of team ideas, and the artist drew sketches and painted our ideas. The farmer only shook his head and grunted yes or no. He had nothing to say.

Our team was given a secret workroom on premises to complete the project. On Wednesday of that week, team members, after several hours of trial and error, brainstorming, and no comments from a silent farmer, agreed that the world needed a better glue dispenser, one that would cut off the glue flow and not smear it, one that would keep the glue off an executive's pinstriped suit, off desks at schools, off children's fingers, off secretaries' hands, and off the reports and documents that become files. One special feature of the new glue dispenser, which the artist contributed, was to angle the dispensing nozzle so it worked in the corners of photo albums and scrapbook corners without the ugly smear of glue. Members of my team were in complete agreement that the new glue dispenser would sell in all countries around the world and especially in all the states of the United States.

Time was running out! From nature, what direct analogy could our team use to create a glue dispenser that didn't leave a sticky mess behind but rather would cut off the glue sharp and clean every time it was used? The artist sketched in minute detail a slow moving snail with a spiral shell. His idea was to reverse a slimy process of the snail. He said, "The snail moves by creeping on a flat foot underneath the body. The band of muscles in the foot contract and expand and this creates a kind of rippling movement that pushes the snail forward. The foot has a special gland that produces slimy mucus to make a slippery track. Slippery tracks can often be seen in the garden. The slime comes out from the front of the gland and hardens when it comes in contact with the air."

Team members didn't think the snail was a good choice for the new glue dispenser because reversing the process couldn't be done in time for the final presentation. Besides, the snail is both male and female, and team members felt that this would be a disaster for any ploy to market and sell the new glue dispenser.

"The clam is the best choice," the writer kept saying. "The clam uses two strong adductor muscles, the clam pulls in its foot and siphons and locks shut in defense. Like the clam, the glue dispenser would have siphons to open when the glue dispenser is in use and close when not in use. To solve the problem of the messy excess glue when the glue dispenser is in use, hair-like cilia would sweep the residue into a part of the dispenser and recycle it for the next use."

Team members liked the idea of using the clam as the analogy but reasoned that it was a complicated idea and would take longer than the two days left to make the final presentation on Friday.

"The aphid," I said, "is a small, homopterous insect that gets its food by sucking from leaves, stems, roots, and plants. It cuts its excreta clean and deposits it in little balls on leaves. Honeydew is the rectal secretion with high sugar content of the aphid feeding on the phloem juices. Phloem is the living tissue that carries organic nutrients, particularly sucrose, a sugar, to all parts of the plant. The aphid provides for its food needs from the dark sugar solution in phloem juice, and, after sufficient intake, excretes the rest. Microscopic fungus and algae emerge on sticky sugary excreta, which may then pass to honey. Honeydew can occur as a drop at the anus of the aphid or it may just squirt off. Honeybees carry this dark sugary substance to their hives and transform it into honey."

The writer quickly frowned and said, "That dissertation was too long but interesting." He continued, "The aphid is microscopic and its size makes it hard to use as an analogy for a new glue dispenser." Other members of the team agreed with the writer and my idea was turned down.

Throughout the week, everyone in the seminar called him Silent Cal. One night, at a late hour, when my team members and I were working frantically to come up with something from nature that could be used as an analogy for the new glue dispenser, the farmer slowly said, "I've got it." My team members and I could not wait to hear the farmer's idea for the analogy. He continued, "My horses had the thin squirts in the spring when they grazed on grass. But the squirt was cut off sharp and clean by the sphincter muscle and there was not a watery mess around their asses each time their bowels moved."

Immediately, the artist sketched a ring of muscle surrounding and serving to guard the nozzle of the proposed glue dispenser. Quickly, the sketch was molded, fired, and polished at the pottery wheel. On Friday, I removed a purple velvet covering from our sales idea and used twelve minutes to present the sphincter muscle of a horse's ass, the creative idea for the new glue dispenser, and ideas for the marketing ploys to distribute the new glue dispenser to a world market.

My team members and I left the seminar with blue ribbons and $400 apiece, the first place prize! From this creative seminar, I gave The Hartford a creative idea for time management based on Mama's method she taught me years ago of make ready, do, and put away.

I worked in the Atlanta, Charlotte, and Memphis offices of the Hartford and also in the Home Office in Hartford, Connecticut. I held positions of trainee, multi-line marketing representative, instructor, and superintendent of the Association Franchise Department at different times over the twenty-seven years until I retired.

1963

1964

Insurance Institute of America

Incorporated

Founded at Philadelphia, Pennsylvania, April, 1909
Incorporated, May 1, 1924.

or having satisfactorily passed the examinations General Principl
Insurance, Principles of Fire, Marine and Allied Lines Insuran
d Principles of Casualty Insurance and Surety Bonding

Ray Paul Douglas Carpenter

is hereby awarded this

Certificate

the Board of Governors of the Insurance Institute of America, Incorporat
on this twenty-fifth day of March, 1964.

A Great Gift—The First Day

T hings change! Catching babies on October 1, 1971, was different. I went to a Lamaze Childbirth Education Class for new parents in room 100, Hartford Hospital, Hartford, Connecticut, for six weeks during the third trimester of my wife's pregnancy. I was there not to learn how to catch babies, but to learn about modern obstetrics and how to apply them to support my wife during her pregnancy and delivery. I walked into the classroom the first time with trepidation! Unexpected things cause me anxiety and uneasiness. Birthing babies was "women's business," I had always believed. Men came back around when they could hold the new baby. No longer.

Filomena Onesti, a beautiful young Italian woman, my Lamaze instructor, was an enthusiastic, competent, highly qualified educator who was an advocate for childbearing women and their families. She taught with zeal! The Lamaze curriculum supported birth as normal and natural without obstetric anesthesia or "twilight sleep."

It covered the gamut of normal labor, birth and early postpartum, positioning for labor and birth, relaxation and massage technique to ease pain, labor breathing and pushing, communication skills, medical procedures, breast-feeding, and lifestyles. I learned those skills of timing, breathing, and pushing that she reviewed before each session so I could be a part of the medical team during my wife's labor and delivery.

Ms. Onesti popped into the room each session with great excitement and interesting quips to help the twelve pregnant women in the class relieve their fear of childbirth. On one occasion she asked me to give the quip she had taught us last session. I was pleased that I knew it and shyly said, "If birth is undisturbed, it never gives you more than you can bear."

The last day of class, she ended it by saying, "Ladies, when active labor begins, your endorphins kick in and your body goes on autopilot. There is no thinking...you just 'do'—and you can do it!" The participants gave her a standing ovation!

For weeks, my wife got up during the night to pee every so often. After a trip to the bathroom around 5:00 a.m. on October 1, 1971, she got back in bed and advised me that she noticed a popping sensation "down below." I was perplexed but not overly concerned. She said, "It's like no other sensation I have felt before; maybe my water has broken."

I felt for moisture but didn't feel any. I made my way back to the bathroom with her. Just as I pulled down her panties, a clear liquid flowed from her body. I called to her, "Zella, I think your water just broke." I groggily asked her if she was sure of what had just happened. She explained that she had not peed on herself and couldn't imagine what else it could be.

Our moment of shock and disbelief passed momentarily, and for the next hour or so I finished packing her suitcase. Knowing that she might not want to eat later during labor, I got her to drink a cup of hot soup for what I thought to be a marathon ahead.

She wanted to rest during this phase of labor but her body wouldn't allow it. She had to keep walking. It just hurt too much to lie down or sit. It hurt her feet to remain upright, but she had to choose the lesser of the discomforts. Each contraction was fairly mild at this point, yet she had a difficult time telling me exactly when each one came and went.

Around 6:00 a.m. the contractions took on a new level of intensity and she could no longer tell me the time between them. It just took too much energy and concentration. I wondered if her water had truly broken; I suspected that it may have actually stayed intact.

Because she was riding each wave so well, I had no idea how far into labor she was. She found comfort leaning on our buffet in the dining room, leaning against walls and door jambs and the vanity in the bathroom as she made her way through the house. Throughout labor and during the final moments at home, she was couraguous even though she was nauisated. Although sitting on the toilet was uncomfortable and intense, her body had to release what was inside. She said that throwing up felt so good; it was a physical cleansing.

About 6:30 a.m. contractions took on yet another level of intensity. In between contractions, I said matter-of-factly, "I see why women give up." At that moment, with contractions coming so closely and with so much energy, I understood how easily women succumb to the comfort of obstetric anesthesia. Seconds later she expressed her need to leave for the hospital. I was concerned about getting there too early but I did respect her request. I loaded up the car and we made our way to the garage. She wedged her body between the door and seat into the bucket seat of our Grand Prix. She leaned over the seat hugging a pillow. As soon as the car was in motion, she felt the urge to push but didn't because she was determined to hold her baby inside until she reached the hospital. She buried her face in the pillow and moaned through each wave.

As soon as I pulled up to the curb, she

expressed her need to push. The contractions were so intense that it took her an extra minute or two to get out of the car. Once on the sidewalk, another wave came rushing through her and she leaned first into the door, then on the brick wall just steps away from the automatic doors. She waddled inside the hospital, still clutching onto her pillow as she passed the reception desk. In between contractions, she mumbled to the ladies behind the desk, and they replied, "I think they're going to keep you and not send you home." It was pretty obvious that she was in active labor. From the lobby to the triage room, she stopped wherever she could to push: against the wall in the elevator, at the counter of the nurse's station, anywhere.

As soon as she stepped into the triage room, she asked if she could push but was told to wait. The nurse wanted to check and measure her dilation. The nurse told her she was fully dilated and moved her immediately to a labor-and-delivery room. The nurse tried to get her into a gown and preserve whatever modesty they assumed she had, but she couldn't have cared less about being naked in front of all those people at that moment. Her contractions were close together and very strong.

The entire medical team and staff, including Dr. Tripp, pediatrician: Dr. Shapiro, cardiologist; and a coalition of nurses, midwives, and doulas were there in her delivery room. A doula motioned for me to go over to a side room and don a green surgeon's gown, a white breathing mask, and a pair of white protective gloves then take a seat beside my wife's bed and hold her hand.

As her labor progressed and the endorphins kicked in big time, her face became smoother and she began to sway her hips. She became calm and quiet.

The lights were low. It was beautiful to watch her labor progress undisturbed. Dr. Tripp sat at the foot of her bed, very observant, and gave us thumbs up! She squeezed my hand to let me know that she was awake and aware of her progress. The nurses and doulas were busy checking charts, and Dr. Shapiro was reading her heart monitors, including the baby's heart rate and breathing rhythms.

I knew everything was going well. My wife was a woman who had thought labor would be scary. But with the things we had learned in class and practiced many times, she found that labor was something she could do. Labor was a challenge that she could meet. She had the mental fortitude and the tools at hand. Birthing her own baby was most important to her. I don't think she'll be scared about anything again. "Crashing though our fears and our cultural myths is what's scary; birth isn't," she later told me.

She was more than ready to push the baby out. She didn't want her baby to be cut out, to be sucked out with a vacuum process, nor to be pulled out with forceps. So, with the nurses holding her legs apart, she pushed with all her might when they told her to push. The baby's head wasn't coming out as quickly as they would like, and the nurse told her that she had to make a small cut. This was the first time in the process that brought on a sense of panic. I thought to myself, "She is not under any anesthesia and the nurse is going to cut her?" I was very concerned. Surprisingly, it did not hurt her at all. She felt the snip, but it didn't hurt. Quite simply, her body was doing its work because it had not been injected with drugs.

Her one final push got the baby out! And then there was that moment, the moment when we crossed the line from fantasy into reality. From two to three! Our baby was born! Skin on skin. A perfect being—all ours. It took us a minute or two just being in awe before we ever thought about the baby's sex. Then cheers go round as we look and see that it's a boy!

Clumsily dressed in that long green surgeon's gown, I stood by the bed in the delivery room now, a man intensely interested in life's processes and keenly aware that life's good is mixed with pain and evil. I saw in the miracle of birth a symbolic truth. I saw human life emerge out of pain and struggle. No sight every stirred me more deeply or excited me more. It was ugly, bloody, messy, horrible—but somehow beautiful. I told my wife later that when I saw the little crown begin to come, then a little body followed as Dr. Tripp yanked him up by the heels to spank him, and he screwed his face up and let out his first yell—a good one—I could not restrain myself any longer. I gave a yell of my own and said, "Come on, baby!"

No one can understand why I got so excited. The ugliness, the horror, the pain were gone now; all that remained was that little perfect child and all the mystery and tragic beauty of life, which seemed greater to me than ever.

The birth of my son renewed my awareness that the lonely, troubled journey of man begins with the birth struggle. Something gathers in my throat and my eyes are wet when I think of all the pain and wonder the little life must come to know. I hope to God those feet will never walk as lonely a road as mine have walked, and I hope his heart will never beat as mine has at times under a smothering weight of weariness, grief, and horror; nor his brain be damned and haunted by a thousand furies and nightmare shapes that walk through mine.

I would never have wanted my son's birth to be

any other way. I am grateful that I was there and supported my wife. Now I know that child-birthing is a man's business as well as a woman's business.

I had asked Mama how I could repay her for her birth struggle to bring me into the world, to give so much of herself to me, and the countless things she did for me over the years. She smiled and said, "I want you to continue to give me gifts at my birthdays, wedding anniversaries, and other special times. Always love me, think of me, and come to see me often. These things are important to me, and I appreciate material things you give me."

We continued working. Clothes flapped on the line as we gathered them. She said in an angelic voice, "But the way you thank me that is most important to me and a great truth that I ask you to pass on to your son, and he to his family, and they in turn pass on to their families, is a simple one: you see dimly with your eyes but clearly with your heart. Everything of real value is invisible to the eyes. Know God and look about; you will see Him playing with your children. Look into the heavens and you will see Him walking in the clouds, stretching His hands in the lightning and descending in rain and snow; and you will see Him smiling in flowers, then rising and waving His hands in the trees."

Earlier, my son won the swimming race, an aggressive race against all female sperms. He came into the world on his own. He set the pace and showed me how important it was to trust nature's way. He still is a beautiful gift!

That's Ray's Boy

Soft and round, a sweet little boy
That's Ray's Boy!
With a cute little nose, blue eyes, blond hair
That's Ray's boy!
Whose constant chattering made my ears ring
And whose mystic smile made my heart sing
That's Ray's boy!

Now he's grown
And on his own,
On his phone, the sound of his voice
Ending with "I love you, Dad"
Makes my heart sing again,
My son!

Cliff and Ray Carpenter-1993

Above: Cliff with Aiden and Autumn—2009
Below: Charlotte with Aiden and Autumn—2009

Cliff and Charlotte Carpenter-2009

Attic Trunk

Old photographs
Across time, across space
A smile still touches the heart

Tatterd Bible
A record of births, deaths
Messages of hope and love

Faded quilt
Moth riddled
Wrapped in the memories of warmth
Crumbling letters
The eternal messages of love.

Epilogue

Through prose, poetry and photography, I tried to conquer the transitory nature of my existence on earth, to trap moments before they evanesce, to untangle the memories of my past and pick up the elusive threads of the lives of many others and some of my illusory recollections. Memory is fiction. I selected my brightest and my darkest memories, and embroidered the broad tapestry of my life story.

Every instant of my life disappeared in a breath and instantly became the past; reality is ephemeral and changing, pure longing. With these pages, I kept memories alive. They are my grasp on a truth that is fleeting, a lifestyle I was a part of that is all but gone, but truth nonetheless. They are proof that these events happened and that these people passed through my destiny. Thanks to them, I can recall moments about my wife, mama, dad, sister, and brothers who have died; my stalwart grandmothers and wise grandfathers; and other links in the long chain of loved ones.

I wrote to elucidate special moments in my childhood, to define my identify, to create my own legend, and to continue my passion for writing and the creative process. Shadows, dreams, furies, visions, and ghosts that haunted me were part of my early life and writings.

I scribbled on in this book about a mischievous wooden puppet whose nose grew longer when he told lies; a wooden sculpture of a weak and gaunt near-death Mary Magdalene; a world-famous architectural faux pas that took over 250 years to complete and still leans an inclination of twelve feet; a fresco painting in the Vatican Museum; a *Pieta* in St. Peter's Basilica; a marble sculpture of a shepherd boy with a sling over his shoulder in the Academia Gallery created by a master sculptor; a painting of a radiant woman in a floral-embroidered garment; a painting in the Uffizi Gallery of a woman standing naked and beautiful on a large shell; a painting of a beautiful woman with an elusive smile in the Louvre Gallery in Paris, France; and a gold merchant at Ponte Vecchio on a bridge crossing a muddy Arno River in Florence, Italy.

I experienced fears, loneliness, tears, laughter, hardships, sorrows, successes, and failures. I lived among mysteries about my purpose here on earth and life, death, and uncertainties about eternity when the ship pitched in stormy seas. I saw fields of pineapples; sunken battleships; fiery sunrises and sunsets; frolicking dolphins alongside the sailing ship; a magical mountain beyond the tea fields and rice paddies wearing a kimono of snow; geisha and pan-pan girls; and countless thousands of people who were born, lived and died on their boats. I celebrated the wonders and beauty of foreign lands and their people with my prose and poetry to decorate the unique land and people with sunrises and to weave valleys delicately with the edging rim of sunsets.

I told my story closer to that of a black and white photograph in bib overalls that I found years ago in a match box in the attic of an old house on a dirt road on Mill Creek. I found scribbles I had written before my formal school years there and knew I wanted to follow my dream to write about the passions of life, death, love, nature's beauty, and all other images of my soul. My scribbles and poetry brought great beauty and joy to my life but also great sadness. I was never sure it was a fair exchange or worthy of my time. To continue my dream to write, I'm working on short stories, and a longer story about honey bees, and I continue to make verse to publish in the near future.

In the end, the only thing I have in abundance is the memories I have woven. Each of us chooses the way to tell his or her story; I have chosen the durable clarity of print and my scribbles. Something in my destiny possesses that luminosity, and I can still find strength to write another poem by isolating one star in a brimming sky, and another chapter in my bee story because butterflies and honey bees still perform their ordained destinies to continue their races even after 40,000,000 years—based on evidence bees left in fossils in the mud flats of the Nile River near Alexander, Egypt.

From my scribbles, I made a base on which the spirit of my dream to write still lives. Around its rim, I wound the strings of my simple and humble life that began in the enchanted forests of Graham County in western North Carolina on a frosty night.

Strings of my life lead me everywhere:to fields I plowed with a horse; to elementary and high schools; to a prayer rail at a small church; to ships, to ports of call, to harbor towns and quays; to a college town when study time was young, when pliant minds were molded by the cold book guage; to a simple plan of do you love me, written by a slender forefinger in hoary frost for two on a cold winter night on the windshield of a blue ford; to an altar where I answered "I do"; to a sailboat where she gave me a gold sailboat pendant with a kiss or two; to a large city where I found a job; to a birth where I heard my son's first cry; to an old house on a dirt road with a mountain tied to its end, blue-humped against the sky; and one special string, just to fool me, led me back home again.

As a beloved scribbler of the evening, I turn my thoughts and scribbles to closure. My one hope is that I didn't pour forth jejune words and useless phrases. I kiss my scribbles with affection— would they were cheeks instead.

Will,
I enjoyed going fishing
with you. Most important,
I wanted to know you better.
work hard and smart when
you play sports.
Enjoy the book.
          Ray Carpenter
            11-26-11
             103/300